A DIABOLICAL LAST
COMMUNITY RESUL...
SPOOF SINCE *A CONFEDERACY OF DUNCES.*

The assets of the surprisingly valuable estate of a small time, eccentric lawyer become the target of the unscrupulous and greedy in the bucolic town of Pine Ridge, North Carolina, setting off a chain of events no one could ever have even dreamed of, let alone imagined. It's almost as if the wily old lawyer is playing one last trick, resulting in a rollicking and unpredictable ending.

When the opposing attorney's masterful oration was over, Jimmy G was actually sweating. His nervousness was palpable.

"Do you wish to respond to that argument?"the judge asked him.

"Nah, Judge, I can't touch that. Even I gotta a'mit it was pretty good. But Judge, ya know, it'sall fluff. Smoke and mirrors. Judge in dis here courtroom we got a Bible." He made a show of picking it up. "But Judge, we got a different Bible here too. You an' me. We got dis one here." Jimmy picked up an unobtrusive green soft cover book and held it high for the judge and everyone else to see. "Judge, dis is de general statyoots of our state." He opened it and made a show or reading to himself, his lips quivering. No one coughed, rustled, or even burped., as if the courtroom had been evacuated.

Praise for O'Halloran's Will

A barely successful street lawyer dies but puzzles the townfolk by leaving an unexpectedly large estate to either a church he never attended or to his dogs. David Tanis uses his experiences of almost half century as a judge and a trial lawyer to craft this story of greed and stupidity by those trying to get their hands on the antique gold coins, the winning lottery ticket and an ancient stock certificate now worth millions. The usual suspects are right out of central casting for a 1930's court house drama. A quick read. This well crafted story will educate and leave the reader smiling and laughing out loud.—*Tom Keith, District Attorney (Ret), Forsyth County, NC.*

David Tanis gets it just right. The small Southern town of Pine Ridge comes alive, and so do the characters.-living and dead. Tanis, a lawyer and former judge, makes the courthouse crowd come alive with a light touch of authenticity. There's plenty of wry humor in this fine novel, along with plot twists and turns to keep the reader intrigued. Oh, yes, there's an element of dark mystery that has one wondering. A wonderful story that readers will find totally engaging. Sit back and enjoy.—*Joseph L.S. Terrell, author of the Harrison Weaver Mysteries.*

"Tanis has crafted a fascinating legal tale. He has constructed a riveting legal thriller that is both smart and funny. Engaging from the beginning until the end, Tanis left me wanting more."—*William B. Reingold, Chief District Court Judge (Retired), Twenty-First Judicial District, North Carolina*

O'Halloran's Will

David R. Tanis

Moonshine Cove Publishing, LLC
Abbeville, South Carolina U.S.A.

ISBN: 978-1-945181-313
Library of Congress PCN: 2018935653
Copyright 2018 by David R. Tanis

To Steffi, my long suffering wife who puts up with a writer with Attention Deficit Disorder.

ABOUT THE AUTHOR

Writing is Tanis's third career. As a U.S. Army officer, Captain Tanis served with three Special Forces groups.  In Viet Nam as an infantry Task Force Commander he was seriously wounded. After his recuperation and graduate school, he attended Wake Forest University Law School. He then pursued a career of over thirty years in the law, serving as a prosecutor, District Court Judge, and trial lawyer in North Carolina, with thousands of trials, over a hundred of them before juries, dozens in Federal Court. After his retirement from the practice of law, he began concentrating on writing novels. He belongs to the Mystery Writers of America, North Carolina Writers Network and Hampton Roads Writers. *O'Halloran's Will* is his third published novel, after *Just Add Water* and *Strange Goings on at Mother Nature's* featuring the inimitable attorney, Hamish O'Halloran. He has also had four short stories published in various journals. He lives with his wife of over half a century on the northern Outer Banks of North Carolina.

For more about the author, visit his website:

http://davidrtanis.com/main.html

Also By
David R, Tanis

Just Add Water

Strange Goings On at Mother Nature's

Things aren't what they use to be and never were.

—Will Rogers (1879-1935)

O'HALLORAN'S

WILL

Chapter 1

As far as sleepy little Southern towns went, Pine Ridge, North Carolina was about as sleepy as you could get. People passed one another on the street and said howdy. Workers in slow motion under the baking summer sun wiped the sweat off their necks with their bandanas, and life was pretty much as it always had been. Down on the corner in the center of town, an old black man in a rumpled suit, a white shirt, yellowed at the collar, and a plain, dark tie, slender, the kind they wore forty years ago, sat on a park bench in front of the drug store just passing the time away. An old white man in overalls came and sat down next to him. They had known each other their whole lives, never had a cross word to say, and just respected each other, respected the difference, you might say.

"Afternoon Reuben," the white man said, as he sat on the park bench.

"Hiya, Missah Jones," Reuben replied pleasantly. "Kindly hot i'nt it?"

"Sho'nuff." Mister Jones wiped the sweat off his brow. "Yer fambly all right, Reuben?"

"Yassah, dey's jus'fine."

Those two men had something you don't see much nowadays. They had respect and dignity. That was a part of the culture of the old South no one talks about much anymore.

Down the shady street lined with ancient elms that had miraculously escaped the Dutch elm blight, at 214 Pine Street, near the edge of town, a wrinkled old man sat in an ancient rocker on the porch of a square house with a big verandah wrapped half way around it. All the houses were big, substantial houses, with wide verandahs, built around the turn of the century when the cotton was king. Pine Ridge flourished then, but not now. It had been twenty, thirty years since any of those big old houses had a new coat of paint.

Next to the old man on the porch sat a boy, crosslegged, not more than eleven or twelve. He was wearing the uniform all young boys wore then; jeans and a ragged old T-shirt. The old man rubbed his rough hands together, quietly kneading the stiffness out of them. His hands were gnarled like the bole of an old oak tree. Arthritis had gotten them good but the man would not cease the fight. Rocking idly back and forth, calmly kneading and rubbing his hands in the vain hope the pain would abate, he continued to rub them together, back and forth, almost absentmindedly as he talked to the boy.

"Gramps," said the boy, "ain't nothin' never happens aroun' here does it." He went on with the proper tone of respect, without waiting for his grandfather to reply. "Ever' day the same thing. People goin' to work, farmers farmin', policemen policin,' storekeepers sellin' and sweepin' their shops. I seen some importan' lookin' men in suits carryin' briefcases goin' inta the courthouse. Some rough lookin' no accounts goin' in there too. Gramps, has it always been so, with nothin' ever happenin' 'roun' here?"

The old man thought for a few minutes, his gnarled right hand stroking his chin awkwardly. "Well, now. Lemme think a minute. Come to think about it there was sump'in.' Yessuh, some time ago right in that very house right across the street there, lived an ol' lawyer. Yessuh. When he died there sure was some commotion 'roun' here for a while. Yessiree. That was some big time aroun' here, it was. Place ain't been the same since."

The boy perked up, his interest whetted. Any trace of boredom disappeared if the old man was going to tell a story. "Tell me about it, Gramps. What happened?"

"Well, Stevie, it was like this. Ol' Hamish O'Halloran, his name was, lived in that house fer as long as ah can remember. He was a strange bird, he was. Always kept to hisself. Never said howdy, jus' nodded a bit. Had three big dogs he kep' in that yard." The old man pointed to the yard, its decrepit old fence falling apart. "Made quite a ruckus, they did, ever' time he came home from the courthouse.

Well one day, long time ago, bout the time you was born, he jus' up an died. No reason, he jus' died right there at the kitchen table in that house."

The boy shuddered. He didn't like to think about people dying. His MawMaw was the only person he ever knew who died and he didn't like to think about dying one bit. And right there in the house across the street! Maybe there were ghosts there. He shuddered as he thought about it.

The people that lived there now were a young married couple. The wife was a bit haggard with her two small kids always running around, sometimes half naked. Her husband was a mechanic who worked down at Jim's Body Shop. When he came home, he worked around the house until it was time to go to sleep. The boy had watched the couple carefully, and he knew. He looked up at his grandfather who was watching the thought process of his grandson, waiting. He smiled and Gramps started up again.

"Well Stevie, it all started when the old lawyer didn't show up fer court one day. Old Judge Harley Martin was on the bench. Everybody in town was skeered of ol' Judge Martin. He was one tough hombre. Always carried a pistol but I never heered tell o' him usin' it. He'd come into Court like God a'mighty and smack that pistol down right there on the middle of the judge's bench. It let ever'body know he meant business. Which he sure did. Well, it was like this...."

Chapter 2

"Where in tarnation is he?" bellowed the crusty old judge from his exalted perch on the bench to no one in particular. "We been waitin' twenty minutes to start this trial."

"I don't know, yer Honor," came the feeble reply from the befuddled prosecutor, a wispy middle-aged man, who respected and feared Judge Harley Martin, especially when the veins on the old judge's forehead started popping out in one of his apoplectic fits.

Assistant District Attorney Billy "Benedict" Arnold had been around a long time and was a decent trier of the state's cases. While not charismatic, no not charismatic at all, Billy well knew the elements of each crime and got them into evidence in a straightforward, unembellished fashion. Juries in the small town of Pine Ridge usually followed his simple, clear logic and gave him the conviction he wanted. But because of his innate insecurity Billy was not arrogant and did not think of himself as God's gift to the State.

"I spoke to him yesterday afternoon, and he seemed all set to try this case."

Billy and Hamish O'Halloran had a strange sort of bond. Both were misfits in the social sense, at least by the criteria of the upper echelons of Pine Ridge's snoot set. They could usually be seen having lunch together, Hamish engrossed in his omnipresent newspaper crossword puzzle, and Billy's eyes wistfully following the trail of some seedy waitress. Neither spoke much, yet there was a mutual respect that each had for the essential legal competence which underlay their unassuming exteriors.

"Sheriff," Judge Martin, whose face was now turning a brilliant crimson in stark contrast to his snow-white hair and bushy black eyebrows, boomed to the now fully alert bailiff, "go find O'Halloran and drag his butt into this courtroom in ten minutes."

With that, Judge Harley Martin stormed off the bench and disappeared into his chambers with a sharp slam of his door.

Billy, looking furtively around at the startled onlookers in the courtroom, sidled up to Mr. Speedy, the ancient courtroom clerk. No one knew his first name or if Mr. Speedy was his real name or just the nickname he was given to underscore his maddening slowness.

"Jeez, I wonder where O'Halloran is. It's not like him to just forget about coming to Court, especially when he's got a trial in front of Judge Martin," said Billy, in a clear but conspiratorial whisper. "I hope the old fart's all right."

Mr. Speedy just nodded, but a worried look creased his forehead in a tacit assent.

The murmuring undercurrent among the spectators died down after a while and a somber mood befell the crowd of onlookers and jurors who were waiting for the trial to start. Watching a jury trial was great sport and just about all the entertainment the posse of retired gentlemen in Pine Ridge had. There were at least a dozen regulars who would congregate in the Courtroom each morning a trial was scheduled, like Romans in the coliseum about to watch the gladiators in action.

When it was polite to do so, the regulars began to file out into the lobby, while the prospective jurors remained, as if nailed to their seats, fearful of Judge Martin's wrath if he should return and they were not to be found in the courtroom. There was a feeling of universal sympathy for Hamish O'Halloran and the awful fate in store for him when Bailiff Burton dragged his butt back into Court.

After half an hour, Mr. Burton had not returned. Judge Martin was now standing at the door, his magisterial judiciousness framed by the black trim of the door jamb at his chambers entrance like an old masters' portrait. He was no longer seething, but stood there with his hands on his hips, expectantly. He, too, was beginning to show signs of concern.

The judge was about to look for another bailiff when Burton burst into the courtroom, in an agitated state of breathlessness.

"He's dead," he shouted unceremoniously from the back of the courtroom to everyone there, and certainly loud enough for Judge Martin to hear at his post at the door to his chambers. "I went to his house and found him just lying there at the kitchen table, dead," he gasped out in spurts. "I called the paramedics and they got there fast but couldn't do nothin' for him."

The expression of shock paused on Judge Martin's scowling visage for just a moment. He purposefully strode to the bench and stood there a few seconds looking out over the startled faces in the courtroom. "Adjourn Court, Mr. Bailiff," he said, in a more somber and subdued tone, "We'll resume business at two o'clock this afternoon."

The news flashed through the courthouse at close to the speed of light. Courthouse personnel thrive on gossip, and when one of their own bites the dust, it is the epitome of gossip-worthiness. There were expressions of sympathy, of concern for their own mortality, but more important, there was an incredible inquisitiveness, with a deep down longing for some evidence of sensationalism accompanying the death of the colorless old lawyer.

The paramedics had dutifully transported the corpse of Hamish O'Halloran to the small local hospital to make sure that he was in fact dead and not faking. There were always stories about how a corpse had once sat bolt upright in the morgue just before an autopsy and scared the bejeesus out of the medical examiner.

But Hamish O'Halloran was in fact dead and the coroner confirmed it. There was a sense of defeat, a strange sadness that wafted over the town, as the notion was realized by the townsfolk that the eccentric old lawyer, with the badly rumpled suits and pee gray pony tail pulled tightly back on his balding pate, would no longer be the subject of gossip in the Pine Ridge courthouse.

Hamish O'Halloran had had few friends, probably no real friends, during his long tenure as the courthouse oddity. But one of those few who respected him was Mr. Speedy. O'Halloran had always acted kindly toward Mr. Speedy, one of the few lawyers who treated the slow moving assistant clerk with any deference. Over the years, Mr. Speedy had come to see through the simplicity of O'Halloran's legal tactics and understand that there really had been a functioning legal mind there.

He collected Molly McMasters, the head clerk, and in that capacity, she was the *ex officio* judge of probate. They somberly walked down the street a few blocks to the end of town where O'Halloran had lived. The house was a weathered, clapboard house of the simple farm house type, commonly built in the area in the 1880's, badly in need of a coat of paint. It had a large roofed porch which wrapped around half the building. A picket fence in serious need of maintenance surrounded the yard. Next to the front door was a crude, hand-painted sign that said simply, "H. O'Halloran, Lawyer."

They walked past a few curious on-lookers who stood in front of the picket fence with jaws agape, as if some ghost was about to appear. Entering the wide-open front door, the two looked carefully around the old lawyer's house.

The furnishings were Spartan, but neat and clean. They were both surprised at the tidiness of the place, because O'Halloran's personal and sartorial habits were anything but tidy. As they went into the kitchen they immediately noticed an official looking document lying open at the kitchen table, the spot where they had been told Hamish had died. Mr. Speedy picked it up and stared at it. "It's a will, Molly. This is Hamish's last will and testament."

"Here, let me see that," the stately middle-aged clerk said as she grabbed for the document. "If it is his last will, I will need it for probate. I wonder who in the world he left his estate to?" she mused, not bothering to read the document but cautiously and ostentatiously sliding it into her brief case sized pocketbook.

The two looked into all the rooms with morbid curiosity, each silently noting the contents and the incongruous neatness of the Spartan furnishings. It was almost as if it had been purposely furnished to look just as it had the day it was built. With few words, they left the house, carefully shutting the door behind them, and slowly and solemnly walked back to the Courthouse. On the way, they passed a few of the local lawyers, notorious shysters, who were headed to Hamish's house to see if there were any crumbs to collect.

Back at the courthouse, Molly McMasters gathered Billy Arnold and Mr. Sparrow, a venerable old lawyer of impeccable reputation, to meet with her and Mr. Speedy in the Clerk's conference room, which doubled as the probate Court whenever this ancient practice was required, the new will statute having all but made it extinct.

"I've asked you here just to witness this document, which Mr. Speedy and I found at old Mr. O'Halloran's house, just after his death," she stated quite businesslike. "It does not appear to be very long, so I'd like for each of you to read it and then we'll see what we should do about it."

Molly knew that Hamish O'Halloran was pretty much a recluse, associated with very few people, and had few friends. She was intensely curious to see how he had disposed of his house and few possessions in his will.

She handed the will to Mr. Speedy who quickly read through it. When he was finished, he muttered, "I'll be damned," and handed the document to Mr. Arnold. Billy glanced through the document, shook his head in disbelief, and handed the will to Mr. Sparrow.

After adjusting his spectacles, Mr. Sparrow carefully read the document. He read it twice, just to make sure he hadn't missed anything, and laid it down ceremoniously before him on the conference table. He glanced up, knowingly, peeking over his spectacles which had slid studiously to the end of his nose, inviting a response.

Molly was beside herself with anticipation and curiosity at the implication created by the subtle and incredulous response of each of the readers of the will who had preceded her. She grabbed the will and said, rhetorically, "What's it say?" She quickly read through the will, and then looked at those around her at the conference table. "I don't believe this. Hamish O'Halloran was never known to set foot in a church."

"I know," said Billy. "Every once in a while we got to talking about religion. He mostly thought organized religion was hogwash, especially the Temple of God. We often talked about the Temple. It just doesn't make any sense."

The will, after all the usual boiler plate language about taxes and debts, and so forth, left his estate thus:

> All the rest, residue and remainder of my worldly estate I leave to the Temple of God, on the condition that said religious institution should be deemed worthy, and if not, I leave said estate to the Institute for the Treatment of Canines Humanely (ITCH) on condition they take care of my dogs and especially, old Caesar, and not put him down until he dies a natural death.

Mr. Sparrow, unlike all the others sitting around the conference table with glum faces, smiled understandingly. After they had just about exhausted their conversation on how incredulous the terms of the will were, he spoke up. "To the contrary, my friends, this is the quintessential Hamish O'Halloran. You must look at the qualifying phrase, "on the condition that said religious institution be deemed worthy... Now just who, do you think, is going to be the judge of that? It seems old Hamish has pitted the Institute for the Treatment of Canines Humanely (ITCH) against the formidable Temple of God in a battle for what we presume to be his meager estate, but I wonder, hmm."

The others began to realize the irony of the terms of the will. The Temple of God was a huge sprawling complex financed by lavish fund-raising activities and telethons. The leader of the flock, the master shepherd, as he liked to refer to himself, was Pastor Ronnie Conner, a charismatic hell-fire and brimstone preacher, with a dyed black, impeccably coifed, pomaded, hairdo. Pastor Ronnie, and his wife Donna, along with their three white miniature poodles, lived in a regally appointed mansion including an overabundance of gilt and ormolu, and spent more time raising funds on their luxurious television productions than in tending to his flock. Despite this obvious ostentatious hypocrisy, the Temple of God was attended and supported by a disproportionately large segment of the citizens of Pine Ridge and had enormous influence over the thinking and politics of the little society, a fact, which if they would all actually take the time to think about it, made the populace a little uneasy.

Molly McMasters, who was a devoted follower of Pastor Ronnie herself, chirped in. "Well, I don't see it that way. Everybody knows the Temple of God is worthy. I say we qualify the executor and let him proceed to publish, pay the debts, and distribute the estate."

"There's the rub," interjected Mr. Sparrow. "Did you notice who he appointed to be the executor of his estate?"

"Izzy Shapiro, so what? He is certainly a responsible little man, even if he is a bit odd," Molly retorted defensively.

Isadore Shapiro was an old merchant who had operated a clothing store on Main Street in Pine Ridge from before anybody could remember. Despite his longevity in the sleepy Southern community, Izzy had never compromised his heavy accent belying some obscure Eastern European origin. His was the only Jewish family in town and they had to travel thirty miles to Greeneburg to attend religious services at the Temple there. He probably was the only person in Pine Ridge who could be the slightest bit objective about whether the Temple of God was worthy or not.

"Well, at the very minimum, I think it's up to Izzy to determine whether the Temple of God is deemed worthy," responded Mr. Sparrow, amicably. Mr. Speedy concurred with a discrete nod of his head, mindful of the religious predilections of his superior.

Mr. Arnold, on the other hand, was more curious." Let me see that again, Mr. Sparrow," he requested, as he reached for the document. Mr. Sparrow slid the last will and testament over to him and he picked it up quickly leafing to the last page where the notary seal was. "This is curious," he stated, signs of his innate prosecutorial inquisitiveness coming through. "It was signed ten years ago. I wonder what it was doing lying on O'Halloran's kitchen table when he died."

Well, they all thought that an odd circumstance, but, nevertheless, after some final pleasantries, broke up the meeting and Molly McMasters began the procedures to probate the will.

Billy Arnold and Mr. Sparrow sauntered across the street to The Legal Lunch. What one might consider a *dive,* The Legal Lunch had been the preferred gathering place for lawyers and court personnel for at least two generations. Hamish O'Halloran, even during his prime if you could call it such, was a habitué of the joint, often relegating himself to a lonely lunch, eaten at "his" table, located at the very rear of the restaurant, where he often hid out for hours.

Sometimes he would wile away his time working a crossword puzzle, sometimes he hand wrote a pleading or motion on a yellow lined legal pad. Over the last half a dozen years or so prior to his death, Billy Arnold and Mr.

Sparrow often joined him, without any express invitation mind you, just a tacit nod of acceptance. Most often, not a word was spoken between them, as they ate their unappetizing lunches. Each engrossed in his own mental endeavor, they were comfortable with their respective presences, without the need for approval from the other, each implicitly trusting their colleagues. They were all members of the legal profession, but uncharacteristic of members of the profession, self-aggrandizement was notably absent in their characters.

Sometimes the three men idly chatted, even gossiped about some odd event which had unsettled the courthouse. When that occurred, they became engrossed in profound discussions, that occasionally turned to philosophical diatribes of the often disturbing nature of mankind. Mostly, they just sat there silently thinking about something. They were an odd trio, the jaded career prosecutor whose sole daily function was to get through the docket, prosecute the day's miscreants, and go home; the wise, gentle and reserved quintessential Southern lawyer; and the quirky recluse.

Lunch for them was a habit. The food stunk. All the meat, whether chicken, beef, or pork, tasted the same. The vegetables were greasy and tasteless, the sandwiches thin, and the burgers were fried to the point they were shoe leather. But they had gotten so used to each other's company, that when Hamish died there was an almost palpable void. On this day, Billy and Mr. Sparrow somberly discussed his death, the strange will, and the daunting task facing Izzy Shapiro as he undertook the administration of the estate.

"It's a good thing he's not a politician," Billy remarked in a wry manner. "He'd get eaten alive by Pastor Ronnie and his voracious flock if he said the Temple wasn't worthy."

Mr. Sparrow nodded his assent. "But, yet," he remarked thoughtfully, "his is a task which may prove to have monumental implications."

"Hmmm. We'll just have to wait and see," replied Billy, as he filled his mouth with a piece of something of a chewy consistency hidden in the brown gravy.

Chapter 3

The next day, when Isadore Shapiro was told he was named the executor of O'Halloran's will, he was taken totally aback. The unfamiliarity of the appointment notwithstanding, he immediately, asked, "Vad iss da fee for dis execudor doing?"

Molly told him the fee was five per cent of everything he took in and everything he paid out. She let this fact sink in a bit before briefly explaining the duties of an executor. He seemed to understand and was satisfied.

She suggested he go through the deceased's papers and make an inventory of his property. She told him, "I've seen his household furnishings. We can either appoint three commissioners to value the stuff or you can just put $1,000.00 as an estimate. That way you don't have to worry about paying the commissioners and getting my approval."

"So vad, den, dad's fifdy bucks for me?" Izzy asked.

"Right," she responded. "Also, see if he's got any bills, cash, bank accounts, stocks or bonds, evidence of any other real property. Things like that. You have to collect the assets, pay the bills. Oh, and look to see if he has a safe deposit box, anywhere. If he does, you and I will have to get a bank officer to open it so we can inventory the contents of the box. Here are the forms you'll need. Do a preliminary inventory first, and then get back to me. Oh, and you will aslo have to put an ad in the newspaper, so anyone claiming O'Halloran owed them money can come forward."

Izzy was not so sure he wanted to do this. He knew Hamish O'Halloran, of course, although the latter, being generally regarded as sartorially challenged, hadn't bought an item of clothing from him in many years. They were just two social pariahs, excluded from the tight knit, mostly

WASP, social hierarchy of Pine Ridge. Their paths occasionally crossed, and they acknowledged one another casually.

No one was more surprised than Isadore Shapiro to be appointed executor of the last will and testament of Hamish O'Halloran, although he suspected that the opportunity might enable him to make a few bucks. The shabby old house, he mused, had to be worth at least $40,000.00, and that was $2,000.00 to him. Big money.

The next day it rained, a steady depressing drizzle. The business at Izzy's store was slow, but with the rain, it was even slower. So Izzy left his son in charge of the haberdashery and went down the street to dutifully inventory the belongings of the late Mr. O'Halloran. If he wasn't going to be able to make any money at the store, he'd see what he could make on this executor thing. But it was also now his duty and Isadore Shapiro never shirked his duty.

Dis iss spooky, he thought, as he cautiously let himself in the front door with the key Molly had given him. He had never been invited to the house and had only occasionally chatted with the old codger upon chance meetings in the small town, but he knew where Hamish O'Halloran lived. Everybody in Pine Ridge knew the old two story once white clapboard house at the edge of town with the sign, "H. O'Halloran, Lawyer," posted next to the front door.

The air within was still and musty, and the tranquility of the house of death was vaguely disturbing to him. Not a thing had been touched since Mr. Speedy found the will, and there was a faint odor coming from the refrigerator. *Oy,* thought Mr. Shapiro, as he realized that whatever perishable that was contained therein had indeed perished. He decided to skip the refrigerator for the time being and combed through the house looking for documents, the tangible evidence of value.

He centered his attention on a battered old wooden desk in a corner of the living room. There was nothing on it but a green banker's lamp and an old pen set in a marble stand. The executor sat at the desk trying to get a sense of the old man. He had the quirky feeling that Hamish was there beside him and approved. He shook off the odd sensation and slowly opened the center drawer.

Everything was neat and orderly. On the left side of the drawer was a folder with the title *Bills,* written in the practiced archaic long hand cursive of the Palmer method. In it were a few unpaid bills, all of which were dated a few days before the demise of the deceased attorney. On the right-hand side were a check book, a savings account book, and a plain key, all neatly placed and evenly spaced from each other. He opened the check book, and in the same neat penmanship, the register meticulously kept, was the balance - $5,024.36. His excitement grew as he roughly calculated the $250.00 in easy fees. He opened the savings account book and was delighted to find that the balance was $7,883.02. Another almost $400.00 he gleefully calculated. *Duck soup*, he thought, as he picked up the key.

There was no indication as to what it unlocked, but Isadore thought that the plainly etched number, 124, was the key to a lock box somewhere. *Rats!* Perhaps he was going to have to work for his fee anyway. He rifled through the drawers, but despite the organized filing systems, there was a paucity of records - nothing to indicate what the key was for. And he couldn't find anything else of value.

He was perplexed. There were no income tax records, no tax notices concerning the house, no records of anything due from clients. There was a four-drawer filing cabinet near the desk that contained client files, some of them rather old, but no accounts receivable and none of the files indicated anything about fees. Granted, some of the files were court appointed cases with the usual, grossly inadequate fee being paid by the state, but those that were not court appointed, said nothing about what the fee was. Izzy wondered how Hamish remembered what to charge his clients. *Oy, maybe he didn't charge some of them anything at all,* he mused.

Disturbed about what he felt were missing relevant records, Izzy decided to see if he could find some. He was not much of a detective, but he felt it was his duty to try. As he was leaving the house it started to rain again. He popped open his umbrella and walked down the street to the Office of the Register of Deeds to check on the ownership of the house and find out whether any taxes were owed.

Izzy plopped the sodden umbrella in the corner, as he went in. The lower portion of his pants legs were soaked so he rolled them up about a foot or so, revealing some pathetically skinny legs. A matronly clerk looked at him aghast.

Walking up to a counter, he was greeted by a small female clerk of indefinite age. She noted the adddress and went to the files to look up the name, 'O'Halloran,' but quickly returned and said. "I'm sorry Mr. Shapiro, Mr. O'Halloran does not own any real property in this county."

"Vad?" he responded, "vell, who doess own de house on Pine Sdreed?"

"You'll have to go to the tax office for that information," she responded pleasantly. "We just don't have that information here."

Perturbed at what he perceived as omnipresent bureaucratic inefficiency, he trudged next door to the tax office, convinced the rain was coming through the umbrella as if it was a sieve. His head looked like he was wearing a wet cat on it. He went up to the counter and peeked over the barrier, chest high. There was an indolent acting, rather obese man, idly talking on the telephone. After a few minutes and more than a few "harrumphs," increasing in volume from Izzy, just to remind the bureaucrat that he was a taxpayer, the large official looked up and said, "Be with ya in a sec."

In what turned out to be rather more than a few seconds, he hung up and laboriously made his way to the counter, quite apparently aggravated at the interruption. "Yeh?" he asked, not attempting to hide his pique.

"I need a know who owns da house ad 213 Pine Sdreed," Izzy asked, pleasantly enough, deciding to give the bureaucrat the benefit of the doubt.

"I thought old man O'Halloran did," came the reply, obviously proud of himself for his extensive knowledge of the town's tax maps.

"No, I don'd d'ink so," replied Izzy, his back up, the benefit of the doubt having been erased. "Nex' door said he doessn'." Izzy jerked his thumb in the direction of the office of the Register of Deeds just to show the man he was one step ahead of him.

"Hmm, let's see, then," said the heavy bureacrat, his curiosity aroused, as he turned and went to a large map of the city. "Block 152 Lot 34," he said to no one in particular, as he went to a large card file. "Geez," he said in surprise as he pulled out the applicable card. "I've never seen anything like this before." He showed the card to Mr. Shapiro. There was a blank after the word owner, but the taxes were religiously paid by Mr. O'Halloran. The tax notices were sent to H. O'Halloran, 213 Pine Street. The tax value was $36,000.00.

"That's all I can tell you, I'm afraid." And with that the big man nonchalantly returned to his desk and picked up the telephone, leaving the damp and perplexed Izzy standing there without an answer or explanation.

The executor decided to check with the First Bank of Pine Ridge, known pejoratively to the locals as "the First and Last." As usual, there was only one teller awake and in attendance. She looked about fourteen years old, with the freshly scrubbed face and innocence of a vestal virgin.

"He'p ya?" she asked using the local argot with the nasal twang common to trendy teenagers.

"Mebbe," he responded. "Vad iss diss?" he asked holding up the perplexing key.

"I duhno, a key?" the girl answered diffidently. "Nevah saw any key like that, before." She looked up at him as if daring him to inquire further into something she had absolutely no interest in. He turned without responding further and left the bank in an irritated snit, venturing out into the mist of the streets of the little town.

Chapter 4

Isadore Shapiro left the bank and began the short, wet walk back toward the end of town, immersed in thought as well as being completely soaked from the rain like a Baptist after a full immersion. The umbrella had proved to be of little use in the downpour. This case was really getting to be aggravating and was now presenting a serious challenge, not unlike an intense game of chess against an unseen master. There had to be some logic in this craziness and he intended to find it.

He contemplated various possibilities, but the evasive answer had not paused long enough in his mind for him to grasp it, by the time he found himself at the steps to 213. He climbed up on the porch and shook the drops off his umbrella. Leaving it on the porch, in deference to the dearly departed, he quietly let himself in, and instinctively headed for the kitchen leaving a trail of wet footprints behind.

He looked at the kitchen table in amazement. There prominently displayed on the pitted wooden table top was a fresh buttermilk pie, the tantalizing aroma beckoning. But his curiosity stopped him in his tracks. Who could have left the pie? Everyone in Pine Ridge must have known about the death of Hamish O'Halloran. The gossip had spread like wildfire.

Giving in to his instincts he bent over to get a good whiff of the delightful pie, which was still warm, when he heard a noise coming from the bedroom. Startled, and just a little apprehensive, Izzy cautiously approached the room and peeked in. He was astonished to see a short, prim, elderly black woman dusting the dresser. She gasped as she saw him and grabbed a vase and held it up menacingly.

"Don' yo' come in heah, Mistah. Now git, come on, now git, ya heah?" she said, not too convincingly, as she took a tentative step toward Izzy, pretending the delicate vase was some sort of vicious war club.

"Who are you, leddy?" Izzy asked, undeterred by the ineffective gesture of the obviously frightened woman," and vad are you doink in Hamish's house?"

"Whatchoo doin' heah, Mistah?" she asked, undeterred. "Dis heah's ole Mistah O'Halloran's house. Y'aint got no rat to be in heah," she said indignantly, lowering the vase somewhat, as she perceived Izzy was certainly no threat to her. "Caintchoo see ah'm cleanin' up for ole Mistah O'Halloran. I duz ev'y Thusday."

"Come mid me to de kuchen, leddy," Izzy said, "I god do dell you something very impordan." He turned and went back to the kitchen and pulled up a chair at the pitted wooden table. She followed him cautiously, with wide eyes and a querulous expression on her face. Proudly, she sat down, but not at Hamish's traditional place where the pie was.

He wiped his brow which was still a little wet from the rain. "I god do dell you dis, leddy," he said, "Hamish is dead. I am da execudor."

"Oh. lawdy," she wailed, "You done killed him. You done executed Ole Hamish. He nevah hurt nobody. Watchoo execute him for, Mistah?" she lamented ruefully.

"No, no," Izzy tried to defend himself from the uncomprehending verbal attack. "No leddy, I din' execude him. He jus' died. I'm here do dake care of his d'ings. Wud you say you're name vass, leddy?"

The elderly woman assumed a pose of importance as she puffed up just a little and faced Isadore. She was still not certain that he hadn't executed Hamish in some vile manner, but she said with a touch of haughtiness, "Mah name's Miss Shan Tilly. Miss Shan Tilly Rice. Ev'ybody calls me Miss Tilly. Ah comes heah ev'y Thu'sday and cleans up a little fo' Mistah O'Halloran. He a nice ole jennamum. Ah been doin' dis fo' twenny yeah. Leaves him a little buttahmirk pie when Ah comes, he lak it so. He leave me twenny dollah when Ah come, fo' mah trubbles."

She paused for effect, so that the strange little man would understand her anachronistic importance in the household. Astonishing him, she jumped up, crying out, "Lawdy! I'ze forgit about dem dogs." With that, she ran out into the back yard, leaving the stunned executor sitting there in shock.

The terms of the will flashed before his eyes. It dawned on him. O'Halloran had three dogs, one of them, Caesar, was set apart in the will. *Oy vey. Id iss my dudy do dake care of dese dogs, doo.* He rose hesitantly and went out after the woman.

The rain had slackened considerably, almost as if God was protecting the old lady. As he watched from the security of the back porch, insulated from the possible onslaught of a hungry unleashed canine, he observed the trim, little woman hefting a large sack of dog food, filling three metal containers under a leanto. These odd cans had a top that flipped over enabling her to pour in the dry food. When it was about full, some hidden mechanism caused a portion of its contents to drop into a feeding trough. Isadore contemplated the interesting man who had devised this obviously home-made contraption.

Two of the dogs were black, scruffy, nondescript, medium size animals of the *canus genera* variety. They were untethered and had the free reign of the yard. The other was a huge, regal looking German shepherd, with pale eyes that made him look like a giant wolf. The dog was chained to a tree stump with just enough slack to enable him to get shelter in the leanto and eat his dinner. On top of the tree stump, a heavy metal swivel-like device was securely screwed into it to allow the dog maximum range in its limited domain.

Isadore contemplated the characteristics of the animal which required this kind of containment. It was a huge muscular brute, with the traditional markings of a German shepherd, and huge muddy paws. Yet there was something about this beast, that wasn't quite right. Its fur was too dark, and its eyes were too light for a German shepherd.

But the dog seemed no threat at all to Miss Tilly, who was cooing and petting the obviously adoring animal after delivering his ration of food. It was only after she walked away, that he dove into his dinner, snarling viciously when one of the other mutts ventured too near.

When she approached the back porch, Isadore asked Miz Tilly about the dogs' needs, feeding, and other things he would imagine would be necessary to take care of the animals before handing them over to the officials of the Temple of God.... or the Institute for the Treatment of Canines Humanely (ITCH). He chuckled to himself, but he immediately frowned as he realized that the responsibility for these animals was his until the decision was made as to whether the Temple of God was worthy.

Miss Tilly was more at ease when they went back into the house. It was still drizzling just a bit, yet she did not seem to have gotten very wet. She left the oversized boots on the porch near the door. She had slipped them on to protect her dainty feet from the ubiquitous North Carolina red clay mud.

Without a word, she boiled some water and helped herself to some tea. She servilely poured Isadore a cup without asking him if he wanted it. He did, and he was increasingly curious about the industrious old woman. There had been no mention of her in the will, and no gossip on the street to his knowledge. No one had ever included a woman of any kind or capacity in the same sentence that Hamish's name was mentioned.

Quietly and covertly, he removed a twenty-dollar bill from his wallet and placed it next to her tea cup. With the utmost decorum, she ignored it and cut a modest piece of buttermilk pie for them both and silently placed the plate before him. "I swanny. Ole Mistah O'Halloran! He dead, yuh say?" she turned to him as she asked the question, her demeanor demanding the full explanation her question didn't.

"Yeah. Dey say he jus' died," responded Izzy, without giving her the details she wanted, because he himself didn't have the slightest idea what Hamish died of. "Righd here at diss dable, dey found him slumped over."

Miss Tilly jumped up in fright and clasped her hands together, looking toward the ceiling. "Oh my! We cain't have owah pie heah at dis table, Mistah. Oh No. We caint do dat. Wudn't be rat. We'uns gots to respect de dead."

She was clearly agitated, so Izzy rose and the two of them took their tea and pie into the living room where they consumed their repast in silence, Izzy sitting at the desk and Miss Tilly sitting in an uncomfortable looking straight back chair, engrossed in the pie, yet doing so with the finest of delicate manners.

After he had finished the remarkably delicious pie, the delectably subtle flavor pleasantly lingering on, he began making conversation. "D'ank you very much, Miz Dilly. Dad vass eggcellent. You know, old Hamish was a sdrange vun. I don' d'ink he ever spend a nickel. I guess he never made much money," he remarked, rhetorically.

"Why you say dat?" she asked, defending the honor of her long time benefactor. "I knows he gots lotsa money."

"Vad? How do you know diss?" Izzy responded, astonished.

Miss Tilly gracefully, but with some effort, rose from her chair and went to the bedroom. She returned in a few minutes, clearly struggling under the weight of what she was carrying. It was a dusty wooden chest of the type used for a fancy silver service. It appeared to be almost too heavy for her to manage. She ceremoniously placed it on the desk.

"He always keep dis unnah de bed," she remarked matter of factly. "Go 'head. Ompen it. Ah'm sure he wun't mine, he dead an' all."

Isadore made no effort to hide his surprise. He cautiously lifted the lid of the dusty box and peeked in. He gave an involuntary gasp as the glint of gold struck his eyes like the flash of a camera. The chest was about half full of old gold coins, American, British, German, Austrian and even some old Russian coins with the image of a Tsar on them. He picked up one of the coins. It was surprisingly heavy, but there was something about the feel of it. He picked up another one, an old British Guinea. In an instant, he understood the deadly allure of gold, that irresistible attraction that made men steal and even kill for the metal. There was something magic about gold.

But lying on top of the gold coins was a 6" by 9" manila envelope. Of course, his burning curiosity would not let him fail to check to see what it contained. He undid the clasp and pulled out a letter written on cheap lined stationary, the kind they provided at the county jail, and read:

Dear Mr. O'Halloran,

I wanted to thank you properly for representing me several years ago. I know I wasn't able to pay you then, and you did a good job for me and kept me from going to jail, and never hounded me about the bill. Now I have a little something I'd like you to accept - as payment for your legal representation. My cousin and some of his friends started a computer company a while back and I helped them with the grunt work. They couldn't pay me in cash so they gave me these shares of stock.

Maybe if I wasn't sick I would not be doing this, but I guess you might call this settling up. The cancer is getting worse and I do not expect to be alive by the time you read this. I just can't think of anyone who could use this more or deserves it more.

Yours,

Ralph Hurley

Isadore slowly unfolded the stock certificate. It was 100 shares of stock in Komputer King, which, Izzy was aware, was the richest, most famous software company in the world, and it was dated thirty years ago. Isadore mused that if the stock certificate was genuine, it had probably split ten, maybe fifteen times in that period. Spurred on by incipient greed, his excitement grew as he realized the certificate had to be worth a ton of money, probably thousands upon thousands.

But as greedy as Izzy tended to be, he was even more devoted to the concepts of honor and his personal responsibility. The fleeting mendacious thought was gone. He now had to figure out how to value these finds. The coins, he thought, might be easy. The valuation of the stocks on the other hand, would be a little more difficult. Although it was publicly traded and the value of 100 shares would be listed in the Wall Street Journal, considering the accumulated dividends and stock splits, the value would probably be much, much higher.

He examined the face of the certificate and was surprised to see the carefully handwritten number on it. It was number 3. He slowly turned it over. The certificate was endorsed by Ralph Hurley, after which it was stated: "Payable on Demand to Bearer." He wondered what the words, "Payable on Demand to Bearer" meant, but it was not an idle thought for he intended to find out soon. He was unsure of the legal significance of the words, but had an idea of their common meaning, and that made him smile.

After she watched the range of varied expressions on Isadore's face run their course, Miss Tilly sighed. "What I gwine t'do, widdout Mistah O'Halloran need'n' mah suhvisses? Ain't nobuddy gwine take on a ole lady to dust up an' feed dem dogs," she lamented slyly.

As expected, Isadore, still under the giddy influence of sweet buttermilk pie, came to her rescue. "Vell, I'm sure ve could use a liddle help in de chop. Vy don' you come see me domorrow und ve can dalk aboud id."

She smiled and stood, extending her hand with a demure coquettishness. "Wah shoo, Mistah Isadore. Ah'd be honudd." He took her hand, bowed, and kissed it gently. She giggled and took her leave, almost skipping down the front porch stairs. The encounter left them both with a broad grin dividing their mostly honest faces.

Chapter 5

Isadore had prepared a list detailing each coin, carefully marking the country of origin, face value, date and his estimation of the condition. He attached the list to the otherwise bleak preliminary, which he had made to be submitted to the Clerk. In the appropriate space on the inventory form for the value of the stock and the coins he wrote TBD, standing for "To Be Determined," as he had he had been advised to do by Molly McMasters. He then proceeded to the library to see if he could find an up-to-date coin book to try to assess a value for them. All the while in his mind he was calculating his five per cent for he knew that some of the coins may be worth as much as $250.00 and there were 127 of them. He wasn't sure about how to determine the value of the stock certificate yet.

The library provided him with the latest coin catalogue and he proceeded to look up the value of each golden treasure. It was a tedious task, taking several hours. When he was finished, he took out a small pocket calculator he had borrowed. He was amazed that the British coins seemed to range in value from $250.00 to $2,500.00. The French coins were worth slightly less, the German gold pieces were worth more, and the Russian rubles were worth between $500.00 and $5,000.00 each. The American coins were worth the most since most of them seemed to be Twenty Dollar pieces from the mid-nineteenth century. There were nineteen American gold coins valued at between $750.00 and $5,000.00. He was delighted as he tallied his fee in his head.

But there were four strange coins for which he could not ascertain the value. The coin catalogue merely had an asterisk by these coins which meant "see dealer." One was a

1795 coin with no indication of the face value and had a scrawny looking eagle on the back. Another was a smallish coin dated 1880 depicting a girl with a modern coiffure and on the reverse was a star with the words "One stella, 400 cents." It was in absolutely perfect condition. The third was a small gold coin with a seated woman holding a staff. It was dated 1870 with a prominent letter "S" under the date and was apparently a three dollar gold piece. *Dree dollars,* Izzy thought. *Dad's a sdrange amoun'.* He smiled wryly as he thought of the phrase, *Queer as a three dollar bill.* The last coin was a huge brilliant coin dated 1855. On the reverse were the words "San Francisco California. Fifty Dollars," surrounding an eagle holding a shield.

Isadore was astounded. The gold coins for which he was able to find a value in the catalogue totaled $171,300.00. Who knew what the four others were worth, but Isadore sensed that the value of these coins alone could be a lot more than all the others combined. He was elated. He was jubilant. He wanted to dance in the streets, but that would be unseemly, and Isadore Shapiro was nothing if not seemly. This meant his fee was going to be in the neighborhood of at least $25,000.00. Oh happy day!

But his elation was short lived, and he quickly become concerned. He would have to find some one to insure this cache until it could be sold. Who would pay for that? Who could he sell this treasure trove to at top dollar, and how would he go about doing that? And the most pressing question was where could he safely keep them?

He went down to his store and initially placed the coins in the store safe. On second thought, checking to make sure he was alone, and having locked the front door, he opened the safe and removed the four coins for which he could not ascertain a value. He carefully placed each in a small plastic bag and put them into a larger cloth bag which he carefully placed in his coat pocket, the one with the zipper, with as much reverence and caution as if he was handling the Dead

Sea Scrolls themselves. Looking around again, to make sure there were no burglars lurking about, he carefully locked the safe. He then went to see Molly McMasters.

At the clerk's office Isadore Shapiro asked Molly if he could use the copier. Only slightly curious but suspecting it had somehow to do with the O'Halloran estate, she acquiesced. *Izzy is too cheap to even pay to make copies,* she thought with amusement. At the copier, Izzy cautiously looked around to make sure that no one was close enough to see what he was doing. He made copies of the front and back of the four coins, each on a single sheet. Meticulously folding the copies, he placed them in the inside pocket of his jacket.

He then made copies of the front and back of the stock certificate. *Curious,* he thought. He had never seen a stock certificate signed by the owner before. Of course, he had seen precious few stock certificates in his life anyway. Then Isadore Shapiro walked down the quiet Main Street of Pine Ridge to the modest office of the local stock broker.

The office had the feel of a bookie joint. Shabby, the small waiting room consisted of a ratty plaid couch, from an earlier era, two chairs with the stuffing leaking out of the vinyl seats, and a stained coffee table which might have been hand made. He found no one in attendance, but he could hear someone talking on the telephone in the back, so he took a seat and idly picked up a year-old financial magazine with the address label torn off, while he waited for the broker to make an appearance. After a few minutes, he could hear the broker finish his conversation, so he stood up and uttered a loud, "Ahem."

The broker, a young man sporting a fashionable striped shirt and yellow silk tie, with slicked back, overly gelled hair, appeared with a surprised expression on his face. He eyed Izzy with just a trace of condescension.

"Oh, I didn't expect you. We don't usually get walk-in clients. What can I do for you?"

Isadore showed him the copy of the stock certificate and asked him what the value was. The broker's surprised expression, which had painted his face when he saw the name of the company and the date on the certificate, evaporated and was replaced with one a little more sinister. He said, "Well it's 100 shares. Let's see what Komputer King is trading at now."

He sat down at his computer and within a few seconds, blurted out, "Wow! It's trading at 32½ today. That means its worth $3,250.00."

Isadore looked at him suspiciously and was about to inquire further into whether the shares had ever split, but some vague warning buzzed inside him, and he just sat there silently for a few moments. He then rose and reached for the copy of the certificate, but the broker grabbed it and held it against his chest. "I'll give you $3,500.00 for the actual certificate."

"Vy vould you do dad," the old haberdasher asked, a shot of suspicion energizing his veins, "if id's only vord $3,250.00?" he asked, again reaching for the certificate.

The broker, a quick thinking young man, who was no doubt ethically challenged, replied, "Oh, I don't know. It's old and I thought maybe I'd have it framed. How about if I give you $4,000.00 for it."

"No d'anks," Izzy replied. "I yam only de caredaker of dis documend. Id iss my responssibiliddy do save dis documend undil I can find oud vad id's really vord."

Once again, he reached for the document and the broker, after a rather lengthy hesitation, gave it one last try, "Four thousand cash! That's a great deal!"

He dodged Izzy's attempt at retrieving the document, and even though it was only a copy, heaved a sigh, lovingly holding it aginst his chest as if it was a new born baby. Begrudgingly, the disappointed yuppie surrendered it to the persistent old man.

Upon leaving the broker's office, Izzy pondered on the greedy behavior of the young stock broker. His mind, normally trusting of his fellow human beings, began to imagine the devious nature of other individuals he would encounter in trying to evaluate these items. The tangible gold coins, he knew from his essential knowledge of human nature, would cause the innate greed of those who might think they had an opportunity to possess these rare oddities to manifest itself in all sorts of inventive ways. He would have to be very careful in his dealings with people from now on.

At Temple on Saturday, in the nearby and much larger town of Greeneburg, he had the occasion to meet an acquaintance who was rumored to be one of the wealthiest men in the area. Despite the man's rather shoddy appearance, and distinctly unfashionable attire, Izzy agreed with the general opinion of his friends at Temple of the immense wealth of this man.

Arnold Schlusselstein was a merchant of some sort, perhaps an exporter, who lived in a huge, ornate, gated home, hidden from the street by a dense array of strange and wonderful foliage. When he was occasionally seen about the streets of Pine Ridge, Arnold was being chauffeured in a large, odd, old car, a black Bentley from the twenties, according to its design, with huge wheels covered by solid discs. This gave them the impression of strength. The stories of his vast wealth grew from the unusual ostentation of his home, from those few fortunates who had been inside, as well as the pervasive secrecy surrounding him.

But at Temple, Arnold seemed to relax his vigilance. He often mingled with the common folk, for despite the vast difference in standing, the people at the Temple were still his people. Izzy found an opening while he was socializing, and brazenly walked up to Arnold Schlusselstein. Izzy got right to the point and asked him how to go about determining the value of a thirty-year old stock certificate.

"Oy," said the quaint old man. "Foist, you don't trust dem stockbrokers. Dey vill trade and trade and trade, taking commission after commission, until you got nuddings left. If it's voith anyt'ing dey will try to schmooze it from you. I vould call de secretary of de company. I don't know how you find out de address, but dat's who youse should call foist." But then Arnold got distracted when a small child ran up to him and began pulling on his trouser leg. He turned his attention to the child and an expression of pure joy appeared on his face. As he patted the head of the urchin, he forgot all about Izzy.

Izzy again pondered this sage advice and decided it made sense. But how to find out the location of the secretary of the company was another story. He wandered out of the Temple and decided to walk into town. He often did a lot of his best thinking when he was walking. As he was strolling down the tree lined avenue lost in deep contemplation, he had an idea.

The following Monday morning he entered the sleazy young stock broker's office.

The young man recognized him, recalling the embarrassing incident of the day before. He watched him intently as if he was a potential thief, as Isadore entered the office. "I vant to buy vun hundred shares of stock in dis company," he announced as he waved the copy of the old stock certificate in front of the young man's face.

The broker was stunned. He was suspicious of this strange request, especially given the fact that Izzy had a much more valuable original issue certificate. The deal was made and Izzy was told he had to pay the $3,250.00 and a small broker's commission within five days. He was still smiling as he left the office, but the stockbroker's expression still retained the hint of his disappointment at not being able to wrangle the actual certificate from the old man.

Izzy got in his old car, a huge colorless boat of a Lincoln, its style characterized by a single straight line demarking the side from front to rear fender. Both doors opened outward from a center post. He still washed and shined it weekly, although there were a few bare spots where the paint had worn off and shiny metal shone through. He drove to nearby Greeneburg, where he knew there was a shop where the proprietor bought old gold and coins. He knew this because his old friend from Temple, David Mann, was the owner of the shop.

His mind was racing as he drove down the highway at his customary five miles an hour under the speed limit to the annoyance of a line of time starved drivers behind him. Eventually he arrived and parked near the store - about two feet from the curb. David was surprised but genuinely glad to see Izzy. "Well, well, well. What brings you here to Greeneburg, you old kvekzer?" he announced rather than asked.

They greeted each other warmly and after exchanging pleasantries and information about the status of their families, Izzy brought out the copies of the coins. David studied them carefully but said nothing. He got out a large catalogue and a magnifying glass and inspected first the copy, then the book, and repeated this action eight times, front and back. Finally, he put down the magnifying glass and slowly turned to Izzy.

"Where did you get these coins?" David asked simply, his voice displaying a hint of restrained emotion as he held up the photocopy.

"Dey are from de old lawyer's esdade, which I am execuding," Izzy responded.

The dealer grabbed Izzy's forearm and, furtively looking around, leaned his head close to Izzy's ear. "Listen, my friend. These things are worth millions. What we could do with 'em!" he exclaimed.

Izzy appeared to be interested and leaned forward, almost whispering, "Millions, you say. I don' believe id. So vad are dey agshully voith, David?"

The dealer hesitated, and again looked around conspiratorially, to see if anyone was watching and maybe try to horn in on the deal. He brought his face within an inch of Izzy's, and Izzy feared David would kiss him. He was known to be friendly like that. "Listen Izzy, they are worth what somebody will pay for them, that's all. They are so rare there is no market value for them. We need to bring them to an auction and advertise it like mad. Get every serious coin collector in the country to come. Some serious collectors will pay big for these coins. Or maybe, Iz, you should leave them with me, you know, on consignment."

Izzy didn't really see David wink, but it was there none the less. They were friends or at least as close to being friends as Izzy would let anyone be. But Izzy kept thinking of that hackneyed phrase, *What are friends for*? (He was only thinking it and he didn't have any accent in his thoughts). Indeed, what are friends for, if not to give one a terrific profit at your friend's expense? David still had a pseudo false grin on his face when Izzy responded, "I'll dink aboud id, David. I'll gif id a lod of doughd. You can bed on id." Of course, with lives fraught with dealing and commercial experiences, they both understood that was the end of it. Izzy had seen through David's feeble ploy. But it was OK. They were friends after all, weren't they?

Izzy had a worrisome thought, "Lissen David, dis has god do be our secred, jus' bedween us, you know. Don' dell any one. You never know. All dad crime. Jus' bedween us old friends, OK?"

Izzy left the store with mixed emotions. On the trip back to Pine Ridge, he pondered long and hard about the situation. David had not given him any real idea of the value of the coins, but he put a festering thought in the old merchant's head. An auction! He wondered if Molly McMasters, the Clerk, would authorize it.

When he returned to Pine Ridge, Izzy went to the office in the haberdashery where his son was busy checking inventory availability on the computer. "Can you find out a secredary of a company and anyd'ing about aucshuning coins on dad ding?" he asked, his voice full of doubt, pointing carelessly toward the computer. Izzy understood the basic concepts of computers but had lingering misgivings about the whole idea of being able to type a few characters into a machine and find out about anything you want.

It took only a few minutes for his son to come up with the name of the secretary and address of the company in the financial district in New York. It took just a little longer to find out information about coin auctions. Izzy was simply astounded and looked at his son with a new-found admiration. He then went to work.

Chapter 6

Meanwhile David Mann was thinking about the extreme rarity of the coins. He was astounded by the immense value of the coins portrayed in the pictures Izzy had brought him. They were worth millions, some of the rarest and most desirable coins he had ever seen, and he knew it would not be easy to get his hands on them. Just the thought of these rarest of coins being so near, and almost available, almost there for him to touch and feel, was about to drive him crazy with avarice. He had been an avid coin collector all his life. The awesome sensation of the rare and priceless coins tickling his fingers was the only thing that truly excited him. And the thought of these coins really got him excited. Titillated, even. His mind raced with all sorts of nefarious plans for obtaining the coins for himself.

He had known Isadore Shapiro a long time, though not that well, but well enough to consider him a friend. He knew him to be honest and responsible. But he also knew that Izzy would not let go of the coins until he had maximized their value, for that was his responsibility as executor and Izzy was nothing if not responsible. David suffered a great conflict in his soul as his conscience told him to be true to his friend, while that part of him that dearly loved gold schemed on how to get his hands on the coins.

David had also heard the rumors about the estate of the eccentric old lawyer. Everyone was just amazed that O'Halloran was leaving his net worth to the Temple of God. But David was acquainted with Pastor Ronnie Conner too. Conner had come into his shop on several occasions with various coins he had received, probably fished out of the collection basket. They were usually not particularly valuable coins, but interesting none the less. Some foreign coins, an occasional buffalo nickel and, surprisingly, quite a few Barber quarters, minted over a hundred years ago. Some old lady must have been saving them up for generations, and now, probably well into senile dementia, started putting them in the collection basket.

Mann knew Conner was the epitome of greed, but he also knew that Conner was not a true coin collector and had no idea of the actual value coins could have. David had usually made a considerable profit on the coins Pastor Ronnie had brought him in the past.

With a nagging sense of betrayal eating subtly at his sense of honor, David called Ronnie Conner. "Hey, church man," he said. "I heard the old lawyer in Pine Ridge that died, had a nice coin collection. Maybe worth some money. When you get it, bring to me, why don't you? I'll see what I can do for you." Thinking back on his conversation with Izzy, Mann could kick himself for suggesting an auction. If he went the auction route, Mann would never see the coins.

Pastor Conner was intrigued. He never really trusted the old coin dealer, but always thought he got a good price for the coins he brought him. *What kind of coin collection could the odd ball lawyer have accumulated?* Nevertheless, Conner assured David he'd bring the coins in when he got them. However, the pastor may have had his fingers crossed behind his back as he made this assurance.

But he thought about the odd telephone call. Why would David Mann be calling him about coins that he had never seen and did not have? The pastor, practiced in the art of greed himself, knew avarice when he saw it. *David wanted to get his hands on those coins because they must be very valuable.* He resolved to find out more about them.

Chapter 7

Izzy went back to the clerk's office and once again made a photocopy of both sides of the old stock certificate. He then wrote a letter in his own strange hand to the secretary of the company explaining his situation as executor of the estate. He wanted to know if the stock had ever split, if dividends that had not been paid out, had accumulated, and what the actual present value of the stock was. After mailing the letter and the copy of the stock certificate he walked over to the Register of Deeds Office.

He asked the duly elected Register of Deeds, a frail older man wearing an imperfectly hand tied red bow tie, to help him find out who owned the house at 213 Main Street. The Register of Deeds, Mr. Arvil Forrest, had worked in the office since he was eighteen and succeeded to the top spot when his predecessor was found dead in the deed vault. It was his sole ambition to be what he was, and he took pride in his total knowledge of the property records under his care.

"Hmm," said Arvil Forrest, when Izzy told him what he wanted, "I seem to remember something odd about the house where Hamish O'Halloran lived." He stroked his chin thoughtfully as he tried to remember. Then, with what seemed like an inspiration, he went to the viewer and put in a reel he took from an indexed film rack. He peered at the viewer as copies of deeds and other recorded documents sped by. After images blurred by, it began to slow as it neared the target address. When it did, the image came to a stop. "Now I remember!" he said. "This was a really strange one. Take a look at this deed."

Izzy looked at the deed. Something seemed strange, but he didn't know what it was. "So vad iss id?" he asked.

Mr. Forrest explained. "When Old Mr. O'Halloran bought this house, he bought it from a circus clown named Mr. Funny Bones. That was his actual name. He had it legally changed from whatever his given name was, and that was the name on the deed when the Rolley family heirs deeded it to him. Old man Rolley built the home around the turn of the century on land that had been in the family for generations. I was only an assistant here when O'Halloran bought the old house, and I questioned Mr. Wood about it. He was the Register of Deeds at the time. He told me it sure was strange, but Mr. Funny Bones was the clown's legal name. The catch is that the clown was a real practical joker. At the closing when he sold the house to Mr. O'Halloran, which was on a Friday, he signed his name in invisible ink. Then he must have handed the pen with the invisible ink in it to the Notary because her signature isn't there either, but her seal is readable. The problem is she's dead now. By the time we sent the deed to be filmed the following Monday, the signature had disappeared and so had the clown. Nobody knew what to do, so we didn't do anything. Mr. O'Halloran has lived in the house ever since and paid his taxes on it regularly, so nobody ever said anything. I don't think the old lawyer ever knew the house was not actually in his name. I guess it didn't matter until now."

"So vad I godda do now?" asked Izzy.

"I don't know. I suppose you'll have to hire a lawyer," was the reply. "Maybe, Mr. Shapiro, you need to get a very good lawyer. This could turn into a real can of worms."

"Oy vey. Iss nod anyd'ing easy wid dis execution d'ing?" said the frustrated Isadore Shapiro, as he left the office of the Register of Deeds, while Arvil Forrest, the dedicated bureaucrat, scratched his head.

Chapter 8

When Mr. Shapiro returned to his store, he was exhausted, mentally and physically. He was not a young man and had never been what you might call athletic, or even close to being physically fit. He walked into the office where his son was once again busy on the computer, and plopped in a very old, very worn, leather overstuffed chair. After heaving a great sigh, he turned to his son and asked, "So how's business?"

The younger Shapiro replied resignedly, "Slow, Pop. Slow. You know what? I don't think it's ever going to get any better. We need to do something. Sell the store. Sell the inventory to a factor. Something. We can't compete with the huge new bargain basement stores, selling all that cheap stuff from China and south of the border. We are almost out of money, Pop"

Izzy gave another sigh. "I know. I know. Dad's vy I'm doing dis execudor d'ing for de lawyer's esdade. Dere's a lod ov money bud nuddings iss easy in id. Every d'ing iss god problems. Problems dad I don' know how do fix. Now I godda ged a lawyer. Oy vey."

He explained the predicament about the estate to his son, the coins, the title to the house, and then he said more prophetically than he could ever realize. "Who knows vad else iss goink do happen to mess d'ings up."

Wouldn't you know it, just then the telephone rang. Izzy picked up the receiver. It was Pastor Ronnie Conner, the high potentate of the Temple of God.

"Mistah Isadore Shapiro?" he boomed bombastically, emphasizing the "dore" in Isadore as if it was the door to Hell itself. He went on without the normal pleasantries two distant acquaintances might be expected to normally resort to on such an occasion. "I unnastan' you got some valuable things that belongs to me – ah – mah church." His speech was loud and slow, and he placed undue emphasis on certain syllables such as 'val'."

It was clear that Pastor Conner was neither a man to mince words, nor allow mere mortals to stand in his way. At first Izzy was taken aback by the pastor's harsh directness. But he had had a rough day, and this hassle was just the icing on the cake. His hackles were raised as he retorted in no uncertain terms.

"Lissen here. Ven I ged de OK from de clerk, you'll ged vad's comink do you. Ride now, I d'ink dad's nudding. I don' d'ink dad Demple of yours is goink do be found voithy. How do you know dese dings, anyvay?"

Pastor Ronnie was stunned by the brazen, heretical response, and all sorts of anti-Semitic thoughts raced through his self-righteous mind. Flustered, he finally settled on a retort. "We'll see about that. Molly McMasters is a fine upstanding member of mah flock. I will have her get in touch with you right away. Good day, suh," he said as he slammed the phone down without so much as a by your leave.

Izzy smiled as he thought of the pastor, red faced, sputtering and fuming to whoever had the misfortune to cross his path at that moment. Then a wave of worry washed over him as he envisioned the cleric calling the clerk to have her do his bidding. Not more than a minute later, well maybe five to be precise, the phone rang again. In a pique of prescience, Izzy knew who it was.

"Hello, Molly," he said without fanfare as he spoke into the receiver he had just picked up.

"How did you know it was me, Mr. Shapiro?" she asked politely.

"Ah, Molly, jus' an ol' man's induition. Mus' have been a liddle boid vad dol' me."

"Mr. Shapiro, we need to have a meeting on this O'Halloran estate," she politely advised him. "Can you come into my office tomorrow morning at, say, ten o'clock?"

"Sure. I'll be dere. Vad I should bring?"

"A preliminary inventory of his estate would be just fine," she replied and after salutations and other meek politenesses, she hung up.

"Sonny, boychik," Izzy said paternally as he looked over at his son who was staring at him with a concerned, questioning look. "You know a good lawyer?"

After a few telephone calls Izzy had an appointment with a lawyer, one he had never heard of. He prided himself on knowing the name and shirt size of every man in Pine Ridge, but he couldn't even picture Mr. J. Riddle Bowes. Nevertheless, promptly at 5:00 p.m. he walked through a nondescript portal announcing the office of Mr. Bowes in small but strong lettering. Mr. Bowes, it seemed, had not been too busy too have a consultation with Pine Ridge's only haberdasher.

Bowes was young. He was small. He was bespectacled in wire rimmed glasses. And he was neat, impeccably neat. Despite the fact he appeared to be no more than a freshman in high school, and his blond hair and pink complexion gave him the appearance of never having shaved, there was something about him that exuded an air of confidence. Izzy smiled warmly as he shook Mr. Bowes' hand and was shown to a serviceable, but not too comfortable leather chair in his office.

After Izzy explained the situation and the need to go armed to the clerk's office the next day, Mr. Bowes smiled to himself.

"Mr. Shapiro, there are a few matters I am professionally required to divulge to you. I do not think they rise to the level of presenting a conflict of interest for me in this case, but that will be up to you to decide. First, it was my own father's brother, my Uncle Larry, who owned that house and pulled the practical joke on Mr. O'Halloran with the invisible ink. I can still remember my father telling me how hard he laughed when Larry told him about his little practical joke. My uncle went by his first initial, L. for Larry, L. Bowes, and everybody called him 'elbows" in school. He was kind of gangly. When he started playing the clown professionally, he thought it an easy transition to go from 'elbows' to 'funny bones.'

He continued on, "My Uncle Larry died a couple of years ago, but I think it shouldn't be any problem to get the deed reformed. The second thing might be a little more dicey. I do not belong to the Temple of God. I am a religious man to be sure, but the church I attend is in Greeneburg. It is a small Methodist church with few trappings, and no ostentation whatsoever. However, my cousin on my mother's side is one of the assistants to Pastor Ronnie Conner, a true devotee, if you will. I am sure he will put pressure on me in any way he can think of, when he learns I represent you as the executor of this estate. So I want you to think about these things before you retain me."

Izzy mused a little bit, but he was still smiling. "Dad's funny. Mr. Funny Bones. L. Bowes. I like dad. So you don' dink it vould be a problem do fix de deed?"

"No," the young lawyer responded matter-of-factly, using his index finger to push back his glasses when they slid almost to the end of his small ski jump nose. "We would have to file an action in Court, a Special Proceeding. There would be no Defendant and I can't think of any one who could claim any legitimate right to object. Even the Temple wouldn't object because if they did and won, they would still have no right to the property. You see, their right can only come through Hamish O'Halloran's ownership. Just think. Who would own the property if not Hamish O'Halloran? Oh, wait," he paused, frowning as it slowly

54

dawned on him. "I would. I am the only heir of my Uncle Larry."

Izzy's smile faded. A wistful expression clouded over his eyes as he realized what the young lawyer was talking about. If the deed was void and the property reverted back to the clown and the attorney was the clown's only heir, Mr. J. Riddle Bowes would own the house, and at least arguably, would have a claim to everything that was in it, the ownership of which could not actually be traced to Mr. O'Halloran. Izzy had no choice. He had to hire some other lawyer.

They parted with a smile and a handshake, but Izzy sensed sadly that the friendly and competent young lawyer had just signed up as his adversary. He walked back to the store even more depressed. Nothing was easy with this estate.

Chapter 9

At ten o' clock sharp the next morning, Izzy was at the clerk's office waiting patiently for Molly McMasters in the small waiting room. He looked around the room furnished with a few puke green vinyl captain's chairs and a magazine table festooned with terrifically outdated copies of Field and Stream and Newsweek. He had not been able to meet with any other attorney, and so he was there by himself, waiting expectantly.

By 10:20 a.m. Molly had still not come out of her office. Izzy got up and started to walk around nervously, finally drifting up to the counter. He was just about to ask one of the deputy clerks for some advice, when the door to Molly's office opened and out walked Pastor Ronnie Conner, resplendent in his royal blue sharkskin suit, a pink and purple Italian silk tie sporting a modernistic design, and a gigantic gold pinky ring that must have weighed three pounds.

Izzy's jaw dropped. Pastor Ronnie ignored him as he arrogantly strode by without the faintest acknowledgment or even recognition of his presence. A few seconds later, Molly stuck her head out of her office and said, "Mr. Shapiro, you can come in now."

He did and without being invited, he sat down in an overstuffed chair sitting directly across from her with only the government issue faux walnut desk between them. It was devoid of files, paper, paraphernalia and other accouterments. He eyed her expectantly.

Molly cleared her throat, then cleared her throat again. She was visibly perplexed, perhaps even upset.

Izzy just sat there with a curious expression on his face and when the silence finally began to be seriously uncomfortable for both, Izzy said, "Vad iss id, Molly? Vad's de madder?"

Molly's eyes were red. She said, "I just don't know what to do. Pastor Ronnie wants you to turn over the assets of the estate to him, now."

"Molly, you know I can'd do dad," responded Izzy dolefully. "Foisd, I haven' even adverdised id yed for de debds, even dough I doub' id, dere iss any. Second, I don' know whad de house is woid or even if id is de lawyer's house. Dere iss no name on de deed. I godda figger oud how do fix dad. Doid, I'm finding new asseds ever day, I godda find de value of. Coins, sdocks, who knows vad else. Und you know vad, Molly, I'm nod so sure de Demple is woidy. I godda figure oud how do do dad. I godda figure oud whad coun's, dere. Here is de lis' you ask me for."

He was about to get up to take his leave, when Molly, almost tearfully, asked him to stay a minute. She begged him, "What do I tell Pastor Ronnie? He is such a good man and he says he needs the money for all the good he has planned for it. I don't know what to do."

Izzy knew what to do. "Molly," he said with conviction, "You know vad do do. You're a good poisson. You godda do vad iss righd." With that he got up and left the office of the distraught clerk. His day was already better than the previous one.

He was about to leave the courthouse, when he ran into Billy "Benedict" Arnold who had just transferred the tedious task of prosecuting plenty of petty misdemeanants to an unsuspecting neophyte prosecutor. He told her it would be great experience, learning on the run.

"Hey Izzy," said the bland Billy, "You got time for a cup of coffee?"

"Sure, vy nod?' responded Izzy, for as a matter of fact, he did not know what he was going to do just then, or where he was going to go.

They proceeded to The Legal Lunch, the greasy spoon that had been the gathering place for courthouse personnel for more than a generation. It was a standing joke among the locals that before 11:00 a.m. the place was universally referred to by the courthouse habitués as the Court House Coffee, because it just wouldn't be right for anybody to eat lunch before eleven. Everything at Court House Coffee was not bad. The food was not bad, the prices were not bad, the waitresses were not bad. Those things were also not good.

They settled into a booth with cheap vinyl seats on both sides of the table, torn and leaking stuffing in an unappetizing manner, so it didn't matter who sat on which side. Billy ordered a cheese Danish and coffee, Izzy, a bagel with cream cheese and tea. Both knew that neither was an adept conversationalist, so they just sat there and munched and sipped for a while.

After a decent, if not prolonged, interval, Izzy, with a full mouth, said, "I need a good lawyer for diss esdade I am executing. You know vun I could hire?"

"Well, Sparrow's out. He and I witnessed the will in the Clerk's office in order to probate it," replied Billy after an interlude in which he thoroughly masticated a bite of cheese Danish. "Maybe that young pup, Bowes," he mused.

"No, I arready dalked do him," said Izzy, his mouth full of bagel again. "Hiss uncle vass de clown vad sold de house to de lawyer. Also, I need a lawyer vad doesn' belong do da Demple of God."

"Well, then, how about, Jimmy G. He's a papist, so I know for sure he's got no love lost for Pastor Ronnie and his group of hair sprayed evangelists," replied the venerable prosecutor.

"Aha. Dad vun's de Eye-dalian boy, yeh?" queried Izzy.

"Yeah, but he's a smart one and a good lawyer. I've had plenty of cases with him. I know," said Billy. "He's just not very impressive to look at. And he has this strange way of ticking off the Judges without half trying. But they still have some respect for him."

Chapter 10

So Izzy made an appointment and went to see Jimmy G, which was short for Giacogiavonni which nobody, but nobody in Pine Ridge, including any of the judges, could come close to pronouncing, hence Jimmy G. Jimmy was a transplant, or more appropriately, a refugee from New York. His escape from that metropolis came about when his family members became embroiled in a caper on the wrong side of the law, that's right, on the Feds side against the "Family." He and his dopey cousins had no choice but to high tail it to the good ole South, where they were safe from the impetuous night dangers of the neighborhood street gangs, drive by shootings, and other forms of inventive strong-arm retribution by the Mafiosi. When he and his family members broke the code of silence, *omerta*, by becoming *cascitunni,* informants, Brooklyn, in fact, the entire New York metropolitan area, was as safe for them as an injured bird in a yard full of cats.

Jimmy could never shake his New York roots. They stayed with him like a coat of paint. He had the most awful Brooklyn accent which was only natural since he was from Brooklyn and went to Brooklyn College and Brooklyn Law School. He even named his kid Brooklyn, but nobody knew whether she was a long-haired boy or a tom-girl because she got in so many fights, and could certainly hold her own, even against the toughest bully.

It was déjà vu all over again for the two iconoclasts, misfits in the *ancien regime* of the old South. They were familiar with each other, at least with the stereotypes of each other, from an age gone by. If the stereotypes held, each thought, they could trust each other to be what they seemed to be. This was a trust that they were both comfortable with.

Izzy explained the case, and Jimmy rubbed his hands together like a kid on Christmas. *The Temple of God, no less. Justice! There is a God after all,* thought Jimmy. But he got awfully quiet when he began to hear about the assets. A house with no name, sort of like the song. Unique coins and old shares of stock. This was not going to be a piece of cake. He would certainly earn his fee, just in trying to figure out the value of these items, let alone having to deal with the vultures circling overhead, waiting for the opportunity to enjoy the ripe feast.

After they agreed on a fee arrangement, Izzy left, comforted by the knowledge that the incorruptible Jimmy G would be flying his banner in the fight against the indomitable Temple of God. A thought had earlier crossed his mind, that it might be easier just to give in to Pastor Ronnie. After all, who was going to object? Certainly, not Molly McMasters.

But Izzy was blessed, or cursed depending on how you looked at it, with an inborn sense of justice. He sensed that beneath that veneer of religiosity, Pastor Ronnie, and necessarily, his entire church, was a powerful force of greed, even if it was widely touted as a powerful force for the greater good. Izzy just couldn't see the goodness that had been so vaunted by Pastor Ronnie. True, the Temple of God was a glorious edifice, dripping with gold trappings, purportedly exemplifying the magnificence of God. Ronnie himself was always attired in the most expensive, if inelegant, outfits. But Izzy was not aware of any actual good that had been done, for he did not consider the self-aggrandizement of Ronnie and the Temple as being an actual good deed.

Izzy contemplated on how he expected to prove or disprove that the Temple was actually worthy, the quirky requirement old O'Halloran had sagely put in his will. He pondered on the meaning of the word 'worthy.' *Something of value,* he thought. But what value? Certainly not necessarily monetary value. He did not think that could possibly be what O'Halloran meant by worthy. Maybe he meant worthy in the sense that the church had to be honorable. If that is what he meant, the estate would surely go to the Institute for the Treatment of Canines Humanely (ITCH), after he got his cut, of course. He smiled at the thought of the ever-increasing value of the percentage he was to receive. He resolved to look up the word 'worthy' in the dictionary.

Meanwhile, Jimmy G dashed off a letter to Pastor Ronnie, and sent a copy to Molly McMasters. Tact was not the attorney's strong suit. In fact, he had often been told that his tactlessness was quite offensive to polite Southern society. But, he had reasoned, he was from Brooklyn. Brooklynites were famous for their straightforwardness. If being straightforward offended some people, so be it. So in the letter, he brazenly told Ronnie to stay away from the clerk's office, and not to try to convince Molly to do anything related to her job for his church.

The Temple was a conditional legatee, the lawyer told the Pastor, and he would just have to wait until the estate was settled and the condition fulfilled before the church could get the money. He hinted in his not so subtle way, that attempting to use undue influence or interference with the proceedings would be a significant factor in the determinaition of whether the Temple was considered worthy, in the final analysis. Jimmy conveyed the distinct impression to the colorful pastor, that it would be he, Jimmy G, the attorney for the estate of Hamish O'Halloran, who would make the ultimate determination of worthiness.

Pastor Conner was irate as he read the letter. He was somewhat decidedly un-Christian concerning certain pejorative prejudices he harbored, and attorneys, Italians, Yankees, and especially New Yorkers, and that despicable sub-class – Brooklynites, fell into some of the various categories upon which his prejudices were heaped.

Consequently, his irateness was multiplied by four when he read the letter. Steam literally poured from his ears, and his face became a hue of red not seen since the Pope's funeral when the world's Cardinals with their bright red miters, gathered in solemn splendor.

How dare that infidel cross me, Pastor Ronnie Conner, leader of the vast and faithful flock of the Temple of God, now quite incensed, thought. *That subhuman papist, I will show him, as God is my witness. I will carry the standard of God, my very own God, into the crusade for right and justice and trounce that irreverent and foul Eye-talian, New York lawyer.* Ronnie was on a roll. He even thought in the overblown oratorical style he had so effectively used in calling the flock to his shelter. Actually, he believed fervently in his invective.

He ordered one of his assistants to gain him an audience with the most competent, most powerful lawyer in the largest law firm in Greeneburg, for the puny village of Pine Ridge was too small and too inconsequential to spawn large and powerful law firms, or even a branch of such an institution. He wanted to trounce Jimmy G, that Italian pissant, and grind him into the proverbial dust. Charitable thoughts eluded Pastor Ronnie when anyone stood in the way of accumulation of riches - for the Temple.

Several days later, Ronnie made a grand entrance into the offices of Armitage, Grace and Powers, LLC, a law firm of 100 mostly Ivy League educated attorneys. They represented all the major players in the area, from the Mayor and the city of Greeneburg to virtually all the major corporations in the area. Sometimes, they even represented one against the other, a policy which often raised the eyebrows, if not the hackles, of objective observers with any ethical sense at all.

The firm had a long-standing policy it used in determining whether there was a conflict of interest in a case. The attorney who had any doubt or question of whether a conflict existed would go to the cemetery and kneel at the crypt of the firm's venerable founder, Arbuckle A. Armitage, now long dead, but whose famous name lives on in infamy, emblazoned on the firm's marquee.

The crypt was a magnificent marble edifice replete with carved stone lilies, angels and seraphim. The attorney would state the facts and then ask for a sign from the esteemed deceased to indicate the existence of a conflict. None would ever be forthcoming, of course. Rumor had it, however, that once, in the distant past, not too long after the venerable lawyer had succumbed and was duly interred, one of the firm's lawyers visited the grave to show his respects. Idly, but perhaps out of a curious respect for the old man, the lawyer asked such a question. A bolt of lightning suddenly erupted, cleaving a nearby crepe myrtle in two, and scaring the wits out of the stunned attorney. *A conflict it is, then, for sure*, thought the frightened lawyer, quickly converted to the ranks of the true believers at the powerful message which could only have come from God. Thus, the rigid ritual by members of the firm for the determination of all conflicts of interest, henceforth, began.

Without having to wait, not even a second, Pastor Ronnie was shown into the cavernous office of one of the firm's partners, an esteemed trial lawyer named B. Swarthmore Fotheringham, III. He insisted on being called by the initials B.F. but as might be expected, other than when one was actually in his presence, and often even then, he was universally referred to by a profane perversion of his first two initials, B.S. No one actually knew what the "B" stood for although that, too, was universally perceived in a profane and pejorative manner. The same kind of respect was handed down to his son, also a member of the litigation team, a swaggering, good looking young man, B. Swarthmore Fotheringham, IV, affectionately referred to as Son of B.

Fotheringham had a reputation as a cold blooded, ruthless, and efficient litigator. Despite his privileged, blue blood upbringing, and his Ivy League credentials, he was a fierce competitor. The niceties of legal ethics were pushed to the limit and often beyond, in his unrelenting quest for victory in the courtroom, and the fine notoriety that went along with it.

An instant kinship was formed between the two, lawyer and client, as Pastor Ronnie entered the grand office in a virtually regal manner. The office appeared to have been transmogrified straight from a princely Victorian library. The huge, ornate, nineteenth century, walnut partner's desk sat on a magnificent red and blue Persian rug, in which solid gold strands had been cleverly woven into the rich, intricate pattern. This opulence was presided over by a high, ornate, plaster ceiling. A superfluous banker's lamp cast an effusive light on an ornately tooled leather blotter on which lay an expensive fountain pen.

The large office was devoid of clutter and papers. Floor to ceiling bookshelves contained ancient, leather bound classics, and even a few rare old law books. The furnishings were of a rich, maroon Moroccan leather. The whole effect of the office was purposely designed to convey confidence and success. The actual result was something different. The reaction of most clients was to immediately reach for their wallets to make sure they were still there and intact. They sensed that whatever was in their wallets would soon be transported to that of the attorney's.

B.S. was a stately man in his early sixties. His silvery white hair rested in a casually coifed example of tonsorial splendor. Piercing blue eyes stared intimidatingly from beneath bushy gray brows over an aquiline nose of which even the great Julius Caesar would have been envious. His slightly cleft chin jutted just enough to show he meant business. His charcoal gray worsted wool suit reeked of luxury, and a contrasting, tasteful red and light gray silk rep tie added to the effect.

Pastor Ronnie stated his case to the attorney as a slight, gray haired stenographer busily took notes, memorializing the conversation in shorthand. B.S. had known of O'Halloran, of course. He made it his business to know everything about every lawyer in Greeneburg and the surrounding areas, especially anything his investigators could dig up which might be used to his advantage in a case.

He wasn't surprised as Ronnie began detailing the assets he had learned from Molly and about the otherwise apparent paucity of the estate. But as Ronnie went on, old B.S.'s jutting jaw dropped. He almost assumed a pose which might be characterized as undignified if he hadn't caught himself as a slight head nod from the stenographer brought him to his senses.

Coins and stocks worth untold millions, an estate whose hidden wealth could be worth a fortune! B.S. began to think mercenary thoughts of intrigue and stratagems as to how to maximize his fee. Even a disgustingly exorbitant hourly rate of $500.00 would not yield enough; a contingency fee was the proper fee arrangement, the arrogant attorney thought, long before Pastor Ronnie had fully and ornately stated his case.

When Ronnie had concluded his description of the case, as he knew it, involuntarily unable to refrain from the excesses of speech and the exaggeration which characterized his whole persona, B.S. responded in a grave and somber manner. He detailed the intricate legal problems inherent in such a complex and difficult matter. He outlined the financial resources of the Institute for the Treatment of Canines Humanely (ITCH) whose infinite and ubiquitous direct mailings had swelled their coffers making them a formidable opponent. In a solemn and articulate voice, with a slight trace of an affected New England accent, a vestige of the prep schools and Ivy League universities he had attended in amassing his impressive educational credentials, B.S. outlined the pitfalls they would undoubtedly face. Difficulties stemming from the executor's attorney, the unscrupulous Eye-talian lawyer from Brooklyn with his unethical street fighting techniques, from the vagueness of the simplicity of the provisions of the will itself, and from the total uncertainty of the evaluation of worthiness and the tribunal that would be deciding the issue. Without saying so, or even expressly hinting of such an evil recourse, somehow the esteemed attorney gave the indication there would be palms that had to be greased, important influential palms, and lots and lots of grease.

At last, with the normally supremely confident Pastor Ronnie groveling in uncertainty and suspicion, B.S. Fotheringham, III, lowered the boom. "This case will demand the vast resources of my firm, which as you know, is the largest and most successful firm in the area. I, and many of my highly trained associates, graduates of Rhodes and Oxford Universities in England, as well as that bastion of American legal education, the Ivy League, will have to spend countless hours in research and preparation in order to assure we will prevail. We will have to do everything that is humanly possible, no, we will have to do more, everything that is absolutely necessary to sway the judges or jury to decide in favor of our position and thereby insure victory. Too much is at stake, for the Temple of God," he paused for effect to make sure the enormity of the situation was indelibly etched on Pastor Ronnie's psyche, "for you to consider even for a moment, any other minimally trained attorney to act on your, er, the Temple's behalf."

He let Pastor Ronnie stew on that a bit, especially at that little hint of a venal path to justice, that kind of justice which would inure to his favor. B.S. sure knew his craft, he did, and the good Pastor, despite being practiced in the art himself, was a real pigeon. After a pregnant interval during which Ronnie pictured, somewhat vaguely, the vast resources of this premier law firm being expended on his, Pastor Ronnie's, own special case, B.S. continued, "Of course, in a case of this magnitude, there can be no defeat. We must have victory for you and the magnificent Temple of God. Therefore, I will link my future, and that of my prestigious law firm, to the success of this case. There will be no fee whatsoever unless we are victorious. But in the event of victory, my fee will be 30% of the proceeds." When Pastor Ronnie didn't flinch at the figure or appear to be stunned, B.S. continued, "40% if the case has to be tried before a jury, and of course, that will only happen if we cannot convince the executor of the futility of a trial." B.S. smiled slightly for he well knew that his chances of convincing the executor of the time of day was minimal and the larger per centage was sure to be his.

"The reason for the increase in the fee is not only the significantly increased amount of time and resources which will have to be expended in preparing for, and conducting litigation in Court, there are the other considerations..." He winked surreptitiously, knowingly, at Pastor Ronnie, a gesture unequivocally understood by the unprincipled cleric.

The stenographer left, and returned shortly, very shortly, with a formal, impressively typed fee contract, printed on high quality rag paper, a document with the contingent fee set forth prominently in bold type. Pastor Ronnie gave it a quick glance, trusting the attorney as a man of prominence and estimation, and heaved a big sigh as he signed the agreement.

As the pastor, bubbling over with confidence and excitement at the thought of the certain victory, was being chauffered back to his manse in his powder blue Lincoln limousine, the one with the gold trim, he began to experience a vague discomfort, which centered, he realized, on the distinguished attorney. He was not sure he liked that contingent fee agreement. He should have negotiated the fee, or used his accustomed influence, his presumed connection with God, to get an agreement that was more in his, and God's, favor. But, he reasoned, it certainly did give the lawyer an added incentive to do everything he could to win the case. And 60 to 70% of that estate was still a lot of money, for the Temple, of course. A nagging thought, simmering in the dark recesses of his mind, questioned whether he needed an attorney at all.

The battle lines were set. Jimmy G had sent his letter warning the pastor to back off. The proverbial ball was now in the Court of the high-priced attorney, senior partner in the esteemed law firm of Armitage, Grace and Powers, Limited Liability Corp.

Just then, at the prestigious law firm, B. S. walked into the office of one of the associates on the litigation team and tossed the record of the interview his stenographer had just transcribed, on her cluttered desk. The associate, a haggard looking, thin blond with bags under her eyes and stringy, unkempt, shoulder length hair, hid behind a massive pile of folders and papers on her desk in her cubby hole of an office. She looked up as the haughty, impeccable senior partner walked into her miniscule sphere of influence, and picking up the papers, looked at him questioningly.

"Get familiar with this, Margaret," he said contemptuously, for he disdained to deal with the wage slaves, "and prepare a complaint." Without any further explanation, he pivoted in a pseudo military fashion, and walked out.

Margaret Ann Young, for that was her name, carefully began to read the record of B.S.'s interview with the pastor. She was an intelligent neophyte, who had gone to law school harboring illusions of grandeur. Her goal then, like so many starry eyed naivelings, imbued with the milk of human kindness, ideas of world peace, ending human suffering, and feeding and clothing all mankind, was to make the world a better place. She had excelled academically, and had significantly participated in loads of do-gooder projects, and was even the driving force behind quite a few of them. She was a real collegiate superstar.

Naturally, upon graduating in the top five in her class, she jumped at the well-paying job offered by Armitage, Grace. Naivete, however, blanketed her idealistic vision, and she was soon relegated to the cubicles, along with dozens of other brilliant young attorneys. Their mission, the same for all of them, was to grind out inane boiler plate legal documents for which the partners would charge boat loads. Upon success in accomplishing these kind of mindless tasks, after a couple of years, they would be promoted to the mind sapping, crushing and boring legal research team, only to have their dreams and personalities erased by the oppressive hours and demands of demeaning work. Legal research was a euphemism. Digging deep enough, any lawyer could find cases to support whichever side of a case she wanted it to.

In time, the diligent and sycophantic, having sold their souls and their individuality, for that matter, to the devil, would be formed in the firm's corporate image, with production, that is, financial production, being their *raison d'etre*. Fading memories of past idealism and working for the good of mankind would be but a halting vestige of their idealistic youth.

Margaret was not yet totally jaded. She still harbored incipient dreams of altruistic service to mankind. She was convinced, in the deep and uncomprehending recesses of her mind, that she, Margaret Ann Young, could actually save the world.

Fueled in part by a slavish, even somewhat sexual, devotion to the head of her litigation team, the charismatic B.S., she continued to sacrifice her being to the firm and its causes. She put down the legal brief she had been concentrating on and read the record of the interview. She knew of Pastor Ronnie, of course, but had mixed feelings about him. Somehow his ridiculous appearance and trappings did not coincide with her mental image of the modern-day saint or savior. She had yet to learn that some people were riddled with some of the seven deadlies, of which avarice was the most popular these days, just barely beating out pride and lust. But she had not made up her mind about him, and still considered Pastor Ronnie Conner, at least potentially, to be a man of God and a good man.

Margaret had not heard about O'Halloran and his estate. She did not know of him as a lawyer and became increasingly interested as she read the report. *This is so odd,* she said half aloud to her self. *I wonder just how this is going to play out.*

After a few telephone calls, she had a copy of the will, the preliminary inventory, and a copy of the entire estate file, courtesy of the firm's well paid contact in the clerk's office, a pimply faced lad who was enamored of the shapely Margaret, who happily faxed them to her. She began to do a little research on the procedural issues such as just what exactly the role of the executor was and when a provisional legatee could expect his bequest. She also set out to find what constituted a determination of 'worthiness,' and just who was to make the decision.

The next day, her intense research completed, and the bags under her eyes significantly baggier, she began a memorandum to Mr. Fotheringham, and prepared a draft of the complaint. The complaint was the document that started the law suit and in this case, did not name a Defendant, but was called simply *"In re Will of O'Halloran."*

When she was finished, she shook her head as she thought about the results of her endeavors. From the maze of associates' cubicles crammed into the attic, she walked down the several flights of stairs to the palatial office of her mentor, a man she wanted to admire and like, but just couldn't bring herself to actually arrive at that state, yet. But she kept trying.

She should have used the intercom, because he wasn't there. "Playing golf," was the terse explanation of his secretary as Margaret handed the elegant and attractive woman the legal brief and complaint.

The next day, Margaret had been diligently and responsibly at work for several hours when the now superbly tanned senior partner barged into her office. "What is this?" he demanded.

"That," she explained defensively and with more than a hint of disdain, "is the complaint you asked for, and a brief on the research I did."

"All this crap says, is that there is no precedent on the issues of the definition of worthy and who is to make the determination," he boomed irascibly. "I want an answer!"

Margaret hesitated and then assumed an air of indignation. *Here it goes, my career with this firm, but I just don't care any more. I can't stand his rudeness, boorishness and inconsiderateness.* She glared at him and said, as if she was talking to a retard, "That is because there isn't one. I am sure you don't want me to invent the law where there isn't any. There is not one damn word defining what constitutes what "worthy" is, and who decides it in any of the case law in the entire fifty states and all the federal jurisdictions. It is simply a case of first impression, Mr. B.S. Fotheringham."

"It's B.F.," he corrected her with an air of perturbation, as he plopped down in the lone straight back and highly uncomfortable chair in her tiny cubicle, the wind gone out of his blustering sails. "What do you suggest we do, Margaret?"

She was a bit taken aback by the sudden change in his demeanor, a slight acquiescence of respect creeping under his supercilious façade. "All we can do is file the complaint and ask that the matter be decided by the Clerk, who is of course the Judge of Probate, instead of by a Superior Court Judge or jury. But it won't take much for opposing counsel to get it before a judge, instead."

"But does a beneficiary have standing to sue before the estate has been administered?" he asked plaintively, surprising Margaret by demonstrating an actual understanding of a legal principle.

"No, she responded with growing confidence, "the Church and Pastor Ronnie Conner do not have standing. If we file a law suit, the case should be peremptorily bounced as soon as they file a Motion."

Fotheringham grimaced as he comprehended the import of what she had said. What he understood was that if he took the course of action implicit in Margaret's evaluation of the case, there was no way he was going to get the fee he had quoted, or any fee at all in the near future for that matter. This would especially be the case if the executor was allowed to plod along administering the estate at his own pace.

He had to think. He had to salvage what he could of that gorgeous potential fee. He looked at Margaret Young, standing there haughtily with her hands still on her hips, glaring at him. He sensed this honest and sensible associate was the first obstacle he would have to overcome.

A ray of sunlight suddenly reflected off her blond hair, recently shampooed that morning. The result presented her in a professional, well groomed, almost angelic manner, a look she had expressly prepared just to impress her arrogant boss in the event she did run across him in person. It was too early for her hair to have become unkempt and oily from constantly running her fingers through it, her agitation and deep anxiety rampant as she nervously pondered some unassailable legal point.

The effect of the soft sunlight on her golden hair though, rather than to convey professionalism, aroused a pleasantly familiar emotion in B. S. Fotheringham, III. All of a sudden, he experienced a new found emoton for the young associate, as an atavistic, baser urge welled within him, giving him a new, as yet unformed, incentive. This, combined with the more devious aspect of his nature, resulted in an unsavory, emerging plan. On an inspiration he said, "Margaret, let's you and I go to lunch today and discuss this case. Have you ever been to the club?"

The associate was astounded, and at the same time beamed at the inherent compliment. Her distaste for her employer vanished as she recognized the change in his attitude toward her, and sensed the undefined, personal nature of his sudden new interest. That's all it took. She was hooked. "No, I've never been. I would like that very much." It was a date.

Later he collected her, and they drove in his snazzy new, candy apple red Jaguar convertible to the exclusive men's club several blocks away. The Greeneburg Men's Club was located on the top floor of a posh office building, housing Greeneburg's largest bank.

As they got off the elevator an attractive receptionist recognized Fotheringham and greeted him warmly. She turned to Margaret, her blue eyes suddenly frosted over, and in a tone, dripping with contempt which held more of a command then a question, asked, "Would you like to sign our guest register?"

Margaret was impressed by just about everything that day, beginning with the enticing smell of the expensive tan leather and the ergonomic luxury of the new Jaguar convertible. Strangely, she was also beginning to look at B.S. in a different light, that pesky personal interest arising in her. She, less than surreptitiously, gazed directly at him. His silver-gray hair flowing casually in the breeze, contrasted by the superbly tanned face, his aquiline nose forcefully leading his strong face forward, conveyed a confidence which gave her a thrill, an emotion that was new and quite surprising to her.

The club was a stereotype of exclusive old men's clubs the world over. A large parlor, generously furnished with dark brown, soft leather overstuffed chairs, was populated with a plethora of the region's barons of business. Despite their variety of sizes and shapes, they all seemed to have a similar appearance, an expression of supreme confidence, of men used to having their commands obediently and unquestioningly followed. They were, she realized, of the same ilk as her employer.

These Titans of the area's commerce were engaged in such mundane activities as perusing the Wall Street Journal, watching the stock market shows on television, and casually chatting about sports. They all eyed Margaret with a feigned disinterest as she, feeling she was on a runway in some fashion show, strutted by. Although Margaret was not your typical beauty, she was possessed of regular features and a slim, yet feminine physique, with appropriate, subtle curves. The eyes of the barons followed her with increasing fascination, even a hint of envy, as she and B.S. entered the club's dining room.

They were presented with menus by an efficient, reed thin young man who eyed Margaret warily. B.S. began with small talk. "Where did you go to school," he casually asked.

Put off by the apparent fact that he didn't know, even though she knew he had been the one to make the final decision to hire her, she responded icily, "Princeton undergrad, Cornell Law School."

"I went to Yale for both," he told her.

"Yes, I know. Bill Clinton went there, too, didn't he?" she replied, the innuendo sailing over his head.

B.S. was quite comfortable despite the unusual situation of having an attractive female guest across the table from him in the last bastion of male preserve. Most of the other men dining in the posh environment did not disguise their frequent stares, some characterized by envy or admiration, but through their sneering glances, most conveyed their disdain at having their private domain invaded by a mere woman.

He drifted into a discussion of the case, starting with what he had learned about the life of the hermit lawyer. He was pausing, occasionally looking up at some imaginary object as he blew smoke from an aromatic cigar into the air. It was an expression of dominance, of power.

Playing the devil's advocate, Margaret made a strong case for the executor, but B.S. kept on as if he was not listening to her. When he had finished presenting his case, almost as if he was practicing his final argument to a jury, he concluded, "So you see, Margaret, despite the procedural and legal niceties, it is in the best interest of the good pastor for us to represent him in this matter, and to file the suit as soon as possible, to get the matter moving, to preserve the estate assets, and ensure, to the extent we can, that the Temple gets every penny that is coming to it."

Margaret looked at him in disbelief. It was abundantly clear to her that the proper administration of the estate would take years, and furthermore, she had serious doubts about the actual worthiness of the Temple and Pastor Ronnie Conner. But she did agree that it would probably take a lawsuit to force a decision of what standards would be applicable and who would determine the issue of worthiness. Carefully observing her boss and erstwhile mentor, she developed a new insight into his character. Like Pastor Ronnie he was obsessed with greed. To B.S., she surmised, this case was about how much money he could get from it. She shuddered at the thought of his undisguised avarice.

That afternoon she returned to her cubicle to slave away as she was accustomed to do, now squarely faced with the horns of this dilemma. Her sense of professional responsibility with respect to the frivolousness of a hurried legal action, clashed with the clearly stated desires of her boss. Nevertheless, she reasoned, it was not up to her to decide what the defense was going to or should do. She looked at the draft of the complaint she had been working on. It was solid, well considered, and given the state of the law with respect to such things, was as good as it could be. Her decision having been made, she heaved a great sigh of resignation and went to work.

The complaint was a work of art. Margaret had tried to think of every possible point she could make in support of a monetary claim, without resorting to base frivolity, and every defense that she could think of which might be able to forestall the suit itself.

The Temple, and thus vicariously, Ronnie Conner, were contingent beneficiaries. Margaret asserted that this gave them standing, especially since they were more than mere contingent beneficiaries, they were virtual beneficiaries, for, she strongly alleged in the masterfully drafted complaint, the Court should take judicial notice of the worthiness of such a paragon of goodness as the Temple of God. She alleged that the haberdasher was not experienced enough in the intricacies of estate administration, and this estate was particularly intricate. He was neither competent nor capable of administering an estate of this size and complexity, that hundreds of thousands of dollars in interest were being lost at the inexcusable delay, and that the worthy beneficiary was thus being irreparably harmed. She asked for millions of dollars in compensation from the executor of the estate alleging that he had a fiduciary duty to the beneficiary to maximize the value of the estate and had failed miserably in this duty.

After determining from his secretary, who also acted as his warder, that he was alone, Margaret walked into the office of Mr. B. S. Fotheringham, III, without knocking. Her presumptiveness in this bold maneuver, she felt, was justified by her newly found devotion to the mercenary cause of her boss, and the subjugation of her professional ethics to mammon.

She brazenly plopped the document on his desk and smugly sat down in the well-padded leather chair facing him. He picked it up and carefully read the document, his frown slowly turning to a wide grin. "This is magnificent, my dear," he said. "I do believe you have out done yourself. Let him try to wriggle out of this." B.S. seemed to segue into a reverie as thoughts of dollars raining down on him filled his avaricious mind. "Let's file this right away."

Chapter 10

It was Thursday and the thought of a piece of tasty buttermilk pie to savor energized and excited him. A piece of pie was more important than carrying out the next item on his "things to do" list that Izzy had had prepared with regard to the administration of Hamish's estate.

He had arrived at the home on Pine Street at the appointed time, but Ms. Tilly wasn't there, and neither was the buttermilk pie. He waited. And waited, and the more he waited the more concerned he got. He had come to rely on her dependability, so after forty-five minutes when she had still not arrived, he walked over to the rundown section of town where the black folks in Pine Ridge lived.

He was aware of suspicious eyes peeking out surreptitiously from behind lace curtains of the seedy homes as he meandered by. There was no one on the street, no one to talk to, no one to ask. He paused before a neat clapboard house of the mill style, built in the early part of the twentieth century when the now defunct textile mill was at its heyday. The house was small but immaculate, with a brilliant garden of asters, zinnias, and daisies frolicking in the sun, inviting him, in stark contrast to the rundown nature of many of the other houses in the area. He strolled up the walk and knocked on the brightly painted fuchsia colored door.

He heard some noise within, some whispering, and after a while the door opened. A skinny young black boy with glasses stared up at him questioningly. Izzy cleared his throat and asked. "Iss diss de haus vere Mizz Dilly lives?"

The boy nodded, deferentially. "She cain't come to de do', Mistah. She real sick."

An expression of deep concern spread over Izzy's face. "Dake me do her now, my boy. Id's impordan' dad I see her. Who iss vadchink her? Who iss dakink care of her?" he demanded, with sensitivity.

"Mah Momma is," the boy responded. "Come on in, Mistah." The boy read Izzy's genuine concern accurately, and thought maybe he could help the strange little man, for he was quite worried himself. He showed Izzy to the bedside of Miss Shan Tilly, who lay there, gaunt and sweating. She was tended by a woman who clearly was the boy's mother, putting cold compresses on the forehead of the ailing woman. Izzy stood at the foot of the bed, looking from the sleeping and obviously sick woman to the gentle caregiver.

Without being asked, she offered the explanation to the questions implicit in his concerned look. "Yo must be Mr. Izzy who Miss Tilly talk about so much. She very sick, Mistah Izzy. She got a powerful fever an' been mos'ly sleeping these past coupl'a days. I put dis col' cloth on her head, but she don't seem to get no bettah. I'se mighty worried about Miss Tilly."

"Vy don' you call de docdor?" he asked ingenuously.

"We cain't do dat, Mr. Izzy. She ain't got no money, no insurance. All we can do is pray to Jesus."

"Vell, I do," he said cryptically and ran out the door leaving the stunned woman to decipher whether Izzy meant he had money or prayed to Jesus.

He was back in a half an hour with, believe it or not, a real doctor in tow. "Here, diss iss Docdor Gold. Led him look ad her." The doctor immediately went to the bedside, felt the pulse of the now awake, but listless woman. He took her temperature and asked the caretaker a few pointed questions.

"We have to get her to the hospital right away. Lady, can you come with me?" he directed his question to the caretaker. "I don't think we have time to wait for an ambulance. I'll drive her in my car."

The doctor, with the help of the angel of mercy, picked up the semi-comatose woman in his arms as if she was weightless and rushed her to his car. The two of them sped off, leaving Izzy and the boy alone in the house. They stared at each other for a few minutes. "Do you haf a place do go, young man?" Izzy asked.

"Sho." The boy answered, indignantly. "Rat cheer. I lives rat cheer."

Then it dawned on Izzy. "So," he said, "Miz Tilly iss your grandmother?"

"Yup," he said. "She sho' is. Mah great gran."

After making sure the boy, who was about eleven years old, was all right, Izzy left and walked back to Pine Street. He was sitting morosely at the kitchen table wondering whether he should go to the hospital, when he became aware that the dogs were barking. He went to the back porch and realized they were barking at him, or at least in the direction of the house. It didn't take a genius to realize they were hungry. Cautiously venturing into the yard, now overgrown with waist high weeds and vines, careful not to step on snakes or hidden pitfalls such as piles of dog excrement, he determined the mechanism was stuck. He scraped a little rust off and a large portion of dog food dropped into the trough.

After feeding the now rather mangy animals, making sure they had water, he went back to the store. On his way, he was thinking about the responsibilities he hadn't considered before. He had to hire somebody to at least bush hog the back yard, and then mow it. It grated him that he would have to spend some of the estate's money for maintenance, but then he considered that five percent.

He pondered what to do with the dogs. Miss Tilly wasn't going to be able to take care of them any time soon, and it was not something he cared to do either, slobbery big dogs not being his favorite pets.

When he got back to his store, he collapsed into the ancient office chair behind the desk in his tiny office. The dogs were still on his mind when, with a sudden inspiration, he remembered the provisions of the old lawyer's will. Impetuously, he called the head of ITCH, explained the situation about the dogs, and arrangements were made on the spot for them to come get the dogs and take care of them. The man he spoke to said he would do that at no cost to the estate. Izzy breathed a sigh of relief and went home to the relative sanctity and comfort of familiar surroundings, forgetting for a while the pressures of executing O'Halloran's will.

The next morning, after a restless sleep, Izzy was busy making breakfast in his kitchen when he heard a thump. Cautiously, he went to the front door and peered out. Laying right at the door on the stoop was a freshly thrown newspaper with headlines glaring up at him. Izzy was stunned. He picked up the paper as if it was diseased. He glared in amazement at the headlines.

TEMPLE OF GOD SUES EXECUTOR of ESTATE of RECLUSE

The subtitle was worse.

Claim of Mismanagement Demands Millions

The more he read of the account, the more irate he became. Furiously, he dialed Jimmy G's telephone number, but stopped when he realized it was only 7:30 a.m. No matter how good or industrious Jimmy G was, Izzy could not imagine the attorney being in his office at that early hour. But at nine sharp he was at the attorney's door anxiously waiting for him when he arrived.

"I know, I know," Jimmy G announced without preamble or even a greeting, waving him aside with a dismissive hand gesture, typical of those of his heritage "I awready saw it. It's crap. Pure crap."

"Vad? Dey can'd do dis, can dey?" Izzy's snit gave way to fear, fear of the unknown which the secret society of the law always seemed to thrust upon the honest citizens of the town. It was only the perennial miscreants and felons, well versed in the myriad courtroom procedures, and familiar with the foibles of the various judges, who had no fear, no anticipation, when it came to legal matters. These criminals figured the worst that cound happen to them was three hots and a cot, TV, and basketball. And best of all, freedom from the horrors of trying to earn a living.

"Nah. Don' worry about it," Jimmy reassured him, unconvincingly. "When da sheriff brings you de suit papers jus' drop 'em off. I'll take care of it."

Izzy was beside himself. He had never been sued before. No one in his whole family had ever been sued. The cavalier attitude of the attorney about such a serious matter, unnerved him almost to the extent of panic. His good name was being vilified in the press. His diligence, which he considered exemplary, with respect to his duties as executor, was lambasted without any care whatsoever as to whether there actually was any mismanagement on his part. How could they print such blasphemous tripe? He, Isadore Shapiro, derelict in his duty? Never. He wondered how he could go about suing the newspaper.

Id's dad greedy Pasdor, he thought, his dander rising, but his frustration began to abate as the practical side of his nature slowly brought about the realization that he did not know how to deal with the situation, and Jimmy G did.

He left after some more ineffective and insincere reassurance from the lawyer. That evening a deputy sheriff did drop off the suit papers, giving Izzy a truly condescending look as he did so. The deputy literally dripped with contempt as he filled out the return and left.

Izzy was crestfallen. He had done nothing wrong, he reassured himself, tears welling in the corners of his eyes.

The morning after Izzy was served with the suit papers he was still boiling with rage and fear. At exactly 9:00 a.m. he trudged over to Jimmy G's office fully intent on raising Cain. But Jimmy wasn't there. It seems that Jimmy had to be in court that morning. He was a trial lawyer, after all, even if he was from Brooklyn.

When Jimmy G returned to his office after lunch, his normally pomaded hair was out of place, and he appeared to have been the victim of a significant spate of running his fingers through it. He was obviously frazzled when he breezed into the office. Clearly, he had suffered the wrath of some Judge whose propriety and sensibilities were offended by Jimmy's brand of tact. Truth be told, Jimmy's courtroom demeanor often did come perilously close to disrespect, even contempt of court.

Hazel, his gray haired, horn rimmed bespectacled secretary, with a bee hive coif sporting a pencil incongruously stuck in it, was none too friendly as the attorney walked in. In a perturbed manner, she motioned to a corner of the reception area where Izzy meekly sat looking like a wet cat. "He's been sitting here all morning," she announced, her disgust with the intrusion into her domain palpable.

Jimmy sighed and said gruffly, "Awright. Let's have it, Iz. Lemme see watchoo got." He grabbed the papers and walked into his office trailed by the totally defeated executor. Once in the office, Izzy began an unrestrained barrage of criticism about the opposing attorney, B.S.

In his typical Brooklyn fashion, Jimmy replied, "Keep yer shoit on. Lemme read dis crap."

Izzy watched intently as the lawyer pored over the papers in silence, surprising Izzy with his ability to concentrate. He said not a word as he swiveled his office chair around and pulled a dusty statute book from the book case behind him.

He studied the tome silently for what seemed an eon, during which Izzy's edginess was increasing exponentially.

Finally, Jimmy G heaved a huge sigh, tossed the statute book on his desk with a thump, and turned and looked at Izzy, a serious expression creasing his visage. After a pause that was way too long, he said, "Dis is a lot of crap. Dey don't have any right to get to foist base on dis t'ing. Don't sweat it, Iz. I'll motion the damn t'ing right outta da sky."

Izzy wasn't sure what that meant, but he had grown to respect and trust the irreverent Brooklynite. He felt he had to, and that he had no choice but to leave the matter in Jimmy G's sweaty hands. He left the document in what he hoped would prove to be his capable care and departed, a curious sense of undeserved dejection overwhelming him.

Things only got worse as the day progressed. On his way home, he passed a newspaper stand that had a tabloid prominently displayed. The headlines of the *Secret Inquirer*, a daily rag whose quest for truth was questionable, but its sensationalism certainly wasn't, prominently displayed a picture of Izzy going into the Pine Street house in the rain, the collar of his seedy rain coat turned up, looking surreptitiously over his shoulder.

What Led Recluse to Trust his Millions to this Man?

Izzy was beside himself. The picture not only could not have been more unflattering, it positively made him look like a burglar or worse, a child molester. Tears formed in the corners of his eyes. It just wasn't fair.

Jimmy G was true to his word. He filed only a single simple motion challenging the Temple's standing. Standing, that necessary legality which enabled a Plaintiff to have a basis to stand on which to support the suit.

Chapter 11

The entire courtroom gaped in awe as B.S. presented his case. He was the epitome of what everyone in the world wanted their lawyer to look like. His tall, regal stature exuded confidence. His powerful build was the paragon of strength and competence. His deep mellifluous voice articulated his masterful words like the highest paid news anchor. He was flamboyant, yet reserved at the same time. He was convincingly dramatic, yet perhaps he was just a tad overblown. But God, he was good. Margaret was simply salivating at his magnificence. She was dripping with admiration. How could the judge not be totally swayed by the very force of that magnificent delivery? Just look at the unimpressive haberdasher. He was virtually quaking in his drab brown shoes.

When the masterful oration was over, and Fotheringham sat down with exaggerated aplomb, smug and completely self-satisfied with the presumptive assurance that the Judge's decision was his, he shot a glance full of contempt at the viscous attorney who was anything but his worthy opponent. Jimmy G was actually sweating. His nervousness was palpable. He was, after all, a New York, Eye-talian lawyer in the deep South. A Brooklynite for God's sake. Even Jimmy G thought he really shouldn't be here. If he got out of this one maybe he'd go back up North and take his chances with the good fellas.

The courtroom was silent. All eyes were on the executor's lawyer as he sat there, nervously perspiring, silently tugging at the sweat stained collar of his lavender shirt. After what seemed like an interminable time, the Judge issued a polite "ahem" followed by a quiet, "Do you wish to respond to that argument?" he asked, the silent word "persuasive" all but understood. B.S. had indeed performed a magnificent oratorio, unparalleled in the annals of Pine Ridge forensic proceedings.

Jimmy stood up and courageously faced the judge, but it seemed to all that the Judge had already made up his mind. "Nah, Judge," he lamely said. "I can't touch that. Even I gotta a'mit it was pretty good. But Judge, ya know, when I t'ink about it, when I really t'ink about what he said and how pretty he said it, Judge, B.S. is all fluff. Smoke and mirrors, dat kind a t'ing. Judge, in dis here courtroom we got a Bible. Right here on dis table." Jimmy made a show of picking up the Bible and letting everybody, curious as they now were, see the Good Book wafting in lazy circles before them. He reverently placed the book back on the table and looked long at it like a loved one viewing the body of the deceased at a wake. He even patted it lovingly. Some of the few Catholics in attendance even imagined he made the sign of the cross.

"But Judge, we got a different Bible here. You an' me. We got dis one here." Jimmy picked up an unobtrusive green, soft cover book and held it high for the judge and everyone else to see. "Judge, dis is de general statyoots of our state." He purposefully thumbed through the pages and suddenly stopped. He read a paragraph to himself, his lips silently moving. The audience was rapt, completely having forgotten about the magnificence of the oratory of his predecessor. Jimmy's simple, honest effect was even more dramatic than the effusive professionalism of B.S. Izzy's lawyer read to the Judge, and it was then just Jimmy and the Judge. The courtroom was as if it had been evacuated. No one else counted. No one coughed, burped or even rustled.

"Dis statyoot says dat an estate representative shall be selected from qualified poissons in dis Order, Judge. Qualified poissons are anybody over 18 who is not a convicted felon." Jimmy looked up to make sure the Judge was paying attention. He was. Boy, was he paying attention.

"Foist, Executors appointed as such in de valid last will and testament. Second, relatives of de deceased in da foist degree. Den, relatives of de second degree. Den, creditors. Last, any udder qualified citizen not int'rested in de estate. De statyoot goes on, Judge. It says who's disqualified. People what breaches d'eir fidooshry duty." Jimmy pronounced fiduciary as if he was a fishmonger in New York's famous Fulton Street. "People what embezzles, felons and such as dat. Nowhere in dis book does it say dat slowness is a felony or a reason to disqualify Izzy. I don't even t'ink Izzy's deliberate woik in trying to find de value fer da t'ings in de estate is anyt'ing but dooo diligence." He emphasized "due" as if a cow was bellowing it.

Jimmy paused. He had made his point. The Judge had slid back down from his basking in the glow of B.S.'s sermon on the mount. But Jimmy wasn't finished. "Judge" he continued respectfully, but with an increasing air of confidence. "Dat ain't de big t'ing. Da big t'ing is dat dis guy and his client ain't got no standing." He pointed accusingly to B.S. Fotheringham, III, who blushed a deep red like a kid caught with his hand in the candy jar. "Judge, he is like a bee-yootee-ful edifice built on a swamp. No, one built on quicksand, and he is sinkin' fast. Dis Temple of God isn't even a beneficiary, not yet it isn't, anyways. Before he can even come in here and make a claim to the goods, he's got to prove he's woithy, Judge. Dat's a condition of de will. What's called a condition preee-cedent. Somebody's got to prove de Temple is woithy. So Judge, I ask youse, who is to be de one to find dem woithy? Is it you? Is it de Executor here, Mr. Shapiro? Is it de newspaper? Is it, God forbid..." and Jimmy actually did cross himself here, "God?"

The judge was no fool. He quickly recognized peril when he saw it. He knew instinctively that his political career was in dire straits if he decided it was he who determined whether the Temple was to be found worthy. His mind raced as he traced the probable consequences of any decision he made, looking desperately for that one miraculous decision that would take him off the hook. He looked at Ronnie and shuddered. He also knew that half the people in his jurisdiction subscribed to Pastor Ronnie's brand of religion. Boy, finding a jury who didn't attend the Temple of God, or whose close relative wasn't a member, was going to be tough. He pitied the poor Judge who....

And slowly it came to him. Form over substance. That age old dilemma that lawyers insisted upon emphasizing when the facts were not in their favor. Procedure! That was the answer. Find the procedural loophole. There was always a procedural loophole. That is precisely why lawyers went to law school and charged exorbitant fees. That is why insurance companies made tons of money at the expense of society's wrongly wounded, maimed, and victimized. Find the procedural loophole!

But the judge looked out over a sea of expectant visages rife with anticipation. The esteemed Your Honor, that dispenser of learned justice, the shining light of society's darkest alleys, had to make some decision, and do it now, to quell the incipient rebellion as the dueling factions waited in breathless anticipation. An inspiration! He knew exactly what he'd do. His abulia, his inability to make a decision, vanished in a flash of clarity!

"I'll take it under advisement," the esteemed Judge pronounced, to the universal groans of all in attendance. Of course, he would take it under advisement. That's what judges do. Deep down in the dark and infinite abysses of their souls, everyone in the courtroom really expected the Judge to do just that.

Leaving the courthouse a step or two ahead of his brooding lawyer, Pastor Ronnie pompously got in to the back of his powder blue Lincoln limousine, the one with the gold trim, with the solicitous and unnecessary assistance of a retainer, and sped off without so much as a word to

Fotheringham or even a glance in his direction. As his two expensive lawyers morosely walked down the sidewalk, Margaret broke the silence. "We're going to lose that one, aren't we?"

"Shut up," was all B.S. Fotheringham, III said.

The mood was different in the opposition camp. While perhaps not rising to the level of downright euphoria, the two were extremely chatty.

"Vad is dis mean?" asked Izzy, energized by the general mood of the folks in the courtroom.

"It means da Judge is gonna t'ink about it. He din't wanna make his decision in front of all dose pipple. I t'ink he's worried so he'll prolly end up doon de right t'ing," Jimmy responded.

"But don't get your hopes up, Iz. Dere's a lotta crap goin' on around here. Stuff I aint got no clue about."

They parted, Izzy's head swimming with the procedural mysteries of the law, and Jimmy's crude but apparently adept understanding of it. Izzy went home and sunk, mentally exhausted, into the warmly embracing folds of the old overstuffed chair with the doily on it.

He woke with a start when he heard an unfamiliar noise, kind of a slap. He was surprised to see his son standing in front of him, looming over the coffee table on which he had just thrown the afternoon paper. "Pop, take a look at this." He picked up the paper and showed his not quite awake father the headlines.

Izzy was stunned. Normally a very private person, devoted to the honest good values and principles inherent in running his haberdashery store, a business based mostly on the reputation he earned over the course of a generation, worshipping at Temple, basically doing what he saw as his duty, his normally placid routine was about to be rocked to its core as he read the words prominently emblazoned across the front page of the local afternoon newspaper.

JUDGE DUCKS A TOUGH ONE

Gold Hoard in Hands of Haberdasher

Mesmerized, Izzy read the story and read it again. It described in detail the estate's inventory, emphasizing the unknown value, probably untold millions, of the rare gold coins.

Izzy was trembling as he put the paper down. Tears were in his eyes as he looked up at his son who was now wearing a very quizzical expression. Nat had not seen as much of the dark side of human nature as Izzy had, and was still rather naïve. Izzy, on the other hand, with the horrors of the war from which he emerged as a child, the tortures, and exterminations of the Holocaust deeply etched in his psyche, looked on everyone with a bit of suspicion, almost asking them to lay bare their true character. He knew human nature. He knew the essential greed of the pompaded preacher. He knew of the innate prejudices of the landed classes, of the threatened classes, and the various shades and tints of bias that colored the views of everyone, even those that ostentatiously purported to be bigotry free. The liberals were always the most intolerant, he had philosophied in his youth.

"What's the matter, Pop?" Izzy's good son asked, curious over the tears lingering in the corners of the eyes of his wizened but wise father.

"Dis! Dis rag of a paper," he responded holding up the headlines for his son to see. Since Izzy's hand was trembling so badly, his son couldn't have read anything but the headlines.

"Dey are delling de whole down, dere is nuddings bud gold in O'Halloran's house. I'm afraid, Sonny. Every dief in de down will be drying do figger oud a way do ged de gold. I godda do someding."

The good son, Nathan, tried to soothe his father's fears. As a kid growing up in a community that hid its prejudices, Nathan had been virtually tortured, but in a good natured way, by his friends who referred to him with the same unfortunate epithet his father used when calling him; "Nad," they called him, and sometimes by the more formal name, "Gonad."

"We can call the cops, Pop. Ask for around the clock security," Nad naively asserted.

"Vy, Nad? Vy vould dey do dad for me. I'm nuddings. Jes' a poor haberdasher. I god no cloud wid de police," Izzy wrung his hands, and you could just see the "Woe is me" waiting to pop out.

But Nat called the police anyway and politely and carefully explained the situation. Despite pleading and cajoling, the best he could wrest from the recalcitrant police, who were a little annoyed at being aroused from their gossip session, was for a commitment for a patrol car to ride by the house every once in a while for the next few evenings.

Not a minute after Nat hung up after getting the tepid assurance fom the police, the phone rang. It was David Mann. Nat handed the phone to Izzy. Without preamble David got right to the point. "Listen, Iz. I saw the headlines. Them coins should be entrusted to a professional, ya know. Somebody who knows what he is doing. I can handle them for you. I got the know how. I'll get the most for you, for the estate, you know." After a polite but non-committal answer from Izzy, he hung up. His suspicions about David Mann were growing.

Izzy was beside himself with worry. He understood the evil impulses in human nature and he knew his own vulnerability. A small, elderly Jewish man, unskilled and unused to the things of violence that had characterized so many societies, he saw himself as a sitting duck. His only chance, he reasoned, as his worry gave way to his wit, was to outsmart them, for he was certain they would come. He was absolutely certain of it.

He thought and thought intently. Nat was a little concerned at the unfathomable expression on his father's face, but he could tell the old man was deep in concentration. He had seen it before. It was like his father was in a trance and it was not a good idea to interrupt him when he was in this state. It usually foretold great ideas, but every once in a while the musings were a prelude to completely loony nonsense. And that made Nat worry.

Slowly, after what seemed an interminable time as the two just sat there, the expression on the old man's face changed and Izzy began to smile. A wry, crooked smile, as if he had just sold the proverbial ice box to an Eskimo, but a smile nevertheless.

"So," he said enigmatically, and that was it. That was all he said as he got up and walked out of the house, leaving his stunned son to decide whether to stay or follow the old man. Typical of Nat, he did neither, watching the old man walk down the street until he was out of sight.

Nat became very worried, himself, for he did not know whether it would be the brilliance or the goofiness that would ensue. Nat went looking for his father, but he was too late. The old man had simply disappeared.

Izzy had been thinking long and hard about what the safest place might be to keep the coins until he could sell them, for Molly had reluctantly given him permission to sell them at auction. When he first approached her with his idea, she hesitated, somehow believing Izzy was attempting to bilk the Temple out of what was rightfully theirs. For some reason, she considered it would be more appropriate for Izzy to just hand over the estate's assets to Pastor Ronnie Conner, and yet inexplicably, that concept did bother her.

Molly, made some feeble excuses, delaying making the decision until she had spoken to her friend, Arlen

Bestwishes, the glad-handing business manager of the Temple, who himself, seemed to have come into quite a bit of money, lately. Arlen, whose responsibilities included investing the Temple's mountains of cash, let her know the coins meant nothing until they were liquidated and the proceeds could be invested wisely in some lucrative real estate development reaping huge profits for the benefit of the Temple. So Molly gave her assent for the executor to sell the coins at auction in the big city, but was adamant about the record keeping requirement, and due diligence concerning the auction house he chose.

In fifty years of immersion in the retail industry, Izzy had certainly learned to understand people. He could read the emotions of desire, the extent that such things as vanity, utility, economy and pride played in a customer's decision to buy something at his store. He refined his shrewdness to the point that he understood extremely well the factors behind human decision making in general. He would have made a fabulous deal broker, but in his culture, you simply were what you were, and he was a simple haberdasher.

Because of his considerable understanding of human nature, Izzy was frightened that the careless sensationalism of the newspaper article would bring out a panoply of greedy predators, and the personal danger that such greed would evoke. It would be not unlike the fervor that caused the mad gold rushes of 1849 and 1896, but on a smaller scale. He felt he had to take immediate measures to protect and defend the gold that had been entrusted to his care.

Once he secured the coins as well as he could, he had to find out the facts behind the strange key with the simple "124" engraved on it. It was Izzy's duty to determine what that key unlocked. He didn't feel there was anyone he could ask who might be able to provide the answer or even steer him in the right direction. He felt the answer was to be found by deductive reasoning. At least it was safer if he kept his reasoning to himself, in his own mind, since there was more than enough danger because of the gold coins. Gold always seemed to bring out the worst in people.

Obviously, the key unlocked something. In all likelihood, *124* was the number of a box or locker that the key would open. One didn't have to be a genius to come to that conclusion. Maybe it was a key to a safe deposit box, perhaps a locker at a train station or bus station, or a locker at a sports facility. All he had to do was find what the key opened. Simple, right?

He considered what he knew. O'Halloran was an elderly man and a recluse. He kept to himself, and except for his lonely walks about town, he wasn't known to work out or exercise. The locker in a sports facility clearly was not a probability. He kept the gold coins and stock certificate in an unlocked box under his bed, so it seemed reasonable to rule out the probability of a safe deposit box at a financial institution. His car, a 1968 Camaro convertible, was always kept under a protective waterproof cover. He wasn't known to drive much, so that might indicate a locker at a train station or bus station. But he was not known to travel so that ruled against the probability of a locker at the train station, and it did not make much sense to keep valuables, if that was what the key was for, in a bus station, especially since Pine Ridge didn't have a bus station with lockers – it was rather more like just a bus stop, and the nearest large bus station was in Greeneburg.

His logic had brought him back to where he started. It might be a locker in a school, perhaps a high school. But that didn't really make much sense. As he thought some more, it slowly dawned on him. The most likely explanation was that it was a key to a post office box.

But why would O'Halloran have kept anything in a post office box? All the mail that Izzy had locatetd was addressed to O'Halloran at his house. And the box at the post office was easily accessible to any post office employee, and with its back open to all the post office employees it wasn't really very safe. He wondered if post office employees had to be bonded.

Shapiro wandered over to the post office not knowing what to expect and unsure as to his own reasoning. Like the police station, the post office was near the courthouse but on the other side next to the bank.

He entered a small vestibule and faced a tiny counter which did not appear to be manned. To his left was a glass door that led to a room that contained a wall with many rows of post office boxes. He entered and scanning the numbered boxes, he quickly located box number 124 on the row just above the bottom. The key was indeed a post office box key, and he smiled as he easily unlocked the box.

There was a lone envelope in the box, a certified letter, return receipt requested, with an unobtrusive, uninformative return address. At first glance, the envelope appeared to have been unopened, but a more careful inspection revealed it had been signed for by Hamish O'Halloran himself, and carefully opened and resealed.

For a moment Izzy was overcome by a powerful feeling of uncertainty. He felt like he was snooping, prying into the dead man's personal business, maybe even committing a felony by opening somebody else's mail. But he rationalized correctly that it was his duty as executor to find out what was in the letter, since there was no one else legally appointed to attend to the dead man's business.

Cautiously, even reverently, he opened the envelope, careful not to tear it. He read the letter that was inside. Isadore Shapiro, haberdasher and executor, gaped. His jaw dropped, his mouth hung loosely open, drool sliding down his chin, as he read the short, two paragraph letter a second time. It was direct and to the point. Just one week before he died, Hamish O'Halloran had won the lottery, a chance on which he had taken years before. It was worth one million dollars and all he had to do was claim it. Why hadn't O'Halloran made the claim?

But there was a deadline. He only had sixty days from the date of the letter to make his claim before his right absolutely and permanently expired, according to the letter. Izzy looked again at the date. He breathed a sigh of relief as he realized he still had two weeks before the deadline.

Izzy was not sure what to do. His first inclination was to leave the letter in the box, for after all it wasn't his, and that somehow, he was doing something wrong just by reading and holding the prize notification. But he had to remind himself again, that it was his duty to represent and administer poor old O'Halloran's estate.

Finally, he decided on a course of action. He took the letter and went over to Jimmy G's office. He was sure the wise little wise guy would have an acceptable answer. He began to calculate, for if it was what it clearly said it was, it meant another fee, this time for $50,000.00. And he hardly had to do anything to earn it! He began to get really excited about that prospect. Wow, 50Gs!

When he got there, Jimmy G was in a snit. Hazel was standing in the door way to Jimmy's office with her hands on her ample hips, glaring at him, her face flushed. When Izzy walked in Hazel casually glanced at him, with the same expression she might have if a fly landed on her nose. She announced to Jimmy rather impertinently, "Mr. Shapiro's here. I'm going to lunch. We'll talk about this when I get back."

Jimmy came to the door, his face red with anger, his hair newly mussed, clearly from another episode of frantically running his fingers through it. He motioned for Izzy to come in. As Jimmy sat down behind his desk, Izzy could hear him talking to himself. His muttering sounded something like, "Sombshing 'sole. Tnkygdwaywidis."

Izzy had an idea that he could translate this invective all right, but he didn't want to know what it was about. Like Sergeant Schultz on the old TV sitcom, *Hogan's Heroes,* his famous slogan, "I know nothing," was more than appropriate under the circumstances.

Jimmy was still seething, and muttering unintelligible sounds, and not very pleasant ones, when Izzy silently placed the certified envelope with the letter in it before him. Jimmy stopped making profane noises as he read the letter. He read it again and started to smile. As he read it a third time his smile broadened to a wide grin and it seemed like his mussed hair fell into place without the benefit of a greasy comb.

"Well, ain't dis sumpin, Iz. Da poor sap wins a cool million an' knocks off before he can even collect. Life's a bitch an' den ya die, but not 'til ya win da lotry." Jimmy laughed to himself.

"Vad I do now, Jimmy?" Izzy was clearly concerned.

"Simple, Iz. You gives me a power of attoiney. I write dem a letter. Include a copy of da det' certificate, letters of administration – make a claim fer da mill. Send it certified." He thought some more. "Where'd ja get dis anyway?"

"Ya know da key wid 124 on id? Id was a posd office box key. Da ledder was in id."

Chapter 12

When Izzy left Jimmy G's office, his exuberance once again gave way to worry as he thought about the gold coins. He feared the probable onslaught of thieves. Probable? Almost certain, based on his understanding of human nature. His house, the store, and especially O'Halloran's bleak, uninhabited house, were ripe targets of the criminal invasions he envisioned.

Izzy feared the effect of malicious gossip in Pine Ridge. These fears were enhanced by the insensitive reporting of the local newspapers. He had seen the powerful, unrelenting effect of such sensationalism before. More powerful than mere unadorned fact, gossip could ruin a man; gossip could cause panic-stricken runs on banks, stampedes, and wreak all sorts of unrestrained havoc. Gossip in Pine Ridge, he considered, would have all the morally challenged in the little community trying to figure out a way to get the gold for themselves.

And the newspapers! Some people really believed everything they read in the papers as if the printed word was gospel. Sometimes, headlines alone were like throwing gasoline on a fire in inflaming the passions of the local populace. Editors often tossed principle into the garbage for the sake of lurid scandal and burgeoning circulation.

So without fanfare, the reluctant executor took the coins from the mahogany box and put them in a cloth bank night deposit bag, carefully insuring the zipper was closed. He put the green canvas deposit bag in a paper tote from the haberdashery, got in his old car and went for a little ride to Greeneburg, worrying about the treasure secured on the driver's floorboard between his quaking knees.

Izzy quietly made arrangements at a small bank there, the Southern Overland Bank, the SOB to its friends and customers, to rent a safe deposit box where he carefully and hesitantly stashed O'Halloran's treasure. He had chosen the SOB over its grander and seemingly more prominent competitors, especially ones with imposing marble columns supporting polished granite façades, because it was quiet and did not advertise. The SOB had been discretely doing business in Greeneburg for three generations. The unstated mantra of the SOB was its integrity.

He told nobody, and certainly not Jimmy G. While he did trust his lawyer, he didn't want to put too much temptation right there in front of him. He took the key and receipt and hid them securely at Nat's house, where, suddenly overcome with fatigue, he decided to stay the night.

That morning, when his good son, Nat, awoke, his father was no where to be found. Nat searched the house thoroughly, but his father was gone. Worried beyond belief, because of his father's increasing strangeness, Nat hurried to the store, in the vague hope he would find the old man there.

A light was already on inside the store, and the front door was unlocked. His concern escalated when Nat found his father sitting in the worn old leather chair in the darkened office with his back to him. Izzy did not turn toward his son, or even acknowledge him. Nat remained standing there, stunned, waiting for his father to do or say something. After a while, still facing the wall, Izzy said somberly, "You know, Nad, sometimes I yam afraid. Not of being slain, but of the awfulness of human nature."

Nat did not ask his father what he meant. He did not ask his father where he had been or what he had been doing. He knew from the expression of serenity on the old man's face, he had figured out a plan, considered, and accepted the consequences. Nat would just have to see what unfolded. It was not that the old man didn't trust him, it was just that Nat knew he would be told when his father felt like telling him.

He went into the little kitchenette in the back of the store to make a cup of coffee. He felt that they both needed a strong a shot of caffeine but had to be able to keep their wits about them. Sitting at the kitchen table sipping the brew, Izzy suddenly said to his son, "Nad. You godda dake me do de airpord. I d'ink I'll go do New Yawk." With that he got up to go home to pack his bags.

Nat was used to the occasionally eccentric behavior of his father, so he said nothing, and just waited to see if his father would come to his senses. In an instant, Izzy seemed unconcerned about the thieves and burglars he had been so worried about just a few minutes before.

Nat drove his father to the airport at a speed which the old man considered to be nothing short of reckless. On the way, he confided to Nat where he had stashed the coins for safe keeping and where he had hidden the key, just in case the plane crashed, and he would not be able to administer the estate due to his death. Izzy was morbidly afraid that any plane he traveled on would crash and everyone in it would be killed, smashed to smithereens as the plane burrowed into the hard earth at four hundred miles an hour.

Nat reassured him, kind of the way a father would reassure his small child, by patting him on the head. Nat left just before the old man was about to board the plane for New York. He was still reeling from the surprise, for it was not like his father to recklessly spend money on a jaunt, especially with so little apparent purpose. Nevertheless, Izzy seemed to know what he was doing and had a distinct aim in mind. Nat just wished he knew what it was.

Izzy only only took a carry-on and within a half hour after he landed at LaGuardia Airport, he was in a cab heading for Manhattan. As it always is in the crowded streets of New York, the traffic was bumper to bumper, horns were honking, drivers were swearing and casting aspersions about mothers, and making all sorts of intriguing gestures, each with a decidedly prurient connotation. Izzy settled back comfortably into the roomy, if less than luxurious, seat of the Checker Cab to enjoy the ride in the familiar and nostalgic territory.

Following his direction, the cab took him straight to Stack's, the huge coin store, universally known to serious numismatists. Once there, he asked to see the manager.

He was shown into a small reception area. The secretary whose domain it was, an elderly woman with horned rim glasses and blue tinted bouffant do, started to snicker at the disheveled appearance of Mr. Shapiro, or so he thought, becoming a bit irked as she held the back of her hand to her mouth to keep from laughing.

He was shown into a luxurious office, and as she shut the door behind him, he could hear her burst out into a loud, distinctly unladylike guffaw. The manager had his back turned to Izzy while he was talking on the telephone, simultaneously typing data onto a computer which was positioned on the credenza behind him.

The furnishings in the office seemed elaborate, but Izzy's practiced eye took in stamped plastic instead of true wood carved decorations. The walls were painted in a forest green and were covered with gilt framed blown up glossy color photos of rare coins.

He just stood there and gaped at the photographs as the manager spoke in a vaguely familiar voice and accent. He put the phone down and swiveled his faux leather chair around to face his visitor.

Izzy was incredulous. He stared at the man sitting behind the large ornate desk. It was like looking into a mirror. I mean the man looked just like Izzy. Without really looking up from some paper on his desk that had caught his interest, the bespectacled little man said, "What can I do for you?"

Izzy collapsed into a non-descript chair, his jaw falling almost into his lap. "Vad iss your name again, Misder?"

Then the manager looked up at him. He was also startled at the appearance of the man seated before him. Granted,

Izzy's sparse hair had been roughed up by a gust or two of New York wind coming off the Hudson River, channeled between the skyscrapers. He looked like a frightened Einstein, but the similarity was definitely there.

The two of them just stared at each other in silence for a few minutes, astonishment on their matching faces. Finally, the manager spoke. "Ya know, you could be my twin brother. You look jus' like me." He stood up and offered his hand. "My name is Melvin. Melvin Levy."

They both just shook their heads in amazement. After gawking at each other for a few more minutes, mouths agape, Izzy took out the folded photo copy of the four coins, and handed it to Melvin Levy without a word, sinking back into his chair, a big grin on his face.

"Oy vey!" Mr. Levy said. "You actually got these coins?"

Izzy merely nodded coyly, as Melvin Levy continued to study the photocopies. He took out a large magnifying glass appearing to almost go through it, as he peered intently at the images of the coins.

Finally, with exaggerated care, he put the magnifying glass and the paper down, almost ceremoniously. "Listen, Mr. Shapiro. I'm sure you know these coins, if they are real and are actually like this picture here shows them, are worth a ton of money. I don't have any idea what I could sell 'em for, but I know at least a dozen collectors what would probably pay a million dollars each for 'em. So waddya want 'a do? Ya want I should sell 'em for you?"

"Nah. Lemme d'ink aboud id. I d'ink maybe an auction. Whaddaya d'ink aboud dad?"

"Sure. I can put the word out. Make up some glossy flyers. Put 'em in fancy folders Let the big money collectors know about it. But if I do an auction, I get a commission you know. Fifteen per cent"

"No. Dad's doo much. Mebbe six."

"I gotta eat ya know. My kids gotta eat. They need shoes. Ten per cent."

"Oy. Your kids are prolly fordy. Prolly millionaires. Seven an' a half."

They settled on eight and a half per cent commission for Mr. Levy to sell the coins at auction, both pleased with the fact that the negotiations would result in a ton of money for each of them. Rare coins and rare big paydays. Levy insisted on seeing them first, though, wanting to assure himself of their condition and perhaps being able to do some research on the provenance. "I gotta make sure they ain't hot, you understand."

Izzy said, "Look, Misder Levy. For some reason, I drusd you. You got a hones' face." He chuckled, thinking how odd it was that they had such a look-alike appearance. His smile faded as an incipient and rather diabolical thought began to take shape in his mind. "Ya know, da commission on a million is $85,000.00. Dwice dad if dey sell for doo million. An dass for each coin. Look, I'll dell you whad. I god a idea. You fly down do Pine Ridge, dake a look. Sday ad my place fer nuddings. You spen' a couple of hunnerd. You mebbe make a hunnerd dousan.' Maybe doo."

Levy assumed a quirky smile as he sensed some more room in this negotiation. "Nah, I never leave the city. Bring 'em here. Leave 'em a coupla days. I can't afford to take time to go all the way down to, where'd ya say? Pine Ridge? Never heard of it. That in North Carolina?"

Izzy knew full well what the man was doing, after all they were almost like brothers, at least from their outward genes. But he stroked his chin as another idea began to take shape. "Look Mr. Levy. Jeez we godda be reladed. Lissen. Wha' dime do you go do dinner, huh? Dey's someding else I wanna dalk aboud." He surprised the numismatist by adding, "Look dinner's on me. Verever yo van' a go."

A couple of hours later they met at a restaurant, not at a real ritzy place, of course, but clean and kosher, nevertheless. The drinks came, and Levy looked down at his napkin for about a minute, then looked up at Izzy.

"Listen, Mr. Shapiro. Them coins is worth a lot more if youse can show a real legit provenance."

"Call me Izzy. Vad's dad, a provenance?" he responded.

"It's like you trace the ownership from the time they was minted to now."

"Oy, vey. How I'm gonna do dad?"

"I duhno, but if you can at least show they ain't hot, they's worth a lot more at auction. These high rollers that buy rare coins at auction don't like it one bit if it turns out the goods they just bought for a ton o' cash is hot."

Izzy slumped back down in his chair. He didn't have the slightest idea how to prove any provenance at all, except maybe going back to the time when Miss Tilly first saw the coins in the wooden box under O'Halloran's bed. But that was far from the time they were minted, perhaps a good hundred years unaccounted for. From what Izzy had learned just asking around Pine Ridge, no one knew anything at all about O'Halloran, or where he came from. He just showed up one day many years ago and had been there ever since.

After enjoying the kosher food, which he sure couldn't find in any restaurant in Pine Ridge, and engaging in a little small talk, reminiscing with someone comfortable, Izzy felt a lot better. He didn't have many friends in Pine Ridge, and this camaraderie was good for him. It was especially interesting when the two men delved into their backgrounds to see if they were in fact related. They were both a little disappointed since they could not find a common link other than their near ancestors escaping the pogroms of Eastern Europe. Then they got down to business. Izzy leaned forward. In a conspiratorial manner, looking around to make sure there were no spies or listening ears, he laid out his plan to Mr. Levy.

Levy had been selling coins in New York a long time, an occupation that had been his only real passion. But over time he had become a little bored with selling and auctioning coins, especially since he couldn't actually get to own any of the really expensive ones. Sure, he was the manager, and could get a pretty good deal now and then. He made a good living, even for New York, but he wasn't actually rolling in dough. He had just put three girls through college, one of them even through law school, and that pretty much wiped out his savings.

The mini-adventure inherent in Izzy's plan, did bring about a level of excitement the coin seller had not experienced since somebody brought in an 1804 silver dollar to sell, ten years ago. A little respite in a bucolic burg far away from the hustle and bustle of New York might be just the vacation he needed, especially since he wouldn't have to pay for it. He agreed to Izzy's little plan with a smirk, and they shook, as the deal was made.

Chapter 13

Levy was dropped off in front of Izzy's store in Pine Ridge by a bored taxi driver, who looked at the meager tip left by the New Yorker with disdain. Levy had been astonished at the slow-paced nature of the town, the downtown streets bordered with cute homemade boxes festooned with pansies. He marveled at the size of the azaleas surrounding the homes in the downtown area, the greenery of the old oaks, elms, and maples shading Main Street like a well-maintained arbor. Looking at the state of repair of all the large nineteenth century Victorian homes, he thought he could make a killing here as a paint salesman.

Levy walked into the distinctly old-fashioned haberdashery as if he was traveling back in time. He looked around the store, with a perplexed expression on his face. Used to the frantic pace of New York, the noise and commotion, the stylish and colorful distinction of men's clothing stores, Levy was surprised to find the store virtually empty. There were no customers at all, and the lone salesperson, a man in his forties, was behind a counter, engrossed in rearranging a display behind a glass front. The salesman looked up casually, and said, "Oh, hi Pop. How was New York?" and went back to work on the display.

Levy was astonished until he remembered his close resemblance to Izzy.

"You must be Nat. My name is Melvin Levy."

Startled, Nat looked up quickly and was taken aback. It was not his father, but a man who could be his twin. "Wow! You look just like my father."

"I know. That's why I'm here. He sent me. Listen, is there a place where we could talk, you know, privately, a little room somewhere?"

Nat couldn't believe it. He stared at the man unabashedly for a few minutes. Levy even sounded like his father, except for the fact that he could speak without too much of an accent, could pronounce his Ts, a little New Yorkese sneaking in. "Yeah. We could go into the office."

With Levy seated in the worn old leather chair normally occupied by Izzy Shapiro when he wasn't busy on the sales floor, Nat was amazed at the similarity between the two men. They even had the same hand movements, and an odd little facial tic evidenced by the simultaneous blinking of both eyes. Nat scratched the thinning hair on the top of his head and said, "What can I do for you, Mr. Levy?"

"Listen, Nat. I met your father in New York. I work for a big rare coin merchant. Your Pop came in and said he had some unique coins for sale and showed me a picture of them. Here, he wrote this letter on the back of one of the pictures." Levy handed Nat the picture on the back of which was his father's distinctive hand writing introducing and vouching for Melvin Levy.

Levy continued, "I am very interested in these coins and I would like to see them for real. But your father also told me about some shenanigans going on here, maybe even some danger. So we hatched this little plan."

Nat listened in stunned silence as Levy outlined the plan. Nat was intrigued. He hadn't known the simple, honest merchant who was his father to have such a diabolical streak in him. But, he thought, as he continued to scratch away the thinning hair on his head, *it just might work.*

Just then the phone rang. Nat picked it up and answered. It was David Mann wanting to talk to his father. Instinctively, he handed the phone to Melvin Levy. As soon as he handed the phone to him, he panicked as he realized Melvin was not actually his father, but it was too late. Melvin looked at Nat strangely as he spoke into the receiver, "Hallo."

"Listen Iz. You listening? I got an idea about dose coins. Listen. Whaddaya say we write a few letters to some big time collectors. Get an idea of deir interest. Whadday say? Iz?"

Melvin hesitated, thinking. But he was pretty sharp, Melvin was, and he caught on real quick. He picked up on David's accent and remembered Izzy's problem with the T sound. "Oy vey. Vad I dink iss we mebbe creade a liddle inderes' fois'. A liddle mysdery. We spread da void dad da coins iss oud dere. You know, comin' on da marked. Nod dell anybody wad coins, jus' real rare vuns. You dink you can doo dad?"

Nat smiled. Melvin was pretty good. He hung up after David excitedly assured him he knew just what to do.

Chapter 14

New York was a strange and intimidating place to Izzy. Even though he had lived there for a few years as a boy, he was always unnerved by the vibrance, filth, and infinite variety of the denizens of the streets. Millionaires in $5,000 suits passed by smelly bums dressed in rags. Izzy had become accustomed to the bucolic little village of Pine Ridge, seeing only an occasional pedestrian on the streets. In New York he was constantly being jostled and rudely pushed by the myriad pedestrians like a steel ball in a pin ball machine. He passed people talking to themselves, speaking in tongues, conversing in some foreign language, some others engrossed in a talking book or enraptured in an unknown music genre plugged into their ears, yelling for cabs or at some acquaintance across a busy thoroughfare. He actually heard some yodelers calling out to each other from across the wide street.

Thousands of people seemed to be in a hurry, walking, running, pushing, intent on reaching their destinations known only to themselves. These destinations must have been very important, judging from the speed they were moving and the intense and strained expressions on the faces of the hordes of pedestrians. Bouncing off a particularly large and sweaty man who almost walked through him, Izzy noticed the entrance to the subway and a stream of serious faced people descending into the gaping abyss like the images of the souls in Dante's *Inferno* descending into Hell.

Joining the stream, he went down, his apprehension rising as he descended into the city's busy underground. At the bottom of the stairs, he saw a line of passengers going through a turnstile, and another line in front of a window.

When he realized he didn't have the required token, he joined the line at the window. He spotted a bored attendant behind the glass and a line of very impatient people fidgeting and griping.

As soon as he joined the queue, a large fat man got behind him uncomfortably pressing his obese girth relentlessly into Izzy's back. As a consequence, Izzy was repeatedly pushed into the well-padded back side of the large black woman in front of him. The fat man stunk unpleasantly, the miasma of garlic and body odor engulfing and almost choking him. The black woman was becoming increasingly perturbed with each bump of the little man's chest into her steatapygous buttocks. Finally, she angrily spun around seething with rage, a rage directed at him. He winced in anticipation of being decked by a powerful right hook from her massive fist. Izzy shut his eyes tight in horrified anticipation.

Instead, he heard the fat man bellow, "Hey! Joley. How da hell are ya?"

The black woman did not punch Izzy, nor even slap him or yell at him. Instead, she said in a loud voice, ignoring the hapless impediment the diminutive Izzy presented in front of her, and said, "Dang, Pete. I aint seed you in years. Whatcha been doon?" They hugged, and it was almost like a threesome as Izzy squirmed to escape the noisome and fleshy embrace.

In a few minutes Izzy was propelled to the window and purchased a handful of tokens, and then committed an unpardonable sin, at least to a New Yorker. He asked for directions.

"Widge drain goes do da Museum, ma'am?" No sooner than the words were out of his mouth than the carping that New Yorkers were famous for began. The fat man, his belly pushing against Izzy's back like a veritable wall of jello, bellowed, "Come on buddy, move it. Yer holdin' up da line here."

The uniformed woman behind the window said curtly, "IRT "A" train." After all, there were hundreds of museums in New York. There must be some museum you could reach on the IRT A. She didn't care. She just wanted to keep the line moving.

Bodies pushed and shoved, undulating like a conga line, as they waited on the platform for their subways. A train approached, roaring down the track and screeching to a metallic halt as the locked steel wheels skidded along the rails, but it was not the A. When it stopped the doors immediately banged open, and a herd of intense and serious looking people were egested from the warm illumination of the interior of the train onto the soot and grime coated station platform. Before the last person had gotten off, people began pushing and shoving as they forced their way into the car. Izzy almost found himself going to Brooklyn, but the subway gods smiled on him and the doors squeezed shut before he was forced into the unwanted journey.

A few minutes later another train roared into the platform and Izzy spotted the welcoming sign of the A on the front of the train. He was both frightened and fascinated as the unrelenting current of passengers swept him on to the train. The doors clanged shut and instantly the train was rocking along at an increasingly rapid rate of speed, the undulations having a soothing, even somnolent effect on the riders. After two stops Izzy saw a white enameled sign with stark blue letters embedded into the white tile of the walls as they approached the next station, announcing simply, MUSEUM.

With great foreboding, he joined the human crush when the doors slammed open and they were spewed out onto the platform. Miraculously, with better odds of actually finding a needle in the proverbial haystack, as he emerged from the bowels of the subway into the slightly fresher air of the city, Izzy found himself standing before the steps of the great museum. He had no idea how far he had traveled underground or where he was in the city, but nevertheless here he was at his destination. Or so he hoped.

He climbed the imposing stairs to the museum and entered between two massive columns. The guards, who had all been to school to learn how to profile art thieves and terrorists, paid the disheveled little merchant no attention as he went in. He definitely did not fit any profile in which they were the slightest bit interested.

There was an information desk prominently located in the center of a cavernous entry hall manned by a short haired woman who looked like a man since she was wearing the same uniform as the other guards.

The bored guard tersely directed him down a hall to an office, and quickly turned her attention back to her sleazy romance novel. Izzy stood in front of the door for a few seconds uncertain as to whether it was the right one, and whether the proper protocol was to knock or just enter. He did both, entering right after he knocked. Upon entering he found a slender, young bespectacled woman behind a large desk with several piles of neatly stacked papers on it. There was a formal wooden name plaque incredulously announcing her name, "Ditzy Ritz, Assistant Curator." Izzy had never heard of any one with the name "Ditzy" before but he had a very good idea of what "ditzy" meant. Instantly he became concerned. *Why on earth would anyone named Ditzy actually advertise it?*

She asked if she could help in the high pitched, childlike, tremolo of the Valley Girls, and of course, that did not fill him with confidence either. Nevertheless, Izzy explained his purpose and she scratched her head in a distinctly unfeminine and unsophisticated manner, pushed her glasses up with her forefinger, and turned to her computer on the credenza behind her. Her fingers flew, various screens and icons flashed on and off, and a few seconds later images of two coins appeared on the screen.

"These two were stolen from the museum fifteen years ago," she announced matter of factly as she printed a color copy of some coins.

Izzy's heart sank as he recognized the four-dollar gold piece, the "stella," and the oldest gold coin, the one with the skinny eagle on it. He carefully unfolded the copy he had made on Molly McMasters copy machine and gave it to her.

"Dese dwo coins, I haf. Dey vere endrusded do me, as execudor of a esdade. Are dese dem?" he asked, pointing to the images on the screen. The assistant curator took the copy and carefully held it up to the screen to compare so the two images of the stella were next to each other. Izzy's mind was racing as Ditzy held a magnifying glass, ironically a square one the same shape as her nerdish spectacles, up to both images and inspected them. He was visualizing two coins with wings flying off into the sky, far out of his reach, and his magnificent five per cent along with them.

But after several hmmm, hmmms, she turned to him, and with a serious, almost angry expression on her face, asked with more than a hint of nefarious intimation, "Where did you get these coins?"

"Dey vere lef' do me by da vill of O'Halloran, da lawyer. I am de execudor."

Another hmmm, hmmm, and another close, very close inspection, followed. Izzy was beside himself with worry. *Dey haf da be da same ones. Wad's de shance dad bod' coins vud show up on de screen? Bud vere's de udder vuns? Mebbe dey ain' god picshers of dem.* Izzy was driving himself crazy with doubt.

The assistant curator abruptly turned back to him. "I'm sorry, Mr. Shapiro. These aren't our coins. But it sure is a strange coincidence you coming in here with pictures of two of the same coins that were stolen. But the pictures of our coins were taken fifteen years ago and they show little nicks and blemishes here and there. Your coins are in much better condition. They don't have the same nicks and and marks

114

that those stolen from the museum have. If you just made this copy recently, why, they can't be the same ones."

Sorry? Izzy was delighted. That meant he didn't have to turn them over to the museum. The coins were not the ones the museum investigator was after. But after the initial wave of elation, his natural pessimism returned. "Dell me leddy. Did you haf an invesdigador lookink for dese coins afder dey vas sdolen?"

"Why, yes. This report of the theft says we hired an investigator fifteen years ago to try to recover them. The museum paid him a $5,000.00 retainer and no one has seen or heard from him since."

Chapter 15

Izzy was nauseous, almost sick to his stomach when he arrived downtown at the Wall Street Station. The constant rocking, starting, accelerating, and screeching to a stop of the subway, combined with the fetid, unwholeswome, underground atmosphere, had made him so seasick that his lunch was on the verge of being delivered to whence it originated. He staggered up the stairs from the rank environs of the subway, gasping for air, not from the exertion, but his lungs crying out for a breath of fresh air, at least something with more oxygen than dirt in it.

At the New York Stock Exchange, he was shown into a waiting room. After waiting about a half hour, during which he had thumbed through all the dated magazines on finance that were laying around, Izzy was just sitting there, a dazed expression on his face, when a young man in his early twenties came into the room. He did not even look old enough to drive a car.

Izzy explained his mission and showed the man the copy of the certificate he had been carrying around. The young man studied it carefully, especially the back where the signature was, authorizing the transfer of the stocks to bearer.

"Hmmm. This is a rarity," the young man said almost as if he was talking to himself. "Let me show this to the boss." He went out the door into the hall and was gone for about ten minutes. When he returned, he said, "Looks like you've got quite a find here. Of course, we will have to verify the authenticity of the certificate, but if we are able to do that, this should parlay into quite a tidy sum. The company didn't pay any cash dividends the first fifteen years or so but issued stock dividends and then the stock split quite often as the share price skyrocketed. On two occasions when the price got up over 300, it split ten to one. In the past year, the company was gobbled up in a stock purchase by the computer giant, Compters R Us, but the officers decided to keep the popular marketing name, Komputer King. They issued two shares of their company for each share of the original Komputer King. The way we calculate it, and you have to understand this is just a rough calculation, you own over 64,000 shares of CRU which traded today at 49 3/8. That's over three million dollars on the exchange.

Izzy just stood there his mouth open, the sunlight reflecting off his gold fillings as if infused with an internal light source. "Dree million?" was all he could manage to say. "Dree million?"

"Yes, but of course it will all have to be verified and the authenticity of the certificate established."

"How do I do dad?"

I suggest you visit the corporate headquarters of Computers R Us and discuss it with the corporate secretary. Their offices are located at..." He punched in a few numbers on his desk top computer, which, Izzy couldn't help notice was a Komputer King model. "Hmmm. Number One Channel Place. That's not far from here. Used to be Canal Street but when they built their conglomerate headquarters they also upgraded the address." The young man snickered involuntarily at the irony.

Still a bit stunned, Izzy thanked the man, retrieved his copy of the certificate and after getting directions, left.

The cool breeze whipping off the Hudson River was invigorating as he left the building, but stung slightly for the wind contained thousands of particles of dirt, blown off the grimy street. Izzy was busy calculating what five per cent of everything was, when an intense sunbeam almost blinded him for a few seconds. An aurous aurora was framing the magnificent building he was walking toward. The afternoon sun was eclipsed by the grand, golden edifice that housed the corporate headquarters of Computers R Us, the largest company in the world, as a golden halo of sunlight auspiciously illuminated the magnificent building from behind.

Izzy was stunned by the opulence of the lobby. It was an indescribable, incredulous display of pure, unadulterated pomp. The total absence of utility sorely offended the simple haberdasher's ethos. Pink marble was everywhere. The floors, walls, and incredibly, even the ceiling were all made of the stuff, and everything was framed by a shiny golden metal. Izzy could not bring himself to think it was actually gold, it must have been polished brass, at least that's what he hoped.

His footsteps echoed throughout the imposing chambers. He began to tip-toe to avoid the discomfort of the reverberations. He cautiously approached a receptionist who obviously had been hired because of her startling beauty.

She looked dubious as he asked for the corporate secretary, almost whispering his request. Her disdain evident, she was about to direct him to an unimportant underling, when he uncharacteristically demanded, "I mus' see de segredary himself, ma'am. Dis iss doo big a deal for anyone else."

Reluctantly, she surprised even herself when she complied with the demand of the odd little man, directing him to the plush sixth floor office of the secretary of the corporation.

Izzy was amazed, even the elevator seemed to be made of gold and pink marble. When the elevator dinged and the doors slid open, he entered into a comfortable lobby decorated with tasteful, expensive furniture. The large windows overlooked the Hudson River, and except for the brownish hue of the water, it was a majestic view.

Again, he waited. After an inordinately long time, a tall, stately, gray haired woman came into the lobby. She looked at Izzy disapprovingly, as if he was a panhandler accosting her on the street, but politely asked if she could help him.

Izzy gaped at her. First of all, she was a good six inches taller than he was. He had never met a woman executive before – a woman of power, and this woman exuded power. Not the Hulk Hogan type of power, but high-level importance type of power. For a minute, he had no idea how to act, for he was truly impressed.

"I yam Isadore Shapiro," he finally said. "I yam sorry do disdurb you, Madam, bud I haf a cerdificade whad is impordan'. I vud like you do dake a look ad id." He handed her his copy without ceremony. The involuntary sneer which had detracted from her efficient good looks disappeared as she examined both sides of the photocopy.

"Yes, we have your letter, which I was quite surprised to receive. I take it this is a photocopy of the actual certificate, Mr. Shapiro." It was not a question but a declaration, an admission. She had the confidence and aplomb of the high position she occupied. Izzy was not exactly sure what a corporate secretary did, but this woman seemed to be the epitome of efficiency and authority.

"Yes, ma'am."

"Please come with me into my office."

He shouldn't have been, but Izzy was quite stunned by the beauty and opulence of the corner office. The rich furnishings underscored the importance of the woman. So did the magnificent view. The office was furnished in dark, obviously expensive, rich walnut furniture. It was extremely attractive, and well designed, without the chintziness of many modern styles, nor the excessive ornateness of the Art Nouveau Nineteenth Century. There was a plush, dark red and blue Persian carpet on the floor and an exquisite lamp on the huge ornate desk.

The corporate secretary's name was Ms. Schuyler. She seated herself in the plush leather office chair with aplomb. Her confidence and unstated sense of authority reflected not only the importance of her position, but her sense of her own importance.

A young man entered the office without knocking, but he was clearly expected by Ms. Schuyler. Izzy had not seen any sign that she had bidden him to come in but suspected there must be some secret buzzer somewhere that she had pressed. Ms. Schuyler handed the underling the copy of the certificate Izzy had given her. "Brian, make several copies of this document. Take it to research and have them check it for authenticity."

Brian returned in a relatively short time, silently handed Ms. Schuyler the original copy, and left with several other copies in his hand.

"May I ask how and where you obtained this certificate, Mr. Shapiro?"

He explained, and she nodded her understanding. In about five minutes, during which they chatted amiably, a bespectacled, slender woman with a bit of a haggard look, entered with a copy of a computer generated ledger sheet.

Ms. Schuyler, ever proper, introduced them. "Miss Schneider, this is Mr. Shapiro, the gentleman who brought the certificate you have just researched. He is the executor of the estate of the man who possessed it."

Ms. Schneider gave Izzy a perfunctory nod. Her slavish attention was directed only to Ms. Schuyler. She delved into her report with an unusual earnestness. "First, Ms. Schuyler, the state has recently made an escheat claim against this very certificate and the funds we have set aside for it. That estate has to deal with this claim immediately or our company will be required to honor the escheat claim and will have to pay the funds over to the state. Secondly, we have recorded each stock split, and dividend including dividends payable in fractions of shares of stock over the past twenty years, which have been reinvested by our company when they were not claimed within the mandatory 180 days. Here are the numbers." She nervously handed the ledger to the corporate secretary. "Will there be anything else, Ms. Schuyler?"

After an almost imperceptible nod of dismissal, Ms. Schneider hurriedly left the room. Ms. Schuyler studied the printout carefully without any expression at all gracing her face. She took an empty file out of the desk drawer and asked, "May I keep this copy," as she placed it in a file without waiting for a response.

Izzy responded nervously for he too was intimidated by the woman's icy authority. "Uh. Wha' da you need id for, Miz Schuyler? Id's de only copy I have wid me."

She was clearly perturbed as she deigned to answer, but for the first time a sense of foreboding invaded Izzy's being. He realized there was actually something sinister about the corporate secretary. Unable to think of any reason to keep the copy until it was formally submitted for redemption, she coldly informed him. "Mr. Shapiro, the escheat claim will have to be dealt with or the certificate will be worth nothing to you. I suggest you have your attorney handle this extremely difficult matter."

She studied the ledger again, this time peering intently at the numbers.

"Mr. Shapiro, I can confirm that this certificate was properly issued, and has now grown to the equivalent of 65,322 shares of stock in the corporation. This growth took place because of the practice of issuing stock as dividends in the early years of the company. Today, the stock last traded at 50 1/8. This makes the gross value of the shares of stock in Computers R Us which this certificate represents, to be $3,274,265.20.

She stood abruptly and excused herslf, telling Izzy to relax, and that she would return shortly. When she exited into an anteroom, she quickly pulled out her cell phone. In a conspiratorial manner, looking around to insure she was alone, she pushed a number. "Sheldon," she said to her boyfriend, "There's a man with an old stock certificate. 100

Shares of the company's first issue signed by the original owner and payable to bearer. He knows it's worth over 3 million what with the stock dividends and splits. But you know what we talked about, remember?"

Sheldon Simowicz was the head of Sykes Software, a Simi Valley company that had the good fortune to hire the quintessential computer nerd a few years back. Not a technogeek, but an honest to goodness nerd. This creature, a troglodyte type, whose entire life consisted of his work which he considered a giant computer game, had just come up with a holographic program which actually printed three dimensional images. The program really worked, and Sheldon had just figured a way to parlay it into millions. He had made an arrangment with his girl friend, Ms. Schuyler, who had engineered the plan, and now the powers at Computers R Us were close to making an announcement. It was the merger between Sykes Software and Computers R Us. Everything was hush-hush, of course, until the due diligence could be completed. But there was a lot of rubbing of hands with the cat that ate the canary expression on the faces of the big wigs. The result would be a block buster for both companies. The stock was expected to skyrocket.

"Can you get your hands on the actual certificate, Sissy?"

"I don't know. The guy's a real schlemiel, but savvy. It's part of an estate that he is the executor for, so he seems pretty cautious."

"Tell him you have to verify the authenticity. Tell him you will arrange to give him cash while you perform the verification which will take about a week. Then you will give him the certificate back for the cash. Over three million you say? I think I can come up with that amount of cash, but it will take a day or so. Do you think he'll go for it?"

"I don't know, but I will give it a shot. Thanks Shel. Love ya." She closed her cell phone and walked purposefully back into her office and, portraying an air of supreme confidence, sat down in her chair.

Ms. Schuyler cleared her throat as she began to speak, and, what is known in the poker business as a "tell," floated across her face. Izzy recognized greed when he saw it. But he suddenly realized the indomitable Ms. Schuyler somehow represented a major obstacle for him. His mind was racing as he assessed the situation.

Shapiro was handicapped by his lack of understanding of the corporate processes, yet he was blessed with a solid dose of common sense. But just then his furious contemplation of the situation was distracted as he observed an old stock certificate in an ornate guilt frame prominently hanging on the wall. The certificate looked identical to the one Izzy had except it had three red lines marked diagonally across it which Izzy correctly surmised meant it was cancelled.

Izzy interrupted the indomitable Ms. Schuyler as she began to speak. "Iz dad de foisd cerdificade of dis company, Ms. Schuyler?" he asked, pointing to the framed icon.

"Why, yes Mr. Shapiro, it is," she said, blushing somewhat. She hesitated, and Izzy had the distinct impression that she was somehow covering something, some emotion. It came to him in a flash. It was her venality. He watched her, waiting for her to expose it.

"Our corporation is now repurchasing up to ten per cent of the outstanding shares of stock in the company. We will be prepared to pay you....," she hesitated and turned to her computer and tapped a dozen keys or so. ".... $3,425,000.00 for the redemption of the original certificate. We will have to verify the authenticity of the certificate, you understand, but we will stand by this offer for one week. If you bring in the certificate I will arrange for the transaction to be in cash, which I will allow you to hold as a good faith gesture while we verify the authenticity of the certificate"

Izzy was flat out astounded, really stunned. He gaped, his jaw dropping, revealing his crooked teeth. Drool began to form at the corners of his mouth. He wiped his chin with the back of his hand.

Almost three and a half million! What is five per cent of that? But then Izzy's instinctive distrust of his fellow man emerged. Three and a half million? Why? Why start with that offer? Was she just an honest business executive, an oxymoron if there ever was one, or was there something else? Something he should know that he didn't, and she did.

Hiding behind his gaping mouth, he vaguely wondered if she was privy to some inside information which would affect the value of the stock. He had been selling suits long enough to be able to sense such things as the relative interest of the customer versus the dampening effect of the price. A little discount here, a bonus there and- bingo-you got a sale! That's what she was doing, she was selling him. Suspicion abounded in Izzy, bubbling over like fulminate of mercury.

Ms. Schuyler continued her spiel. "We have been aware of the existence of the certificate for some time now, of course, but we deemed it lost. You, and your estate, are very fortunate, very fortunate indeed, that the original owner has endorsed it in blank. That makes it payable on order, and, it appears, Mr. Shapiro, that it is up to you to make that demand. It would be very difficult for all of us and would involve numerous attorneys, if the certificate had passed to your decedent without that endorsement. How soon can you provide me with the original?"

So that was it. She wanted the original certificate. It was payable to bearer and if she had the original she would also have her own claim to the 3 mill and could just cut him out of it.

There was no dickering, for that was obviously not her style. Nor did it appear to Izzy that he had any other option. He took a few seconds to consider what he knew. The young man at the stock exchange had said it was worth just under $3.3 million. This lady offered $3.425 million in cash. He presumed the stock repurchase plan would be public knowledge, so the price would be rising until the quota had been met, but it would probably fall after the corporation stopped buying up the stock. He was about to agree to the deal when he had an inspiration.

"Dad's very generous of youse, leddy. But foisd I godda dalk do my cousin. He's a big shod wid anudder compuder company. Mebbe you know id, Muldi Dech?"

Multi-Tech! Ms. Schuyler gasped. The primary competitor of Computers R Us. "What would happen if Multi Tech suddenly became the owner of a block of shares of stock this big with the insider information she knew was about to happen? She shuddered at the thought. Nevertheless, she calmly and composedly reminded Izzy of the offer and the need for quick acceptance.

Ms. Schuyler stood abruptly, quickly reaching her full, quite impressive height. She wore an expression on her face which only could be described as a sneer, yet Izzy, practiced in gauging customer's reactions, noticed something else. Was it fear?

The interview was over. Izzy politely took his leave, a mixture of confusion and elation swirling through his uncomplicated mind. Based on her behavior, he figured if he waited a bit, just a couple of days, the stock might increase in value significantly maybe go as high as four mill. It was a gamble. He smiled as he left the headquarters of Computers R Us, a big, broad, complacent smile on the face of the man who virtually never gambled.

It was time to head back to Pine Ridge. Izzy had done his due diligence and he could now begin the process of liquidation of the assets of the estate. He could have Melvin Levy arrange for the coin auction. He would contact a lawyer and arrange to have the shares of stock and the dividends reissue evaluated. Then he would offer the stocks for sale, a thousand shares at a time, through a reputable brokerage on the New York Stock exchange, if there was such a thing, after negotiating the lawyer's fee and stockbroker's commission, of course

Chapter 16

Hazel, his bouffanted secretary, bounced onto his office and informed Jimmy G that he had to be in the courthouse at 2:00. The Judge was prepared to announce his decision in open Court on Jimmy's Motion To Dismiss in the O'Halloran's Will case. Jimmy got on the horn and desperately tried to round up Izzy. He called everywhere he could think of and couldn't reach him. The best he could do was to reach Nat, and he frantically explained the situation. Izzy just had to be in court at 2:00 p.m. After his conversation with Nat, he hung up the phone, perplexed. *Dat was damn strange,* he thought. *Dat kid is normally pretty straight, but dat was one fishy excuse. I wonder where de ole man is? Anyways, he tol' me he'd go find him an' get Iz in Court.*

It was almost two and Jimmy was pacing behind the lawyer's table, running his fingers nervously through his hair, wiping residual grease on the handkerchief he held crushed in his hands. But at two minutes before the hour, Nat rushed into the courtroom followed by Izzy. Or what looked like Izzy. Jimmy scratched his head as Izzy came in. He seemed to be awfully spry. There was something odd about him, something different, but he didn't know exactly what it was. Jimmy had spent a lot of time with Izzy, and thought he knew the old man pretty well. *Maybe it's some fancy new vitamin,* he thought.

Judge Martin entered the courtroom amidst the usual fanfare at exactly 2:00 p.m. Sounding like he was singing an aria in a Wagnerian opera, Bailiff Burton opened Court. Ever the politician and the epitome of what a judge should look like, Judge Harley Martin decided to formally announce his decision in open Court. He was confident his brilliant decision would bring him accolades. His wisdom would also bring him some relief, however temporary, from the discomfort of having to choose between his loyalty to his constituency, most of whom were devotees of the Temple of God, and what he felt was right. Since judges were elected in North Carolina, pandering to the preferred voting blocs was always in the back of their minds.

The packed courtroom of hastily assembled townsfolk who were rabidly interested in the case, and the regular septuagenarian court watchers, noisily rose to their feet in unison at the mellifluous command of the singing bailiff, who coincidentally, was the lead baritone in the choir at the Temple of God. The Judge entered with his customary regal authority and took his seat.

He got right down to business. The Judge's voice, sounding as if it boomed up from the bottom of a well, was the epitome of judiciousness. "Ladies and gentlemen. I have reviewed the record in this case and have carefully considered the persuasive arguments of the able counsel." As he paused for effect, Jimmy G was thinking to himself that the Judge's statement probably applied only to the Judge's good friend, Mr. B. S. Fotheringham, III.

"But," the judge continued, and those in attendance who were knowledgeable, emitted a collective, but silent groan, as they sensed the decision to delay that was about to be delivered, "I cannot rule on this motion until all the necessary parties are before me. Therefore, I am ordering that the other contingent beneficiary, the Pine Ridge Institute for the Treatment of Canines Humanely (PRITCH), be brought into this case. When this has been properly accomplished and the Pine Ridge Institute for the Treatment of Canines Humanely (PRITCH) has had sufficient time to file their response, I will reconsider this motion." Smugly, Judge Martin stood, tacitly challenging those who disagreed with him. The bailiff adjourned Court and the Judge swept out of Court amidst a cacophony of loud murmurs.

Jimmy turned to the man he thought was Izzy and said, "Dat ain't bad. A' least we din't lose, eh?" He reached out and shook Melvin Levy's hand, gave him a pat on the shoulder, and walked out of the courtroom, leaving the bewildered numismatist in the care of his ersatz son.

A few days later, the proper Order having been prepared and signed by the Judge, the Institute for the Treatment of Canines Humanely (ITCH) was officially a party to "In re Will of O'Halloran." Jimmy was in his office a little early, scratching his head over a legal conundrum, when Hazel, impeccably coiffed as usual with the help of a good quarter can of hair spray, knocked on his office door and peeked around it. "Ahem. Mr. G. There is a man here claims he is the attorney for the Institute for the Treatment of Canines Humanely (ITCH). Would like a moment of your time. Uh, Mr. G, he has a dog with him."

"A dawg, huh? Dere's always a foist time. Aw right Hazel, send him in."

Jimmy almost guffawed as the man came through the door. He looked like an honest to God collie. He had a long sharp nose, deep set eyes under orange gray bushy eyebrows, and long hair that was the most unusual color, a strange mixture of orange, black, and gray. And walking in with him was a well behaved, well groomed collie. He haughtily introduced himself to Jimmy G.

"Good Mawnin,' suh. Mah name's Rex Chase, from neahby Greeneburg. Ah represent the Institute for the Treatment of Canines Humanely (ITCH) in the matter of the Estate of Hamish O'Halloran."

After the pleasantries were exchanged and each of the lawyers had sized up the other in the seven seconds that nature allotted to humans to form their first impressions, he continued.

"Ah have reviewed the will, a devilish instrument containing some unique legal conditions, wouldn't ya say?" Without giving Jimmy G a chance to respond, or even to nod his head in assent, he asked, "How much would y'all estimate the preliminary value of the estate ta be, Mr. uh, G?" he said, looking at the foot and a half long name plate which announced, "James F. Giacogiavonni, Attorney at Law," and realizing he didn't have the first clue as to how to pronounce the name.

Jimmy thought that was a legitimate question from the attorney for the potential beneficiary, but he was not about to stake himself out, here.

"Dat's hard ta say. Prolly a leas' a mill, mebbe two, even t'ree. Who knows? We ain't had a chance ta have nuttin' appraised yet." Jimmy shrugged, and Chase's jaw dropped revealing his shiny big canines, as in his mind he translated Jimmy's Yankee argot to the only true language-Southernese.

Chase stammered a bit as he asked his next question. "Um, uh, um, and wheah might these animals be, the one's mentioned in the will?"

Jimmy had a stunned expression on his face. "Cheez, Rex. I dunno. Lemme ask the ol' man. I'll get back ta ya on that one." He had never considered the dogs, and never even met them, or given them the opportunity to lick his hand or smell his crotch.

They chatted briefly, and as Chase got up to leave, Jimmy said, "Ya know, Rex, Mr. B.S. Fotheringham, da Toid, represents dat Temple, which is de udder contingent beneficiary."

"Ah, yes, Mr. G. A worthy opponent indeed. However, it remains to be seen whether his client is so worthy after all, doesn't it?" Rex said, as he slyly winked.

Rex Chase was obviously an inveterate dog lover, as he left Jimmy's office with his collie proudly trotting after him. But Rex was sorely perplexed. Jimmy G was a city boy and knew virtually nothing about the dogs, including Caesar, so prominently mentioned in O'Halloran's will. But Rex Chase, dog lover, extraordinaire, was determined to find out about them. Since Pine Street was only a few blocks away he decided to start there. He slowly drove by the darkened, somewhat eerie looking house, and observed a sturdy chain link fence in back. He parked his car and got out, walking up to the fence searching for the dogs. The yard had been newly mown, so the vegetation was relatively short, except for several bale size piles of recently shorn vegetation.

Rex Chase experienced a cold chill running through him, causing an involuntary shiver. Like his dog, all dogs for that matter, he could sense changes in the weather and circumstances when things were very wrong or when danger was afoot. The dogs were obviously somewhere else, perhaps having escaped through some crater dug under the chain link fence. There were three well built dog houses, a sheltered feeding trough, and a well-worn path running along the fence. He could see a chain big enough to moor a battleship which began at a tree stump and ended in a good size D-ring which had been torn off the dog's collar, languishing empty in the mud. But the chief distinction of the yard was the ominous silence.

Rex returned to his office and made a few phone calls as he attempted to locate the dogs. He had eliminated several options and shuddered as he suspected what had actually occurred. With a lot less enthusiasm, and a whole lot of consternation, he got back in his car and drove to the kennel operated by the Pine Ridge Institute for the Treatment of Canines Humanely (PRITCH), a subsidiary of the multistate charitable organization, (ITCH).

He was overcome with a sinking feeling as he was directed to the local office of the Institute for the Treatment of Canines Humanely (ITCH) and saw a small man seated behind a desk with a cat coiled comfortably in his lap. This was not a good sign for dog lovers. The cat was purring loudly in response to the man's patient stroking. Rex inquired about the O'Halloran dogs.

"Hmmm. Let me see. O'Halloran, did you say? Seems like I remember something." He looked in a large index card file. "Nothing here. Let me look in the "U" file."

"The "U" file?" Chase asked.

"Yeah. You know. "U" for euthanized. OK. Here they are." He plucked three cards from the file. "Let's see. O'Halloran X-1. mixed breed, 60 pounds, black. U dated only a few days ago. Initials BH. Then on this card, O'Halloran, X-2. Mixed breed mostly Lab. 48 pounds, black. U the same date, same initials. The last one, O'Halloran, X-3, German shepherd, 125 pounds, whew, big one. Aggressive! Bit Billy H. That's strange. There's no disposition, and no initials, but it's in the U file. I'll have to ask Billy what happened to the big shepherd when he comes in."

Chase was despondent when he left. If the man was right, two of the dogs that had been left in the care of the Institute for the Treatment of Canines Humanely (ITCH) had been put to sleep. The Institute was supposed to take care of them, not kill them. He wondered if Caesar was still alive, and if so, could he still collect under the will if only one of the three dogs survived. Speaking out loud, and with genuine concern, but only to himself, he muttered, *I wonder what did happen to the big one. I'll bet that's the one called Caesar*

Chapter 17

The old house on Pine Street was empty and unlit, but the moon shined its colorless light, casting hundreds of eerie shadows among the tree lined street. If a house could look forlorn, the old lawyer's house certainly did. Not only did it appear cold and uninviting, it looked sad and afraid. The house itself seemed to shiver as a slight breeze, sifting through the trees, caused the shadows to quaver as they fell on the house.

O'Halloran's old home was a simple two-story farmhouse, the type that was commonly constructed in the great financial boom of the 1880s. It had ten-foot ceilings and big, elongated windows which gave it a certain aura of coldness, perhaps even heartlessness. To say that it was ghostly would not be an overstatement.

By ten o'clock in the evening, the stodgy residents of the neighborhood had all gone to bed, ignoring the laughtrack lures of latenight Leno and Letterman, and had turned out their lights. Except for the insignificant glow of a night light or an unattended computer terminal, all the houses on the street were dark.

A non-descript sedan of Japanese manufacture, (they all look alike, don't they), slowly crept along the street. The driver, unrecognizable since he was dressed all in black, including a black ski mask and toboggan, was clearly canvassing the area. Almost surreptitiously, he parked his dark sedan, perhaps it was black, navy blue or dark green, a couple of blocks down the street under the undulating shade of a stately elm.

Sneaking along with the stalking gait of a nightfighter, the driver circled around behind the house, clinging to the protection of any tree, shrub, shadow or anything else that provided cover. He finally arrived at the rear of O'Halloran's house, where he hesitated, looking around to make sure there were no prying eyes watching him. There were, of course, for the night is filled with all sorts of fauna invisible to humans in the sun light. A rat here, a cat there, even that universally detested and omnipresent omnivore, the opossum, eyed him warily.

Cautiously, he vaulted up on the porch rail with the agility of a spider monkey and clambered up on to the roof of the back porch. Blending into the shadows, he quietly jimmied a window and crept inside.

The man was an expert second story man. He wore lycra gloves, for he did not want to leave any incriminating fingerprints. He pulled out a miniature hooded flashlight and slowly swept the tiny shaft of illumination back and forth across the empty bed room. Silently, he examined every drawer of the dresser, got on his stomach and carefully searched under the bed, felt each slat for some hidden treasure, felt between the mattresses, thinking there might be some cash, a hidden wallet or even a gun, and carefully looked in every nook and cranny of the room.

About the same time, a uniformed policeman, guardedly walking the beat, approached the house. Looking around like a cat burglar, which of course he was that night, the policeman tried the front door. Just in case anyone happened to be looking, he could claim he was checking the security of the premises. He turned and gave a quick, but thorough glance at all the houses in the neighborhood. Everything was still; nothing moving except the shivering leaves on the trees. Finding the front door locked, he sneaked around to the back door.

The sneak thief in the black attire of the professional burglar had heard the muted sounds of someone sneaking about, trying the door, approaching. He decided that discretion might be the better part of valor, if a burglar could be valorous at all, and made his way to the back window to effect his escape. Quietly, he had just lifted his leg to depart through the open window when he observed the surreptitious movements of the policeman below him. He carefully retracted his leg and with the utmost caution, padded about looking for a suitable hiding place. He reasoned he would patiently wait until the intruder had left.

Finding the back door locked as well, the policeman took a small metal spatula from his trousers, the kind a baker uses in professionally icing a cake. The feeble lock on the old door gave virtually no resistance, and the policeman was inside in an instant. He found himself in the kitchen and began looking into each drawer and cabinet. Although he tried to be as quiet as he could, the contents of the kitchen drawers rattled as he pawed through them. As furtive as a feral cat stalking its prey, he searched the entire downstairs in the hope that the coins would turn up, making him instantly rich.

The man in black was now aware of the presence of the burglar in the house downstairs, but of course, he didn't know the intruder was a policeman. There were no closets in the bedrooms in the old house, an architectural anomaly common to that era, a fact which he found to be curious. He located the only closet on the floor, a large storage closet off the hall at the side of the stair case. Quietly opening the door just enough to slide in, the burglar vanished into the depths of the closet, wedging himself into the very rear corner, carefully concentrating on controlling his breathing, the epitome of silence and concealment.

Suddenly, a car driving quickly down the street came to a screeching halt in front of the house. The doors to the car squeaked open and a second or two later, loudly slammed. Animated by the fear of being caught inside the building, the policeman looked out the parlor window and saw three men running toward the house. Panicking, he ran up the stairs three at a time. Frantically looking about in the dim light, searching the upstairs for a place to hide, he was frustrated by the grotesque shapes and shadows thrown by the eerie light of the moon. He noticed the outline of the hallway closet. He thrust himself inside just as the front door noisily banged open, as the three clumsy felons put their shoulders to the old front door.

At first, the policeman, who was perhaps just a tad overweight, if one wants to be kind, was gasping for breath. He concentrated desperately on getting his heavy breathing under control, afraid the gasping noise would expose him. Slowly, he regained his composure, and could hear the unrestrained and clumsy activities of the burglars downstairs, as they laughed, talked, and noisily searched throughout the house.

After his breathing began to settle down and he had regained his composure, the policeman gradually became aware of another presence in the closet. A cold shiver sent a metallic tingle down his spine, settling in his groin, as his consciousness leapt to this conclusion. He slowly turned to inspect the closet when a gloved hand clamped over his face scaring the bejeesus out of him. A familiar, warm puddle formed at his feet. The man in black whispered, "Don't say a word. Maybe we can sneak out of here without being caught."

Just as they were about to open the closet door to make their escape, the two conspirators and all the clumsy felons on the first floor heard another vehicle loudly approaching the house. Clearly audible was the slam of the car door followed by the thud of heavy shoes climbing the steps to the front porch. The upstairs conspirators snugly tucked away back in their closet, shelved their anxiety for a moment as they snickered at the chaos of the three stooges, downstairs. They could picture their trepidation as the clowns on the first floor noisily scampered around, in a futile effort to avoid compromise, but the amusement of the closeted criminals turned to panic as they heard the trio clambering noisily up the stairs in terror, as they tried to escape the detection of this new unknown intruder.

The latest uninvited person to visit casa O'Halloran that night was the chief of detectives himself, ostensibly having come to inspect the O'Halloran premises for his own edification, if anybody asked, and if he just so happened to discover a box of gold coins, ah well...

As the detective sergeant approached the front door, which was slightly ajar from the machinations of the inept burglars, he noticed some splinters of wood on the floor, a fact that he found to be most curious. Giving the door a nudge with his size 12 EE's, it gave way, and he edged his way in.

The careless and now quite frightened trio, running three abreast, had somehow gained the top of the staircase erect. Looking around in a virtual panic, one of them spied the hallway closet door, and noisily jammed himself inside, quickly followed by the others, just as the chief of detectives entered the house.

It was a comic sight, but fortunately there was not a trace of light in the closet. The three gasped as they found the closet already occupied, not a difficult discovery since they were wedged in like sardines, with not an inch of room between them to move. Packed like sardines was an appropriate cliché lacking only the salt and oil.

The cat burglar and the policeman quieted them with a lot of *shhhs*. A quick whisper warned them to be alert to the presence of the detective, although they did not know at the time, that the intruder downstairs was the chief of detectives himself, committing the same felony of which they were all guilty. After some panicked whispering, they all settled down to listen, the various efforts at controlling their excited breathing becoming a virtual muted cacophony.

The heavy clomp of the detective's size twelves clearly marked his location downstairs to the inept and frightened burglars huddling in the closet. A couple of seconds later, having managed to control their heavy breathing to a state close to normalcy, they were riddled with fear as those footsteps began ascending the stairs, the thud of each slow and careful step virtually reverberating throughout the house.

The blare of loud sirens unexpectedly pierced the air, and the screeching of brakes panicked them all. Fearful of a full-scale police raid, they burst out of the closet in an effort to escape from virtually certain discovery by the police, just as the chief of detectives reached the landing at the top of the stairs.

The herd of criminals burst forth from the closet, a tangle of bodies falling to the floor amid the grotesque and eerie shadows thrown by the brilliant moon. The escaping burglars crashed into the chief detective. A flashlight fell to the floor, its beam illuminating shoe tops and casting weird and distorted shadows. Below, doors were banged open, the ominous sound echoing throughout the house.

A squad of uniformed policemen, legitimate cops responding to the neighbor's frantic call of a break-in in progress, kicked in the front and back doors almost simultaneously. Chaos reigned as the criminals ran wildly about on the upper level as each sought to escape the virtually certain arrest, as the policemen, themselves quite frightened by the tumultuous clamor, cautiously climbed the stairs, with guns drawn, not knowing what calamity they were about to face.

The burglar in black, the calmest of the crowd, attempted to crawl out the same window he had come in. He was solidly pushed from behind, as the large policeman barged his way through the window just after him. Attempting to maintain a semblance of balance, the burglar in black stumbled along the slanted porch roof, tripped, falling face first into a big hawthorn bush a full story below. The unforgiving twigs mercilessly tore his ski mask and scratched his face like an angry cat.

The policeman panicked and ran headlong across the roof. Not realizing the roof had ended, he soared through the air until a substantial maple tree branch, unfortunately forked at just the right place, caught the officer right in the neck, flipping him so that he landed with a disgustingly loud thud, flat on his back, knocking the breath completely out of him.

Each of the others in their panic driven haste, sought a closed window as the preferred avenue for escape. Bursting through the shattering glass on the merest of hope, if any thought at all was given that a non-fatal landing would result, they tumbled to the unforgiving ground. But the twelve-foot fall onto the thorny bushes below was the least of their worries. The glass, which took just a little effort to shoulder through, slashed each of the burglars in numerous places as they flew to their freedom.

Meanwhile, the legitimate policemen, ever cautious, having gained the second story, were relieved to find they were alone on that now deserted floor, yet terrified at the commotion that had preceded their arrival there. Looking out the broken windows into the distorted shadows thrown by the moonlight on the grey-green ground below, the officers could see silhouettes of some moaning and injured perpetrators hurriedly limping off in various directions, leaving behind some seriously crippled and maimed shrubbery.

The next day there was a curious spate of unexplained injuries among a good number of the townsfolk. Jimmy G's cousins each had gotten into their pickups and raced to the emergency room in Greeneburg to have their profuse bleeding stanched, gashes stitched, and bruises tended to. The felonious cop was barely able to stumble to the sanctum of a neighbor's shed where he hid until dawn, struggling for a decent breath as the swelling of his thick neck almost choked him. The next morning, his neck swollen like an inner tube, and his back radiating with piercing pain, the policeman hobbled into the chiropractor's office for a manipulation, and some hoped for serious relief.

The man in black, who was in fact a private investigator hired by the museum long ago, had for many years harbored obsessive designs on the stolen coins he had been hired to recover, and had long ago cut his ties with the museum. He was now a freelance thief. He treated his injuries himself with the aid of a mirror and a healthy supply of hydrogen peroxide, gauze bandages, and anti-biotic salve. When he was done, he looked like a mummy.

The detective sergeant, Sergeant Peter Richard O'Malley, whose first two names were never, ever, to be spoken aloud because of their phallic intimation, was under a lot of scrutiny himself. He was the sergeant because, in fact, he was the only detective on the Pine Ridge force. His boss, Captain Collins, came into his office, and stared at his cheek for an inordinately long time, his silence accusatory. The window glass, shattering as he jumped through it, had slashed the detective's cheek like a Heidelburg dueling scar. Collins was no fool, so deep within his suspicious policeman's heart, he knew, but he just couldn't bring himself to believe that his own detective sergeant had stooped to such shenanigans.

To him the whole idea was funny, it really was, and he couldn't help emitting an involuntary snicker. But quickly gaining his reserve, Captain Collins coughed into his hand, and said, "Detective O'Malley, I want you to interview everybody who showed up in town this morning with a suspicious injury, the kind one might get jumping out of a second story window. Connect them to that break-in at O'Halloran's, and if you get any bit of evidence at all, charge 'em."

As he walked out of the room, he couldn't resist calling back over his shoulder, "And don't forget to interview yourself, too." With that, he burst out laughing, the cackling continuing long after he had walked out of earshot,

Within hours, Jimmy G's cousins had been arrested, and charged with felonious breaking and entering, but not burglary since the house was not technically occupied by a resident. Apparently, occupation by second story men did not count as an element of the crime of first degree burglary. They appeared before the judge and were soon out on bond. Curiously, the policeman with the swollen neck, and the Detective Sergeant himself had escaped arrest, but each looked upon the other with great suspicion.

When Jimmy walked into his office, his three cousins, bandages and all, were waiting sheepishly in his reception area, guarded by a stern visaged and vigilant Hazel, who was obviously disgusted at having the three wounded ruffians sully her waiting room.

It was a strange symbiosis: the impeccable but unstylish Hazel with her horn-rimmed glasses and blue-gray, hair-sprayed beehive, piled high on her head, and the small typically unkempt, sweaty and harried Brooklynite. And yet she did her very best to protect Jimmy from the demons and pitfalls inherent in his field of the Southern style practice of law in Pine Ridge. After all, when one deals only with thugs, drug dealers and pathetic addicts, the morally challenged, and the emotionally unstable year after year, one can't help but be affected. Perhaps that is why the best of that ilk of criminal attorneys attends church regularly in the faint hope that they will thereby be cleansed of the filth that accumulated on them during the work week by their associations.

But Jimmy had his own set of standards and principles. His mind was quick and sharp, and he fully understood where he fit in the social hierarchy of Pine Ridge. Basically honest, he had occasionally given in to the pressures and perhaps might have bent a little, but he always sprang back straight, if not tall.

So when he walked by his pathetic looking excuses for cousins, he just motioned them into his office without a word. When he shut the door behind him and sat at his his desk, he said to the trio, without asking, but knowing nonetheless, "Geez. You t'ree gotta be da dumbest chumps around. Wha' da Hell were youse guys t'inkin'?"

The three dumbest chumps around just looked down at their feet, guilt virtually engraved on their wrinkled, olive complexioned foreheads. Salvatore, the most intelligent of the trio, but just barely, was the regular spokesman. After too long a period of silence, Sally, as he was usually called, said, "Geez Jimmy. I'm sawry. It's jus', you know, da gold. All dat gold jus' sittin' dere all alone. Jeez Jimmy, it was a opportunity."

"Bull. Youse guys are class A dopes. Youse t'ink anybody keeps a bunch a gold jus' lyin' aroun' in a empty house? Even I don' know where da ol'guy keeps it stashed. An' I don' wanna know. So wadda youse guys charged wit'?"

Sally sighed and responded, while Pasquale, who was usually referred to as Squally, fidgeted and stared intently at his toes. Ottorino just sat there, impossibly slumped in his chair, almost like he was a blanket. "It's just a B and E, Jimmy, maybe attempted larceny, too. You know, da usual."

"Sally, youse guys, ya know yiz're supposed to lef' dat crap behind when we came down here. Reeno, Squally. Wadda youse guys got ta say? Nuttin' as usual?"

Squally fidgeted some more and Reeno was about to slump completely out of his chair onto the floor when he caught himself, and, with considerable effort, lifted his body into an approximation of a sitting position. But as usual, they didn't respond.

"Can ya get us probation Jimmy? Huh? Can ya? Ya know, like last time?" Sally knew there wasn't a chance of probation, but hope springs eternal.

"Now youse guys listen and listen good. Here's da deal. I represent de estate of da ol' lawyer, right? Dis here estate-dat's my client. An' youse chumps broke in ta da house what's part of de estate. Ya unnerstan'? Dat's a confict o' interes'. I ain't gonna represent any of youse. Yiz are all on yer own. Have da Court appoint yiz lawyers. Now git outta heah."

Chapter 18

Detective Sergeant Peter Richard O'Malley was exhausted. The stressful events of the night before had not only robbed him of his normal good night's sleep, he was fretting over the cloud of suspicion that hovered over him, too. It could mean his pension if he was caught. *What a stupid thing to do,* he thought, *all for a potential few bucks. Okay, maybe a few million bucks.* He smiled to himself. God, the stress of the events of last night sure made him tired. He put his feet up on his desk, closed his eyes and thought he'd just catch a few winks.

When he awoke there was a man sitting in front of him. He was a thin man, almost gaunt, sporting an old-fashioned crew cut, the kind that was popular in the fifties. He wore wire rimmed glasses and his smallish head sat atop a long thin neck. He wore a black suit, a plain white shirt and an unstylish slim red tie. He sat erect waiting for the detective to acknowledge him, his steel blue eyes piercing through the detective's façade of somnolent unconcern.

A look of fear swept across the detective's face for he instinctively knew the man was a cop himself. "Whatta you want?" he asked brazenly to cover up his concern.

The man unsettled Detective O'Malley by not answering right away. Another surge of trepidation engulfed the detective, as the man quickly reached inside his suit jacket pocket. Instead of a gun, he pulled out a federal ID badge. "I am Agent James Smith," the man responded with authority. "I am an investigator with the Internal Revenue Service."

James Smith. Sure. Of course, that was his real name. An IRS agent named James Smith. But still, O'Malley was frightened although he didn't know exactly why. Guilt has a strange way of having this effect. It would eat away at you until you gave in to it and confessed to anyone who would listen. The agent was used to this reaction, for IRS agents were more feared than the Mafia, serial killers, and five hundred-pound gorillas. As a rule, they were friendless sadists, delighting in the uncontrolled squirming of their interviewees, who were usually their suspects and were usually quite guilty of some tax infraction, or sometimes, a financial felony of mammoth proportions.

It is a universal truth that everyone cheats on their income tax returns. IRS agents know it and exploit it. Under withering interrogation, the agents often obtained all sorts of information ranging from confessions of drug smuggling to embezzlement to kiddie porn as mitigating explanations for the perpetrators' tax evasion.

But this was something different. Detective Peter Richard (Peter Dick to his friends) O'Malley was not a suspect. "It has come to the attention of the service that Mr. Isadore Shapiro has come into possession of some extremely valuable articles on which the appropriate tax has not been paid," remarked the officious agent, eyeing the detective's stitches with suspicion.

These people are like vultures, the detective mused. He imagined that the IRS had a bunch of hungry agents just sitting around reading obituaries, looking for evidence of sizable estates just sitting there waiting to be seized by the omnipresent tax man.

"By the way, what happened to your face?"

Regretting his answer as soon as it involuntarily escaped forth from his parched lips, but being oddly compelled to be truthful with the investigator, who was after all a federal agent, O'Malley said, "I fell through a window." Agent Smith merely nodded, like a fellow conspirator.

They discussed the situation of the estate, the coins, and the common knowledge in Pine Ridge that the dearly departed had been virtually impecunious during his professional life, barely eking out an existence at his less than stellar pursuit of his profession of the law.

After picking Detective Sergeant O'Malley's brains to the point where the big cop wasn't sure he had any left, Agent Smith asked, "Now where can I find this elusive estate executor?"

O'Malley, responded, "Well, to tell the truth, I ain't seen him in a while. His store is on Main Street, but I usually see him marching to the courthouse just about every day. Hmmm. Not for a while though."

Detective Sergeant O'Malley walked Agent James Smith out of the police station to his car in a feeble effort to ingratiate himself with the agent, but in reality, he was trying to find out more about what he considered the competition, for they were both after the same thing, weren't they, the coins? O'Malley thought back on the fiasco the night before at Casa O'Halloran. It was just a temporary setback in his quest for the pot of gold at the end of the rainbow. He was still scheming about how to get his hands on the gold coins, but now his immediate attention was how to get rid of the stiff IRS agent.

That pair of stalwart protectors of the citizenry stood by the agent's car, a black, of course, large styleless sedan with the traditional silver government plates on it. It might as well have had a neon sign on it announcing: *Fed.* O'Malley couldn't help but notice it was parked brazenly in a handicapped parking space.

The cop pointed out the harberdasher's store, just across the street and a couple of doors down. The meticulous agent, his slender briefcase in hand, fedora tilted, stormed across the street to confront the mercenary merchant.

As Detective O'Malley was walking back to his office he met a zealous rookie, Patrolman Louie, coming out of the station. Louie was about as bright as a twenty-five watt bulb, and O'Malley suspected his last name came from an immigrant ancestor who thought the more chummy name of

"Louie" would be more acceptable to the established citizenry of America than the formal "Louis."

"Hey, Louie," O'Malley called in a tone indicating he was the patrolman's best friend, "There's a black sedan parked in a handicapped space right outside the station. It ain't got no handicap placard or license plate. Why don't you go throw a wheel lock on it?" The detective smirked as he went back into his office to grab a little shut eye.

Chapter 19

With an arrogant air of superiority, Agent James Smith, of the Internal Revenue Service, entered the establishment of I. Shapiro, Haberdasher. Izzy's son was standing at a counter idly talking with a customer. Well, he wasn't really a customer. He was a lonely old codger who often spent the day entertaining himself by watching the daily court proceedings, which were the only action in the sleepy little town. When court wasn't in session, the old guy would wander over to the store and find someone to strike up a conversation with about the good old days.

Agent Smith was about to interrupt them, when he noticed the office door. He spied a small bespectacled man seated in the beat up old leather chair reading a newspaper. The door was open for how else could he have seen the man? Smith, smug in the supposition of his superior powers of deduction, barged into the office without so much as an "ahem."

Resulting from decades of closely inspecting coins and stamps, Melvin Levy was more than a little bit myopic and kept the paper only inches from his face as he pored over the mundane and often sappy news of Pine Ridge. Smith rudely pulled the newspaper from in front of Levy's face and announced, "I am James Smith, special agent with the Internal Revenue Service. My agency has recently received information that you have come into a fortune in gold and have not paid the applicable taxes."

Levy, although a small man with thick glasses, was, after all, a New Yorker, and therefore not about to be intimidated by this brash twerp of an IRS agent.

"Look pal, if I had a fortune in gold do you think I would be sitting in this pathetic excuse for a store, in this podunk town, reading this rag of a newspaper?" Levy said it with so much defiance that Smith, who thought he was talking with Isadore Shapiro, a meek haberdasher, was completely taken aback. Involuntarily, he took a small step backwards, and with that, he had lost his advantage.

After that, the conversation was ineffective and went downhill for the agent. Levy pressed his advantage spewing righteous indignation. Levy was by nature a close talker, perhaps due to his myopia, and his nose was just inches from the agent's face. The agent, who was an obsessive clean freak, could not stand the spray and spittle, and quickly backed away from the extremely perturbed little man.

The result was a total loss for Smith. He learned nothing about the coins, failing completely in his normal practice of intimidation that went along with his official title. He walked back to his car in an addled state. But when he saw the wheel lock on his car he was furious. He stormed into the police station and confronted the desk sergeant, berating him as if the burly man was an errant child.

But the desk sergeant was used to public tirades and affected a bored, unconcerned manner. Nonchalantly, he explained that parking in a handicapped parking space brought with it a hundred-dollar fine, and the wheel lock was an additional $75.00 to have it removed. "And you sure don't look handicapped, Buddy," he added, just for good measure.

That was it, no argument, pay $175.00, or get lost. The agent's vociferous protestations fell on deaf ears as the sergeant ignored him. His important stature as a federal law enforcement officer meant little here in Pine Ridge.

"I want to talk to your superior," Agent Smith demanded authoritatively. The desk sergeant pointed down the hall, where a name plate protruding from over the door announced, "Captain Collins."

James Smith stormed into Captain Collins' office without knocking. Collins looked up from a report he was reading, and said icily, "Can I help you?"

"I am Special Agent James Smith of *the* Internal Revenue Service. I just had a wheel lock placed on my car by one of your men."

"So," responded the Captain. "Were you illegally parked?"

"Well, um, well yes. But I am a special agent of the Internal Revenue Service."

"Well, do you have a letter from the governor, or the president, or even a papal dispensation which says you can park illegally? I would accept any of those. Especially, a note from the Pope," he snickered.

Smith stuttered. He stammered. He turned beet red so that the close-cut orange-red hair seemed to stand out on his pink skull. "Of course not."

Collins ended the discussion. "Well, Mr. Smith, you can't park illegally here in Pine Ridge. It's against the law."

Smith made a last-ditch effort. "But I saw a police car parked illegally," he protested.

"Yeah," Collins said, "I know. He has a letter from the governor."

"Crap," Special Agent James Smith of the Internal Revenue Service muttered to himself as he pulled two hundreds out of his wallet to pay the fine as he walked back to the desk sergeant.

"I don't have any change here," said the desk sergeant nonchalantly. "You'll have to go to the clerk's office or the bank next door."

Banks were smart. It really got down to a means to reduce the robbery rate, for a bank to put up an establishment next to the police station, and it even had a nice effect on the rate of worthless checks as well.

Smith's ire was only fueled by the blasé attitude of the desk sergeant. He thought the cop even had a conspiratorial smirk, which aggravated him even more, as he stormed out of the police station, and stewed on his way to the bank. You could almost see the steam coming out of his ears as he slapped the hundred on the counter in front of the bank teller, asking for change.

The teller was a very young girl, impeccably groomed, who exuded a mind-boggling neatness. There was a name plate on the counter announcing her name, Misty Dawn, an appropriate appellation in this case.

She greeted Agent James Smith with a vapid pleasantness. She politely took the bill and Agent Smith noticed her white porcelain fingers and perfect nails. The teller took a special marker and perfunctorily slashed the bill with it. Suddenly, her cordial facial expression vanished as the marker reacted with the bill.

"Um, could you wait just a minute?" she said, rushing off to take the bill to the bank manager, as the startled IRS agent stood there, dumbfounded. He had seen the telltale change in color as well, but he was transfixed. This could not be happening to him. In an instant, the bank manager, a short balding man with a bad combover, stood before the agent, the teller standing slightly behind him.

"I'll need some identification, sir. This bill is counterfeit and will have to be confiscated and sent off to the Secret Service."

Smith was beside himself, but since he was essentially law abiding, he handed the bank manager his IRS Special Agent ID card. The bank manager said, "Hmmm. This is interesting," looking at the ID card. He returned it after making a copy. "I guess you can go, sir. The Secret Service will probably be in touch with you. I have to confiscate this bill, though."

Red faced with both embarrassment and anger, Agent Smith turned and stormed out of the bank, as the manager carefully wrote down his description, even though the bank's security camera had duly recorded the whole transaction.

"I have got to get the hell out of this burg, fast," thought Special Agent Smith as he headed back to his car. He groaned as he looked at the wheel lock again, realizing he still had to get change for a hundred. He looked into his wallet, relieved to see another C-note.

He walked into the nearby McDonald's, waiting on line for the impossibly slow-moving clerk to get to him. When she finally did, he curtly, asked for change of the C-note.

"Ah'm sorry, suh. We not allowed ta make change. Ya gotta buy sommit."

The aggravated agent asked for a cup of coffee, black. His impatience was working on him as the clerk shuffled off in slow motion to get the coffee. When she returned with it, he slammed the hundred on the counter, so perturbed, he was about to explode.

The clerk merely pointed to a sign which informed Agent Smith, *"We cannot accept currency in amounts greater than $20.00."* His fury was now boundless having exponentially increased at this latest development. He scraped together the requisite $1.19 in change, threw it on the counter, and spun around, bumping into a four hundred-pound man, who obviously could not fit into a bathtub. The fetid aroma surrounding the giant man squelched Smith's desire for the coffee, if he ever had one. He tossed the cup of coffee in the trash on his way out.

But as he stormed out of the restaurant, he stopped in his tracks, his jaw agape. His car was gone! "Double shit," he yelled, tears forming in the corners of his eyes. More irate than ever, if that was at all possible, he went back into the police station, but seeing the indifferent desk sergeant sitting there, engrossed in a dime novel, a western at that, a sudden wave of understanding came over him. He was defeated. Surrender was inevitable.

"Excuse me, Sergeant," he said politely, with an air of resignation. "I guess my car got towed, right?"

"Yep. You can retrieve it from Pete's Garage. Towing fee is $135.00," he said turning back to his intellectual pursuit.

Pete's Garage turned out to be a good mile away, just past the outskirts of town. As he walked in the general direction, where he had been told he could find the garage, it started to rain. Not just a little mist, mind you, but a true Southern gully whumper. He was soaked through and through as he sloshed into the office of Pete's an hour later. Like most such offices, it was filthy. Everything anybody touched was smeared with grease. But at least they took VISA.

The next day, Special Agent James Smith, special investigator extraordinaire for the Internal Revenue Service, walked into the office of his superior, quietly and with exaggerated reverence, laid down his gun and badge on the desk, and with neither fanfare nor explanation, walked out of the office of the Internal Revenue Service, and headed for a life as a woodsman in the wilds of Idaho.

Chapter 20

It was after lunch. For O'Malley, that was a huge burger with everything at the cops' favorite hangout, a real dive just outside of town on the Greeneburg Pike called Lefty's Loft. Ironically, Lefty was a frail, effeminate, bespectacled sort, with a high pitched, squeaky voice, who undoubtedly created the best burgers in the region, that is, if you had an appetite like a horse, or perhaps an angry grizzly. The place was actually a biker bar catering almost exclusively to cops, and believe it or not, bikers, of the Hells Angels, Pagans, Outlaws, and other tattooed, bearded, leather vested types, with chaps. The cops and bikers mingled in a kind of Rousseauian harmony.

The one-pound, Southern style burger, loaded with mustard, chili, slaw, and onions, dripping with three or four slices of cheese, had its desired effect on O'Malley. He couldn't keep his eyes open, let alone think about clues and criminals, so he caved in to habit. Resting his size twelves squarely on the middle of his desk, O'Malley closed his eyes, leaned back in his chair with high expectations of enjoying a desperately needed siesta.

After a few moments, a black cloud darkened his subconscious. It was guilt, subconscious, pervasive guilt. He was just about to exit the land of Nod to flee from this inescapable sense of good old fashioned Catholic guilt, when his conscious senses registered the flatulent sound of escaping air. He was quite familiar with the origin of the sound - someone sitting on the vinyl cushion of the straight back chair in front of his desk.

Cautiously, he took a peek, opening one eye just a tad. There was a small, slender man, prissy, if one can use that word to describe a man, not even 125 pounds. He had quietly, perhaps even bravely, taken the liberty of seating himself in the detective's office. He wore wire rimmed glasses, and had well coiffed, sandy hair, graying around the temples. He looked like an accountant, or perhaps more aptly, a librarian. He didn't say a word, but just waited patiently.

What now? Can't a man even take a little nap, without every twerp around coming in? Detective O'Malley thought. Without opening his eyes, he asked, "Whadda you want?"

The little man took it in stride. "My name is Augustus Seay. Do not ever call me Gus. I am employed by the museum to locate stolen artifacts. We feel that the coins which appear to be part of the estate of Mr. Hamish O'Halloran, were the same ones that were stolen from the museum a decade ago. I am here merely as a professional courtesy, to inform you of our inquiry, and our investigation in this area. And I have some questions about the recent break-in at the O'Halloran house, Detective Sergeant O'Malley, if you would be so kind."

Crap, O'Malley thought. *More, competition for those coins.*

Seay continued, "In your investigation, Detective Sergeant, who have you determined was actually involved in breaking in to the decedent's house?"

O'Malley hesitated. Sure, there was supposed to be professional courtesy, and this little twerp purported to be a private investigator, after all. But there were suspects and then there were suspects. "Well, there's those three dopes, cousins of that wop lawyer."

"And… I am certain there were others, Officer. Do you know who?"

Involuntarily, O'Malley's hand went up to his face and stroked his own facial wound, a pretty good tell if Seay was the poker playing type. "Yeah. We got a couple of other suspects who I can't name right now. We haven't interviewed them yet. And one other unknown perp. He was seen at the scene dressed in black wearing a black toboggan. But nobody who saw him can give any real description of him, except he was average size and build. But we think he was injured too, although it doesn't appear that he was treated at the little hospital here in Pine Ridge, or the county hospital in Greeneburg. At least I don't think he was." O'Malley hoped that would be enough to satisfy the little worm, as he unconsciously stroked his healing scar.

"Thank you, Detective Sergeant O'Malley," said Gus Seay, as he rose from his vinyl chair. But as the fastidious little man was about to leave, he turned, a la Columbo. "Just one more thing, Detective Sergeant. How did you get that scar?"

Reacting a bit too angrily, O'Malley snapped his by now stock answer. "I was working under my car and dropped a wrench and it sliced my face."

"Just as I thought," said Gus Seay with a bit of a smirk. He turned and left, but not before giving a very obvious glance to the officer's lily white, perfectly manicured, unsullied fingernails.

Without taking his feet off the desk, much to the chagrin of the persnickety Mr. Seay, O'Malley directed him to the haberdasher's store. He closed his eyes once again, to indicate to the bothersome intruder that the interview was over, and he needed to get back to his true calling. Unlike the hapless IRS agent, Mr. Gus Seay was a pretty smart investigator, unburdened with pesky hubris. First, he inquired at the clerk's office to which he had been directed by persons he first encountered as he entered the courthouse. He was ushered in to talk with Molly McMasters, the beleaguered head clerk.

Molly had never actually seen the coins, but there was a photocopy of all of them in the file. She allowed Mr. Seay to have a copy, upon his showing his P.I. credentials, explaining his mission, and showing her the letter of authorization from the curator of the museum. Molly could add little information about the deceased lawyer. Like everyone else, all she knew was that he was odd, reclusive, and that no one knew much about him. She did not have any idea where he might have gotten the coins.

Next, Augustus went to the Register of Deeds Office, figuring that a quick property search might lead to a little lateral help in tracing the origin of the coins. He was quite perplexed when nothing at all turned up as having been owned by O'Halloran, not even his own house.

Seay walked over to The Legal Lunch for a cup of tea to stimulate his investigative senses, and to help him think. He observed a well dressed distinguished looking older man in a dark blue suit, white shirt and red tie. *The lawyer's uniform*, he thought wryly, and walked over to the table where the man was reading his newspaper.

"Pardon me for intruding, sir. You are no doubt an attorney. I would like to ask you some questions unrelated to any of your cases, nor am I seeking legal representation. May I have a seat?"

Mr. Sparrow eyed the slender man with a great deal of curiosity. He nodded toward the seat, indicating his assent, for the slight little man certainly did not appear to be unscrupulous or dangerous. Augustus introduced himself formally and stated his occupation and reason for being there.

Mr. Sparrow told him, "I suppose I knew O' Halloran well, or as well as he allowed anyone to know him. He had no social life at all that I knew of, nor any close connection to anyone in town. Now that I think about it, he never even mentioned where he went to law school, or even if he did. Now that is curious. Hmmm." Mr. Sparrow reflected in silence for a few minutes. "You know, Mr Seay, O'Halloran is a unique name in these parts, but I seem to recall that many years ago my friend mentioned something about having an aunt who lived around here."

Augustus Seay thanked Mr. Sparrow for his insight, gratuitously paid for his lunch, surprising the elderly lawyer, and left. At least it was something. He wasn't sure where it would lead him. He decided to start with the town library.

The Pine Ridge library was in a small, old clapboard house, more of a branch than a real library. There were the the usual assortment of magazines and newspapers, best sellers, and classics, and some reference books. But it did have a computer, and he was able to get on line.

Because of his diligence and methodology, Augustus Seay had proved to be a superb investigator for the museum. He had made some almost miraculous finds as he checked the provenance of a suspicious artifact or relic or followed the spoor of ingenious art thieves to recover invaluable paintings.

He was not the tough, hard bitten private investigator, who talked out of the side of his mouth, chomping on the stub of a cigar, as typically portrayed by the film industry. Instead, he was precise and persistent, and these qualities, along with a quirky intellect that enabled him to completely understand the dark side of human nature, made him the most effective investigator in the industry. Of course, he did not go by such a prosaic term as private investigator. No, Augustus "Gussie" Seay, was the world's foremost artifact recovery expert.

But perhaps more important than his widely respected personal attributes, was the fact that the computer was his friend. Gussie knew and understood computers. It was as if he could get inside the computer's mind – become one with the cyber side, so to speak. Using his awesome cyber skills, he could find anything there was to find, electronically at least, as his delicate, feminine fingers flew, and his excitement grew as he electronically homed in on his prey.

The library computer quickly responded to his adept commands. Within seconds he had enlarged, incredibly clear images of the museum's stolen coins on the screen before him. His excitement rising, he pressed print, and almost ran to the librarian behind the counter, where the printer was housed. Paying his quarter, he retrieved the glossy, photographic quality, color print. Trotting back to his computer, he took a magnifying glass out of his brief case.

Seay meticulously examined both copies of the coins. His euphoria faded, though, replaced by a frown. The coins stolen from the museum twenty years ago were not the same as the coins depicted on the image he had obtained from Miss McMasters, he was certain of it. First, the museum had never had the San Francisco $50 gold coin. In fact, he had never heard of anybody who had this particular coin in their collection, it was that rare. Second, the coins from the O'Halloran estate didn't have the tiny little marks, almost like scratches, that the coins from the museum showed. Even though the museum's coins were rated uncirculated, the estate coins were in better condition. Rare as they were, and as unbelievable a coincidence as this appeared to be, they were just not the same coins.

But what caught the detective's attention was a newspaper article written when the museum first reported the theft. As part of an agreement with the company which had provided insurance coverage for the museum, back then the museum had engaged the services of a private investigator. The particulars of his hiring were not given, nor was the investigator's real name. Augustus stroked his chin as he contemplated that bit of information, of which he had not previously been aware. Perhaps he might learn something by investigating the investigator.

The newspaper article did give a name, well sort of. It appeared to be a pseudonym to Augustus, who was a bit of an etymologist, and prided himself on his knowledge of the origin of names. Because of his wide-eyed appearance, his few friends often snidely referred to him as an amateur entymologist, a scientist who studies insects. When the name *Ike M. Sucher* came up, it rang a discordant tone with him. He had a rudimentary knowledge of German and wondered at the name, meaning seeker, especially with the initials I. M. *A punster's joke*, he thought, *I'm a Sucker.* Seay took out his cell phone and called the assistant curator who had hired him.

"Cedric, I need a favor. This is a tough one. I want you to see if you can retrieve a copy of the check that was issued by the museum about, let's see. About June 24, 1987."

"I say, Gussie," the curator said in his affected British accent, "you don't want much of a tired old museum curator, now, do you?"

Cedric Barrington was one of the few people who could get away with calling Augustus Seay, "Gussie," a name which he truly despised. In some spare time once, Seay had done some background check on Barrington. He found that despite his fancy British sounding name, old Cedric was born and raised in South Boston. He just invented himself, probaby as a means of escaping his lower-class Southie roots.

Seay waited while the curator pulled a film from the archives and inserted it into the viewing machine. The machine whirred and after a couple of minutes of annoying whirring, Seay heard the machine slow to a crawl. Then he heard a "Eureka!" as Barrington found the microfilm copy of the check, front and back. "Check number 6327. Written on June 23, 1987. Made payable to I. M. Sucher. The endorsement is a bit of a scrawl, old chap, but my trained eye makes it out to read - A., probably Arnold, Pott, no that's Potts. Yes, definitely Arnold Potts."

"Cedric, my friend, you are remarkable."

"At your service. Any other arcane requests, Gussie, old boy?"

Barrington just had to add that "Gussie" just as a little dig to the sensitive artifact retrieval expert.

It wasn't easy. This character really knew how to hide, but after using several search engines and tapping into a restricted source or two, Seay turned up the man who he was pretty sure was the right Arnold Potts. He even had a driver's license photograph of him, which he enlarged, and once again used the library's excellent printer. The photograph showed a blond-haired man with a crewcut, some lines around his eyes indicating an outdoor preference, piercing blue eyes which pierced even in a traditionally lousy driver's license photograph, and a condescending grin, no, more like a smirk. Even the DMV photographer could not photo shop that smirk.

Chapter 21

Izzy was irate with Jimmy G when he learned that it was his lawyer's own cousins who had participated in the break-in. "How'd dose thugs know aboud de money, Jimmy, How? Dell me? How? I drusded you, Jimmy, I drusded you."

Jimmy was virtually dripping with apology. "I'm really, really sawry, Iz. It musta jus' slipped out when I was wid dem creeps, or maybe it was de article in de newspaper, I dunno. Jeez. My own people. Honest, Iz, I never t'ought dose dopey guys woulda did somet'in' like dat."

Jimmy figured he had to somehow divert Izzy's attention from the break-in. "Lissen, Iz, we still gotta do sumpin' about da house. Youse jus' can't ignore a whole house in da estate. But Iz, I gotta tell ya. I ain't never done no real estate case like dis before. Look, nobody owns dis house on Pine Street, right? Dere's no record in da Register of Deeds office. Dat clown sure pulled a fast one an' it's gonna be tough to fix. But what I'm t'inkin' is dis. Dere ain't no defendant. Nobody ta sue, ya know what I mean? So what I'm t'inkin' is we file a case, maybe a special proceeding. We put a ad in da newspaper, wait a mont' or so. See what happens. We weed out da kooks an' crazies dat'll make odd ball claims, den we get a coupla affidavits from guys what knows da ol' lawyer, mebbe one from da tax guy, submit a order to da Judge. Bingo! Da house is owned by da estate. On'y t'ing is all sorts o' stuff can go wrong. Maybe da Judge wants ta take it under advisement, ya know what I mean? Takes forever, ya know. But Iz, we gotta a'leas' try. Whadda ya t'ink?"

"I dink mebbe you vanna jack up da legal fees, is vad I dink." Izzy sighed and looked at the earnest expression on Jimmy's face. "Bud vad else I'm goink a do?"

He sighed again, and slumped back into his chair, an aura of defeat encircling him. By now he trusted and even respected the odd little iconoclastic lawyer, but when would all this legal nonsense be over? Before he was appointed executor of this estate his life had been simple, serene, and if he wasn't rolling in dough, at least, he sort of enjoyed his placid routine. He had never even had occasion to go to the courthouse, but now he virtually lived there. He should have turned down the appointment as executor. *Could he have even done that, could he still do that, or was he just stuck?*

But two things impelled him onward on this difficult course. One was his ingrained sense of responsibility that always directed him to do what he had to do and do it right. The other was that magical effect that money had on him. And he could picture that five per cent as clear as a bell. Five percent of the house, the coins, and the shares of stock. It could easily be worth a couple of years work at the store, maybe even be his retirement.

Izzy sighed again. Jimmy sat there curiously watching him as Izzy went through his convoluted thought process. Jimmy saw the look of resignation and knew that Izzy was hooked like a striped bass on a Hopkins lure.

Leaving the lawyer's office, Izzy was still aggravated, muttering to himself as he walked out. But he was thinking deeply, and even scheming. He felt he had taken sufficient steps to protect the assets of the estate but was still worried. Hiding the assets from the myriad crooked predators out there, who had learned about the surprisingly valuable estate, was not something he knew much about. Like wildfire, gossip over the inestimable value of the estate, especially, the gold coins, had torn through the community, with that deadly sin, greed, affecting everyone from the highest class of society, to the basest rabble trying to figure out an angle to grab something for themselves.

Izzy still had to figure out how to liquidate the estate assets. Gold coins and stock certificates were worth nothing until they were converted to cash, top dollar. Then and only then could Izzy get his five per cent fee, actually ten per cent when you considered the five per cent in and five per cent out. He shuddered with excitement at the thought. But there was still the perplexing matter of the ownership of the house on Pine Street to straighten out. And then there was the even more troubling problem of determining who the beneficiary of Hamish's will was going to end up being. Still, just the thought of that executor's fee kept him going.

A dark cloud descended over him as Izzy considered the beneficiary issue. The Institute for the Treatment of Canines Humanely (ITCH) was probably out of it since they most likely disposed of Hamish's dogs. But what if the Temple of God was not found to be worthy? Who would get the estate then? And who was to make that determination? He supposed it would be up to him to appoint some one who was disinterested to make the decision, or would it end up being up to the Clerk, Molly McMasters, to make the decision or the appointment? Despite her basic honesty, her devotion to the Temple could end up being dicey.

Izzy ruminated about who he might appoint if it turned out that task was up to him. He chuckled to himself as he thought of the commotion which would result if he chose the good Rabbi in Greeneburg to make the determination. Pastor Ronnie, the schmuck, would go apopleptic. The thought of Ronnie's bursting veins on his forehead, steam coming out of his ears, fuming and sputtering at the very idea of having to brown-nose the Rabbi absolutely delighted Izzy.

But who could he find that could actually make a fair determination? Who in Pine Ridge or even Greeneburg, for that matter, would not be influenced by the awesome power of the Temple of God? This thought was perplexing, for who indeed? Molly was a devoted member of Pastor Ronnie's flock, and clearly under his influence. Just about everyone else in Pine Ridge would be afraid of offending the powerful prelate, just in case he did have the connection with the Almighty that he claimed. Jimmy was the only one who didn't seem at all fazed by the charismatic pastor, but he couldn't be the one to judge the Temple, for he was Izzy's lawyer. It looked like the best he could hope for was a rational decision from an impartial jury, if one could be found.

Obsessed with worry himself, Jimmy G was fully aware of his shortcomings before a jury, especially the heavily biased, traditional Southern jury, the kind he was sure to face if the trial was held in Pine Ridge. And these deficiencies would be magnified when he was up against the imposing B.S. The silk stocking lawyer looked like a highly sought after actor portraying a lawyer. He was quite tall and had beautiful silver hair with a handsome wave in it, piercing steel blue eyes, and a sophisticated demeanor. He wore thousand-dollar suits and expensive Italian silk ties with impeccable taste. And worst of all, Jimmy thought, his booming baritone voice would captivate any jury, especially the women.

Jimmy, on the other hand, was short and sweaty. His greasy black hair was long enough, and usually damp enough, to make the back of his sport coat noticeably wet around the collar. To make matters worse he usually sweated so profusely under the arms that it would soak through the sport coat leaving an unappealing white ring of salt at the edges of the sweat.

The Temple of God! Jimmy mopped his brow ineffectively with a sweat soaked handkerchief when he even thought about the daunting task ahead of him. He pondered hard and realized that the first issue to be dealt with was whether it was he that had the burden of proof. Would it be he who had to prove the Temple unworthy, or was it the arrogant and unflappable B.S. who had to prove that the Temple was worthy? A tie would go to whoever did not have the burden of proof. He knew if it was he who brought the law suit, that burden would be his.

If he lost this preliminary issue, and he was pretty sure he would, it would mean that it was up to him to put on evidence to show that the Temple was indeed unworthy. What would that evidence be, and who could he get to testify to the Temple's unworthiness here in Pine Ridge, where more than half the citizens were devotees of Pastor Ronnie and his ostentatious and magnificent Temple?

The more he thought about it, the more he sweated and got himself worked up into a state of clinical depression. He pulled out the soaking wet handkerchief and was absent mindedly wringing it out when it struck him. What if he prevailed? What if he did prove the Temple to be unworthy? What would happen to Pastor Ronnie and his flock of devoted sheep? What about Ronnie's huge televangelist empire? Ronnie would be ruined. But so would Jimmy G! It would have a devastating effect on his business, for a good many of Ronnie's flock, imbued with the unseen protection of God that Ronnie fatuously promised, felt free to go out and help themselves to the largesse God provided, even if it belonged to somebody else. Jimmy would lose most of his practice, the community would be devastated, and so would life in Pine Ridge as Jimmy had come to know it.

No matter which way it went, Jimmy G was toast.

So Jimmy pondered this awful dilemma. Should he throw in the towel and concede the worthiness of the Temple of God? A wave of nausea engulfed him like a stinky fog at the very thought. Jimmy was a lot of things, he knew, but despite his background and a somewhat skewed sense of honor, Jimmy had always slavishly followed a strong inner compulsion to do what was essentially right. And the Temple of God, to him, was plain wrong. He would fight and let the chips fall where they may. *Wherever did that expression come from, anyway*, he thought?

Jimmy had been involved in hundreds of scrapes as a young man, from childish shoving matches to full fledged fist fights. Even though he was a little guy, he actually enjoyed the fist fights. After having had his butt handed to him a dozen times or so, he began to develop some pugilistic smarts. He learned to spot weaknesses in his bigger and stronger opponents and to take advantage of them. He almost never overpowered his antagonists, but he did learn some tricks and began to win a few fights, usually resulting from well placed shots to the opponents unprotected and vulnerable spots, even if that might be considered a little outside the Marquess of Queensbury rules. He decided he would fight, see what he could learn, and trust that it would all work out. What he was doing was hoping to out-God the Temple of God.

So what were the Temple's weaknesses? He pondered the question, absentmindedly rubbing his chin as he contemplated this essential legal defense. He focused on the leader of the flock. Pastor Ronnie was vain and avaricious. He lived with his caricature of a wife in a huge, garish mansion with its park-like grounds, festooned with gaudy, almost obscene, statuary. He had several tasteless limousines, including a powder blue Lincoln, and a chartreuse stretch Hummer. He sported ridiculously ornate clothes and jewelry, which included a pink pinky ring that was so big and heavy he had to use two hands to wave howdy.

How could he expose the already publicly exposed Pastor? *Indecent exposure!* Jimmy chuckled to himself as he thought about the pun. Why, Ronnie virtually flaunted his avarice in the name of God. And the flock, like the true sheep they were, bought it, lock, stock and barrel. No, he would have to look a little deeper, find something about the purported man of God that was so reprehensible that even those sheeplike true believers would be unable to justify following him.

Just then, as if to underscore the overwhelming obstacles facing him, the chartreuse stretch Hummer ostentatiously drove by, the reflections of sunlight magnified off the plentiful polished brass decorative trim, almost blinding all the awestruck onlookers.

Jimmy watched as the Hummer sped by. *A Hummer, of all things,* he thought. *It's probably to demonstrate the pastor's connection with the earth, with the farmers whose back- breaking labor and eighty to one hundred-hour work weeks enabled the elaborate and gluttonous feasts that graced his opulent table. It was a slap in the face to the dusty camouflage colored Hummers, driven by courageous soldiers, whose sacrifices in blood and sweat enabled the very freedom which permitted him to be able to pull off these scams.* Jimmy was disgusted at the crass hypocrisy as the obscene machine sped out of sight, sucking up a gallon of gas a minute.

Jimmy realized that it was not the obvious that needed to be exposed to show that the Temple was unworthy, it was the hidden machinations of the whole operation. *If he could find some nefarious connection to some criminal activity hidden below the surface of their ostentation and expose it in such a way that it would not be connected to Jimmy,* he thought he just might be able to pull off proof of unworthiness.

Jimmy had grown up on the periphery of organized crime. He knew how the wise guys worked, how the Dons thought, how they operated. They had a general lack of respect and concern for the victims, who were mere pawns in the general criminal activity waged for the benefit of "Cosa Nostra." The bosses preyed on the fears and avarice of their victims.

Pastor Ronnie also preyed on the fears of his victims, but it was more the indirect fear of God. He preyed on the term God-fearing, the lack of self esteem of the flock, or perhaps more accurately, the insecurities of the flock engendered by their uncertain understanding of the afterlife, and what God wanted of them. By convincing them of his direct connection to God, and his self-proclaimed knowledge of exactly what God wanted from them, with the hint at the salvation that only he, Pastor Ronnie Conner, could insure, he made millions while advancing the goodness of the Temple. *What a scam,* thought Jimmy with an unabashed sense of admiration for the pastor and his operation.

Slowly, as he thought through the dilemma using his simple logic, the veil of uncertainty was lifted from Jimmy's indecision. Pastor Ronnie was but a pawn himself in the operation, for he couldn't produce this massive spectacle without help, without a fabulous organization. Ronnie just didn't seem smart enough to be able to stage it all by himself. And the truckloads of money brought in from the church's televangelism, the Sunday and Wednesday services, the revivals, the theme park and all the other magnificent revenue producing extravaganzas, made Pastor Ronnie and the other organizers filthy rich. Ronnie, as the most visible of the Temple's protagonists, living the strenuous life required by all that pomp and circumstance, couldn't be the one making the major decisions. Someone had to be pulling his strings. The dark element of Jimmy's criminal mind which looked for illicit activity in every little thing was busy at work.

When the flash of sunlight reflected off the Hummer as is sped off, Jimmy was struck by a flash of inspiration. *If something seems to be a certain way, that's the way it is.* Jimmy could picture his wise old grandfather sitting in his large, pastoral yard, at the table at his house in Sicily, bedecked with a checkered tablecloth with a jar of wildflowers on it. The old man was sipping a glass of chianti when he pronounced that simple pearl of wisdom in his heavy Sicilian accented Italian. He seemed like he was not directing his speech to any one in particular, but Jimmy was the only one around, and the teenaged boy took in and contemplated every word as if it was the true gospel.

The Temple seems like a sham, and therefore it is, he thought. *Just look under the surface, under the face that it presents to the people.* "Hazel," he said walking out to the fussy secretary's desk, "can youse pull up de records o' de propitty owned by de Temple?" He loomed over her desk as her fingers flew, and screen after screen appeared on the computer.

She quickly printed a sheet of paper. The only thing owned by any entity called the Temple of God, or anything with any name close to it, was the actual property the huge edifice was located on and that was owned under an assumed name by a limited liability company, Temple of God, LLC. While he was examining the document, Hazel printed out a second sheet.

"This is getting interesting, Mr. G. The only member of the limited liability company is Pastor Ronnie Conner. And he only filed one annual report – three years ago."

"Whad about de house an' cars. Who owns dem? Can ya fine out on dat t'ing?"

"Here's the tax info on the house. It's owned by a non-profit corporation called Little Sixes, Inc.," she said. "Wait a minute. I'll check with the Secretary of State to find out about that corporation."

She rapidly typed out a string of data. "Hmmm. There is no listing there. Let me check other states." After a few minutes she said, "It doesn't exist, Mr. G. There is no corporation anywhere by that name. No listing with any secretary of state, no tax information, no annual reports, no property listings, nothing."

"So we got a house owned by a bogus, non-existent corporation, huh? Can ya soich da title, Hazel, fine out who sol' it to dat Corp?"

Hazel loved the computer age. She could do anything online, from searching a title to finding out your shirt size.

Her innate curiosity, some would call it nosiness, led her to become an absolute expert on the discovery of information online. After a few minutes of frantic typing, she made her report.

"The land the house is built on was deeded to a grantee named the Little Sixes Corporation a few years ago by one Alvin Rolley and wife, Belvina. Hmm. Alvin seems to have gotten it from his father's estate, but there's a problem there, Mr. G. I remember Alvin Rolley. He was a farmer and as pious a man as there was. He was one of six brothers and sisters, but there is no one else who signed the deed as grantors. That means they each should still have a one-sixth ownership interest in the property if the property passed intestate to his heirs at law. I can't find any deeds showing that the siblings granted their interest in the land to anyone."

Hazel's fingers flew once more and after a few seconds, the printer whirred again. She wordlessly handed Jimmy a couple of sheets of paper. The Hummer and Lincoln were owned by Pastor Ronnie, but that was not a revelation. But it caused Jimmy to think a little bit.

"Hazel, is dere any way you can pull up his tax returns?"

"Well, Mr. G. I'm really not supposed to, but yes. There is a way. It will take a few moments though."

Jimmy went back to his office thinking. *Little Sixes, Inc., huh? That's really odd. Six was the devil's number. And it's a nonexistent corporation, is it?*

In about five minutes, during which Jimmy's inquisitive mind was jumping all over the place and he was attempting to fathom this legal mess, Hazel buzzed him and announced she was ready. He came back out and hovered over her shoulder again, anxiously.

"So what yer tellin' me is, foist, da deed to da corporation is void 'cause it's a bogus corp, which doesn't exist anywhere, an' even so, da estate of ol' man Rolley, or da heirs, still owns five sixths of it, am I right?"

"Yes, that seems to be the case, all right, except that it if Alvin and Belvina's deed isn't valid because the grantee doesn't exist, that means their estate still owns all of the property. Alvin and Belvina can't transfer land that they don't own, can they?"

"No, dey can't, 'cep' dat good title passes by adverse possession after seven years if dere's a deed. Hazel wha's de date on dat deed?"

"It appears to be...hmmm. Let's see, hmm. Six years ago. Oh, wait. Here's something interesting. Here's another wrinkle. There's an option to purchase on that real property. Let me print that out for you."

Jimmy read the document with interest and put it down. He immediately picked it up again and read it once more. At least three "Whadda ya knows," came out of him as he read it.

"Hazel, you a choich goin' lady?"

She blushed a nice shade of fuchsia. He had never inquired of anything personal about her life during the entire time she had worked for him. "Why, yes, Mr. G. I am very religious. I attend church regularly."

"Jever t'ink maybe God looks down and laughs at us, Hazel?"

She blushed again. "Why, I don't know, Mr. G. Why do you say that?"

"Dis here option is old, Hazel. It's signed by a man named Roland Rolley and wife Bella. It's dated twenny years ago, but listen, Hazel, here's da good part. Dis option is to be exercised by Mr. Hamish O'Halloran, attorney, his heirs or assigns, at any time so long as the loan owed to him has not been paid and this option cancelled of record. Hazel, da option price is one dollar. Does it say anywhere if dis option was ever cancelled of record?"

"Uh, let me see." Her fingers flew. She peered intently at the screen, once again delighted with the computer age.

"No, Mr. G. I don't find any record that it was ever cancelled."

Jimmy started to giggle. "Hee hee. Hazel, le's t'row a monkey wrench in dis t'ing. Write me up a check from da estate account fer one dollar an' make it payable to da estate o' Roland Rolley an' wife Bella Rolley. Put a notation on da memo line – exercise of option in da Temple o' God propitty. Le's see wha' happens."

Chapter 22

Jimmy took the check for one dollar and looked at it closely, for he saw in it special significance in addition to a symbolic exercise of the option. He just couldn't suppress the giggle that bubbled up to the surface. Then he wrote a nice polite letter to Molly McMasters. He could just envision the expression on the harried face of the poor besieged clerk when she received the letter and the check for one dollar, along with the Motion to Re-open the Estate of old man Rolley and his wife. He giggled again, but it sounded almost like the cackle of a witch.

Thinking it over a bit, Jimmy decided to hedge his bets. He would deliver the letter and the documents directly to the clerk himself and get her to time stamp it. He wanted to insure she couldn't claim she didn't get it, but more importantly he wanted to examine the estate file.

When he arrived at the clerk's office, the door to Molly's office was shut, and he was informed she was closeted with some other attorney on another estate matter. While he waited, he asked one of the assistant clerks to bring him the Rolley estate files to review. After several minutes, she did. There were two of them, one for each of the deceased Rolleys, but the files were woefully thin. There was only a single last will in each file of the old fashioned one-page variety.

That was cute, Jimmy thought, *each of them left everything they owned to the other, and each was the executor of the estate of the other.* Mr. Rolley died first, but only by a few months. Alvin Rolley, their son, was appointed administrator of both wills by the Clerk. The brief inventories mentioned a single bank account with just enough to pay the expenses, and a single parcel of land.

Jimmy recognized the description of the land as being the same piece transferred to Little Sixes, Inc.

Jimmy studied the deed. The tax stamps indicated the corporation didn't pay much for it, and the signature of the grantor was just "Alvin Rolley," not "Alvin Rolley, administrator." The signature of Alvin's wife, Belvina, was there, transferring whatever interest she had, which of course, was none.

He wondered about the insignificant amount paid by the corporation for the land. Maybe there had been a house on it and maybe not. Maybe it was just a decrepit old mobile home that wasn't worth anything. Maybe it was mostly a gift, or maybe the corporation was just supposed to be only getting the one-sixth interest that Alvin did inherit. In any event, from what he could determine, there was no such entity as Little Sixes, Inc., so the deed was void, pure and simple.

The door to Molly's office opened and a breezy youngish woman with a single, long braid dangling down to her posterior, wearing an ankle length peasant skirt, sort of flowed out of the office. Jimmy recognized her as a relatively new lawyer, the wealthy daughter of a couple of ex-hippies who had made a mint as environmental consultants to major corporations. She sneered at Jimmy as she wafted by him. No doubt about it, a real first class, contemptuous sneer.

Jimmy granted her a little smile, making a mental note of the slight to insure he put her in the same class as B.S and the others of the arrogant lawyer group, to be trounced in court the first opportunity that presented itself.

He went to the door of Molly's office. She motioned him in, an expression akin to fear lingering on her pure, naïve face. "What can I do for you, Mr. G? I only have a few minutes. I have another appointment soon. Do you know that lady?" Molly was referring to the lawyer that she had just met with. "She can be so inconsiderate."

174

He calmly explained the situation to Molly and presented her with the Motion to Re-open the Estate of the Rolleys, handing her the estate file he had been reading. As she looked it over, a quizzical expression crossed her face. Jimmy then handed her a copy of the Option to Purchase and the check for $1.00. The reaction could not have been worse if he had connected with a left hook square on her nose. The Honorable Clerk of Superior Court, the Judge of Probate, started to cry.

"Oh, Mr. G. This is awful. You can't really do this, can you? What will Pastor Ronnie say?" Jimmy really felt sorry for her, but after all, this was just business.

When she had calmed down a bit, Jimmy tried to console her as if he was an old uncle, saying, "There, there, now." But Brooklynites never, ever say, "There, there, now," do they? What they say, and what Jimmy really said was, "OK, Molly, dis is what ya do. File da motion. I'll send a copy to Alvin Rolley, if I can find him, an' you set a hearin' date in about a mont'. You don' even hafta tell da Pastor about it, but I guess ya will. But dat's OK, too."

She cried some more. When she regained her composure, she asked, "You don't mind? I mean, if I tell the Pastor?"

"No Molly, I don' mind. But youse should call his doctor too, in case he has a heart attack when he hears about it. What's de date fer da hearing, Molly?"

Still sobbing, she clocked in the Motion on her time stamp, and set up a hearing date. Jimmy jotted it down, thanked her, and simply got up and left.

Ten minutes later when he walked into his office, Hazel handed him a slip of paper with the name of B.S. Fotheringham, III, and telephone number on it. "He sounded awfully angry, Mr. G. He was actually spitting and stuttering as he spoke. What on earth did you do to him?"

"Nuttin', Hazel. I jus' filed da motion and option in da Rolley estate. Cheese, it didn't take long fer da woid ta get out."

Jimmy called Fotheringham back. After a full minute of fuming and sputtering and listening to Fotheringham spew vile invectives and profanity, Jimmy interrupted. "Cheese, always da professional, ain't ya B.S? Tell me what I did, I ain't got a right ta do."

"You slimy, Yankee worm. (This was followed by a string of words which are just too harmful to your sensitive ears to be printed here, gentle reader.) You are trying to steal the Temple of God. You will incur the full wrath of its flock, Pastor Ronnie, even God, himself. This powerful firm will crush you, you greasy shyster, and grind you into fine lubricating oil."

Jimmy was actually having fun as long as B.S. didn't cross the line with respect to his honored nationality, but he was getting close, now. There were just some names you didn't call an Italian without some serious repercussions. When B.S. was temporarily out of breath, Jimmy cut in.

"Listen here, ya creep. Dis is jes business. Ya unnerstan' business, dontcha? Money, dat's all it is. I don' give a damn about da crummy Temple, da phony Pastor, an' his flock o' sheep. I gotta liquidate da estate, pay some bills, clear up da loose ends. An' yer phony operation what calls itself a choich is a loose end. In a mont' dat estate is gonna own dat phony Temple. Maybe it gets it back, maybe it don't. Do yer best, B.S." Jimmy hung up during a spate of sputtering, a smirk on his face. He had never been happier.

Chapter 23

Jimmy G came to the conclusion it was time to do a little real lawyering. He decided to let the rules of Civil Procedure work for him for a change. That night he stayed in the office late, working on the case, concentrating as hard as he ever had on the intricacies of the law, especially the arcane aspect known as civil procedure.

A couple of days later, Mr. B.S. Fotheringham, III, was quickly scanning the day's mail. He picked up a packet of papers which included a terse, bland cover letter from his adversary. The expression on his distinguished visage abruptly changed. Almost violently, he punched the intercom and ordered his beleagured secretary to get Margaret Young into his office at once.

Less than a minute later, a disheveled Margaret breathlessly entered his office and gasped out, "Yes, Sir?"

"Margaret, what is this tripe?" said B.S., as he slammed the packet of papers in front of her.

She picked up the stack of papers and inspected them. "Discovery, Sir. These are Interrogatories, Requests for Admissions, Requests for Production of Documents, and - ooh, he's not going to like this - a Notice to take Pastor Ronnie Conner's Deposition."

"That rotten little weasel," B.S. thundered. At first Margaret wasn't sure whether he was referring to Jimmy G, or Pastor Ronnie. "He's not going to get away with this, for God's sake. Look at this one. He wants the Temple to produce records of its income and investments. And this one. He wants the Temple to show what it paid Pastor Ronnie and its other employees."

"Uh, Sir," Margaret interrupted. "These all look like they're perfectly legitimate discovery requests."

"Well, you figure out a way to stop him. Ronnie is going to blow a fuse when he sees these papers. Go ahead and notify Pastor Ronnie but do something so that we don't have to respond to this garbage." Of course, this is the polite version of what B.S. really said. What he really said was so hot it would cause the spontaneous combustion of this book if it was to be actually written down here.

Margaret got out of B.S.'s office as quick as she could, and went back to her tiny cubicle with a new-found respect for Mr. Jimmy G. She realized from the implications of the discovery request that Jimmy G had done some research and if those implications were well founded, Pastor Ronnie and the Temple of God were going to have some serious problems. But so was she, for she didn't think there was much she could do to avoid having to respond. The best she could do was stall for a little time.

Margaret dashed off a letter to the Pastor making sure to inform him of the date set for his deposition and including a copy of the discovery requests. Seeing the pastor's reaction was going to be fun, she thought. But she made sure to direct the pastor's attention to her boss for his response.

Then she got down to the business of trying to figure out some legal way by which she could avoid having to respond to Jimmy's devilish discovery. She looked over the papers very carefully. Well, she could begin by stating her objections to the interrogatories, but the rule required that the reason for the objection be fully set forth. Maybe she could somehow figure out a way to rely on the priest, penitent privilege exclusion. *These are really good interrogatories,* she mused. *Each one is designed to prove or disprove some aspect of the Temple's worthiness, or at least lead to evidence or witnesses that could do so.*

Jimmy's assumptions seemed to indicate the Temple was a sham. *Was it really?* she wondered. *What is this Little Sixes, Inc?* She got on her computer and began to do a little investigating herself. It wasn't long before Margaret was following the same route on the internet that Hazel had and making the same rather astonishing findings.

Her social life had fast disappeared with her employment at Armitrage Grace. She worked long into the night, finishing the project. The next day there was a report lying on the desk of B.S. Fotheringham, III, when he came in to work, fashionably late.

Curious, he picked up the thick document and began to read it. He did not like it one bit when things were not going his way, for he was used, very used, to having things go the way he wanted. And things in this case were not going the way he wanted. No, not at all.

Chapter 24

Back at the police station, four policemen had gathered around the coffee machine. A new pot was being brewed, and the conversation drifted to the recent break-in at O'Halloran's, as the cops waited for their cup of joe. Pine Ridge never really got much excitement, so it was a big topic of conversation, even speculation among those entrusted with the safety of the town and its citizenry. Detective Sergeant O'Malley sauntered into the break room, his empty, stained cup dangling from his forefinger. The dueling scar was still a livid reminder of his transgression, but at least the stitches were now out.

At first there was a little snickering from those waiting at the watering hole. However, one of the older cops, a long-time friend of O'Malley's, attempted to defuse the situation. "Ya know, I wonder where old Iz does keep them coins. Sure as Hell ain't at O'Halloran's."

The other officers immediately turned their dubious attention to him, but he rescued himself from their suspicions by adding, "In case there's another attempt at grabbing the gold, we need to be ready for them. Ya know, lying in wait so's we can grab 'em."

Well, the seed had been planted. They continued their idle conversation, speculating on the identity of the perps that got away, but now they were thinking about when and where they would strike next. But just as each of us dreams of what we would do in the virtually impossible event that we won the Powerball lottery, each of the cops privately let his mind wander to what he would do if O'Halloran's treasure happened to secretly find its way into his grasp. Human nature, you know, pot of gold at the end of the rainbow, when my ship comes in, and all that.

There were subtle smiles on all their faces as the talk turned to the store. The consensus was the old haberdashery would probably be the place where Izzy would have stashed the coins. Maybe the store had a safe. There was no factual basis for this speculation, no logic behind this thinking, it was just an idea someone had thrown out and seized upon. No one had offered a better idea, so the suggestion just became adopted by default. As the meeting broke up each of the erstwhile detectives had convinced himself that he knew where the golden hoard was hidden but wanted to keep the secret for himself.

It was a strange night weatherwise in Pine Ridge. There was an eerie mist which moistened the town, leaving a coat of dew on everything glass or metal. The moon cast its colorless light giving the little town the appearance of a set in a Jack the Ripper movie.

Each of the cops had some weird thoughts that night. Maybe it was the moon. They were all strangely affected, like the witches in King Lear, as if some spell had been cast on them. Normally honest and wholesome men, the thoughts of O'Hallorans's gold twisted their integrity like a pretzel, as they schemed, each man individually letting his imagination wander, devising greedful plans.

It must be a man with extremely strong convictions and values to be able to disdain the opportunity to score millions, when all one has to do is sacrifice a little integrity. It's done all the time, just look at the likes of Michael Milken, Ken Lay and Bernie Madoff. Unfortunately for them but fortunately for our story, some of the cops who attended the little impromptu meeting in the police department break room had a fairly loose hold on their own integrity.

At night, the full moon illuminated the store front to give it a forlorn, almost abandoned look. Of course, there was no one in the store during the wee hours after midnight. The mercantile establishment was equipped with a burglar alarm, which had been installed at Nat's insistence. It was monitored by the tattooed and seriously anorexic nineteen-year old son of the security company's owner in Greeneburg, whose practice, when lazily pulling the all-night shift monitoring the idle businesses under the security company's contract, was to enjoy the eroticism of some sleazy porn flicks, while toking on a joint or two. Nothing ever happened at night in these establishments anyway. Needless to say, his attention was not particularly focused on the quiet blackness of the screens depicting the numerous stores in the security company's monitoring room.

Officer Philby, the beat cop idly walking the placid, damp streets of Pine Ridge that night, knew all about the security systems that the various stores employed. He also had keys to the various stores, including the key to the haberdashery that the trusting Shapiros had left with the police department to minimize the need for any glass breakage in the event the police needed to gain a hasty entry.

The beat cop had heard all the rampant rumors about O'Halloran's gold and the episode in which there was strong suspicion upon those in the know, that a few cops might have been involved. But the weird thoughts that proliferate in the wee hours, perhaps because of the effect the moon has on tides and even a person's blood circulation, began to find their ways into the beat cop's head. *It won't hurt to just take a little look see,* he rationalized to himself, *as part of my duty. After all, I am supposed to be vigilant, and that will give me a plausible excuse if anybody should ask.*

Silently, he turned the key in the lock and entered the front door of the store, just to have a look around, you know, make sure everything was safe and secure. He figured he probably had a good fifteen minutes before the security service responded, if it did at all.

As anyone involved in the criminal justice system knows, the full moon brings out all sorts of inexplicable weirdness in that segment of mankind that operates on the fringes of society, resulting in a huge spate of crimes the next few days thereafter. It must be that the gravitational pull of the moon warps the thought processes, or maybe disrupts the normal flow of blood to the brain.

Maybe that would explain the fact that at about the same time the beat cop slipped his key in the store's lock, in preparation for his precipitous slide into crime, two other policemen were at the back of the store, checking just how strong the lock to the basement was. It wasn't. The lock was old, and rusty, and the hasp was older and rustier. A few turns of the screwdriver blade of the older cop's Swiss Army knife, and the lock, hasp and all, were lying on the ground. The lock was nothing more than a psychological deterrent to illegal entry.

"Magic," said the cop, a bored old veteran named Corporal Hadley Boggs, in a stage whisper, as they snuck into the store's dank and dusty cellar.

There were no boxes of clothes, no inventory of items of haberdashery stored in the basement, which was so musty it hurt the cops' eyes, causing them to water. The place was narrow and crowded with all sorts of shelves, old counters, carts, storage racks and other gear that is associated with displaying and moving merchandise.

It appeared that the miserly old owner had never thrown anything out. Apparently, when he bought a new fixture, he just consigned the old one to the basement. But it sure made it difficult for any good sneaking around, for every move they took, it seemed like, the officers, turned felons, bumped into a rack, or counter, causing a rattle or clank to echo through the basement. Of course, although muffled and distorted to to a degree, the clatter could be heard up in the main part of the store.

Officer Philby, after searching in a few likely looking drawers, opening a few boxes, looking behind a few doors, found his way to the office. He was in there when he first heard the indecipherable sound of a clothes rack being jostled. He froze. The officer's first reaction, illogically, was terror, fearing that the place was haunted and that the sound came from a ghost tugging around a heavy chain. He cupped his ear, listening for a moan as fine beads of sweat glistened on his face. Still as a corpse, he concentrated intently, anticipating another sound which would explain his uncertainty. It came, of course, another unfamiliar sound, this time a thump and a prolonged squeak as one of the perpetrators bumped into an old counter, sliding it a few inches across the concrete basement floor.

Philby jumped a foot in the air, panicked, and started to run out of the office. As he did so he bumped into the door jamb dropping his flashlight which remained lit, casting bizarre and ghostly shadows at foot level throughout the store.

At about the same time, the older officer who had broken into the basement, Corporal Boggs, had just reached the top of the stairs. He froze when he saw the weird shadows on the floor and heard the clatter. Philby picked up the flashlight holding it tight to his chest in fear, but in doing so the light shined straight up, presenting his face in a frighteningly ghoulish light.

Burglar Boggs, seeing this ghastly visage, screamed, turned, and ran back downstairs just as the other intruder, Officer Carrico, had almost reached him. Carrico was holding his lit cigarette lighter high for a little, albeit flickering, illumination. The two fell awkwardly back, crashing down the wooden stairs, the unexplained clamor sounding even more eerie. The cigarette lighter, still flickering, fell to the side, which, as luck would have it, landed right on top of a pile of old rags.

A conflagration erupted as the dry rags ignited, fueled by the vestiges of some alcohol based cleaning compound they had been soaked in long ago. The wooden basement stairs quickly caught fire and a tunnel of air, flowing from the open basement door up the staircase and into the store, created a back draft which fed the fire so that it quickly engulfed the store.

Officer Boggs and his partner in crime, Officer Carrico, lurched out of the smoke-filled basement through the same door they entered, gasping for breath, the acrid smoke tearing up their eyes to the point where they could barely see.

"Jeez, that was close," said Boggs, in between gulps of fresh air, his throat burning from the acrid smoke.

His partner was bending over, holding his knees, gasping for breath. Carrico looked up at Boggs, still panting. "Holy smoke," he said appropriately, "Your pants are on fire!"

Sure enough, Boggs had not quite gotten out of the inferno unscathed. The seat of his pants was indeed in flames. Fortunately, it had only progressed to the point where his rear pockets were blazing. Carrico ran up to him and said, "Hold still. I'll put it out."

Instinctively, Boggs bent over as Carrico started smacking his rear repeatedly, in an inartful attempt to extinguish the flames before it was something more serious than a case of hot pants. When his initial onslaught on Boggs' bum proved less than effective, Carrico's reaction was to smack harder, with more vigor.

Mrs. Quigley, a neighbor, hearing the commotion, cautiously peeped under the shade of her bedroom window to see if she could determine the source of the to do. In the distorted light of the full moon, she saw the officer smacking Officer Boggs' butt, hard. She immediately stood up aghast. Torn between morbid curiosity and abject fear, after a few seconds had elapsed, she bent over and peeped out through the curtains again, but the two men were gone. However, this time as her astonished eyes searched for the two men, she noticed the smoke billowing out of the basement of the haberdasher's store, so being the good citizen that she was, she naturally dialed 911.

Officer Philby, uncertain of just what had occurred and blindly reacting to the clamor of the two men falling down the stairs, followed by the whoosh of the blaze, ran back into the office and slammed the door. Reaction without thought is never a good thing, as Philby soon learned. The door was the kind that automatically locked behind him. His reactions were undoubtedly motivated by fear, and perhaps an unreasoning desire at maintaining his anonymity, and thus his innocence.

After just a few seconds, securely ensconced in the windowless office, he smelled the smoke. With the cold realization that where there is smoke there is fire, Philby felt it might be the better part of discretion to make his escape. As he turned the knob, that sinking feeling overtook him when his senses informed him the door was locked. Philby desparately turned and pulled the doorknob to no avail as the old door lock held firm. Finally, as a desperate last resort, he put his shoulder to it with all his weight.

The door jamb, now thoroughly engulfed in flames and weakened, was no match for his bulk. The door, casing and all, fell forward onto the flaming floor, with the hapless Philby prostrate on top of the door, the flames flickering up all around, like a Viking funeral pyre. Rather than make the one-way trip to Valhalla, he quickly got to his feet and sprinted through the burning store to the front door, reaching it at exactly the same time as a fireman, in full fireman's regalia, summoned to the scene by the frantic 911 call from Mrs. Quigley, snatched open the unlocked door.

Philby, with the inertia of his panicky sprint, bowled the fireman over. As luck would have it, or perhaps a form of perverted justice, both landed in a heap at the feet of, who else, but Detective Sergeant Peter Richard O'Malley, who had just happened on the scene. He looked at Philby, the prostrate patrolman, and just shook his head in mock disgust.

The fire department used its high-powered water hose to quickly put out the flames and prevent the whole town from burning a la the Chicago fire, but it was too late for the mercantile establishment of I. Shapiro, Haberdasher. Between tons of the fire department's water and the consuming habit of the hungry flames, the old wooden store and everything in it were ruined.

The 911 dispatcher, after sending the fire department on the call reporting smoke in the store's basement, had contacted O'Malley, who fatefully, was the duty officer on call that night. The dispatcher had roughly described two men in what the caller felt was strange and depraved acts of public lewdness taking place in plain sight at the rear of the old haberdashery.

O'Malley told the embarrassed Philby to let the emergency medical technician check him out, and to report to him at the station the next day at noon. The detective then went to the hospital, sat down in the ER waiting room, picked up yesterday's newspaper, and waited.

The hospital in Pine Ridge wasn't much of a hospital. It only had seven beds, an ex-Army medic and a tired old nurse who should have retired years ago, on duty at the site, but had a real doctor on call. You can just imagine the kind of medical practitioner who would be available at midnight in Pine Ridge. The doc wasn't used to much action at night and had imbibed a few nips too many. Not having planned on being able to be contacted, he had gone to bed.

Now reading the latest John Grisham paperback while lounging in the hospital waiting room, Peter Dick O'Malley looked up as two filthy men dressed in black hurried in complaining to the medic on duty of burns on the bum. Their gas heater had exploded, they explained, but since it was August this fact alone caught the detective's attention. Casually peeking over the top of his paperback, he was surprised, no, actually when he thought about it he wasn't so surprised, to see Corporal Boggs and his hapless partner, Officer Carrico.

Boggs, it turned out, had some second degree burns on his rear and wouldn't be sitting down for a while. His partner, who was actually crying, had his hands roughly bandaged in an old towel, which he held to his chest. It looked like an old-fashioned, ladies' muffler.

O'Malley walked up to them and shook his head disapprovingly. With great feigned disdain, he told them both to report to his office at noon the next day. Each of the burned men looked at him curiously, suspicious of his own fresh scar, for they had heard the rumors themselves.

When Izzy was told of the fire and the massive damage to the store, he was both irate and disconsolate. That quickly passed, and he became distraught as he thought of the ruination of his life's work. Nat consoled him as best he could. "Don't worry Pop, it will be all right. The store wasn't making any money selling clothes anyway. We're insured and now we can sell the property to Mart-World. I hear they are planning to buy up all the property on the block and put up a mega store which would probably have put us out of business, anyway. This way, at least we'll come out with a little something, Pop."

Izzy moaned pathetically. "Oy vey! Mard-World. Dad's my woisd fears, Nad. Wad's happenink do us, Nad? Nuddings of value is valued anymore. Da pipple only buys cheap goods made in China or South America. My poor sdore. My life's woik, Nad. My life's woik, gone."

But as he thought about it, Izzy calmed down. Nat was right. The store was insured. And it wasn't making any money anyway. Maybe the fire was Providence at work. Maybe he could take a breather now. Go on a cruise when this executing mess was over. Maybe go to Miami in the winter, and re-establish old acquaintances. All of his old friends from the neighborhood, had made it in the mercantile business and moved to Miami. But, still, tears filled his eyes when he thought about the store to which he was so emotionally attached and to which he had devoted so much time and effort.

At noon the next day O'Malley walked into his office and faced the three officers who were already there. Two of them were seated uncomfortably on simple wooden straight-backed chairs. The third, Corporal Boggs, was standing, of course. The three of them seemed crestfallen, clearly embarrassed at their predicament, although when they looked up at O'Malley and saw his livid scar, they were reassured a bit as they recalled the rumors floating about.

"You all got an explanation for last night?" O'Malley asked them.

No one answered.

"So?" O'Malley persisted, but it was definitely soft ball. Nerf ball even.

Corporal Boggs, being no fool, said, "Sarge, I think maybe I should call the PBA attorney, what do you think? Guys? Get a little idea of what's going on?" he asked, turning his attention to the others.

His partner, the less than intrepid Officer Carrico, started crying again.

O'Malley said, "Oh, shut up. Yeah, that's probably a good idea. I should arrest the lot of you fools." He turned away, so they wouldn't see his smirk, but he was too late. He started to guffaw, and after a stunned minute, so did the three of them.

Chapter 25

Izzy duly reported the fire to his insurance company. The next day the Old Rome Fire and Casualty Company sent out an adjuster. The insurance man was way too obese to even attempt to go into the ruins at some disaster site to actually inspect the damage. Accompanying him was a young man of no more than seventeen with pimples and spiked purple hair, who he introduced as his assistant, and who constantly took notes.

The adjuster, whose name was Bill Drill, met Izzy and Nat in front of the store. It was pretty clear at the outset that Bill "Fire" Drill wasn't about to go into the scorched premises and get his hands dirty. Not only was he clearly not agile enough to step over the detritus resulting from the fire, he simply made no move to go into the store. Instead, he asked, "Where's the books? I'll need to take a look at the books. That's the only way I can determine how much the loss is."

Izzy glared at the adjustor, but Nat merely stated, "They're in the office. Everything is in there. He pointed to the charred remains of the store.

"You don't have a second set of books or a copy?" the adjuster asked, a leer appearing where his mouth had been.

Izzy erupted, "Vad's a madder mid you? Da whole place boined. Everyd'ing is jus smoke an' ashes. You van a see da books? Go indo da office. See da books. Oy vey!" Izzy slapped his forehead with his palm as an expression of the contempt he had for Mr. Bill Drill.

The adjuster was bored as he waited for his assistant to come back from rummaging through the charred store taking photographs. He already knew that the three people apparently responsible for the fire were policemen. It was pretty obvious to him and to everyone else that the fire had destroyed everything in the store, including the records. He wasn't going to have to work too hard to deny this claim, but he had to at least go through the motions.

More than ironically, the adjuster smoked a couple of cigarettes as he waited, throwing the still smoldering butts on the ground near the store's entrance. When the kid emerged from the ruins, he was positively black with soot. Drill shuddered as he thought how much the kid absolutely loved to get dirty. Drill would never go into such a place. He would never take the chance that the burned floor joists might not be able to support his substantial weight.

Fire Chief Willie Griffin had been a fireman for twenty-five years. He was a quiet man, not by disposition, but because nature had endowed him with a fabulous stutter, and he became sorely embarrassed when he got stuck on a syllable for a minute or two. Not only did it make him embarrassed it made everybody within earshot highly nervous, as they almost physically tried to coax the next syllable out of him. But he was a competent fireman, a college graduate, and fortunately could write well, especially when it came to his reports.

He knew the big deal about the fire in this store, for he had kept up with all the local rumors and gossip. After his crew had extinguished the fire, except for a few smoldering beams, he had ordered his men out of the store.

Chief Griffin and his assistant chief had then gone back into the store to perform a detailed inspection. He was adamant about using the buddy system during an investigation after a fire and would never even consider going to perform a post-fire inspection alone.

Other than an old timey fireproof safe, the size of a double refrigerator and as solid as the rock of Gibraltar, there was no evidence of any coins, nor evidence of anything of value which might have been salvaged. He tried the combination to the safe, and then looked around for some evidence of the combination, for as strange as this may seem, people often leave the combination to a safe written on a piece of paper in the vicinity of the safe, sometimes even taped to it. He had even come across situations where the owners had kept a note to the combination to a safe securely locked within.

But everything was burned and charred and there wasn't a scrap of paper that was readable. If the coins had been in the safe, they were still there, probably as an indistinguishable lump of molten metal, much to his consternation.

Not trusting the charred stairs, Chief Griffin and his loyal assistant went around back and entered the basement where they quickly determined the origin of the fire. In the middle of the ashes which had once been the pile of rags, Chief Willie found the burnt and twisted remnants of Officer Carrico's cigarette lighter.

When they emerged from the burnt store, they found a dejected Isadore Shapiro quietly standing at the door to the store, tears staining his wrinkled face. The haberdashery had been his domain, and he had been very proud of his store. He thought about all that he had lost. At the time of the fire, the store no longer had the large and varied inventory it used to have. Some of the shelves were bare, and customer traffic was significantly less these past few years. But it had been his life, his creation. Emotionally, he was devastated as he stared blankly into the burned mess.

Izzy looked at Chief Griffin, his eyes begging for an explanation for the disaster. He gave a little nod toward the interior of the store. Chief Griffin nodded in response, and said, or at least tried to say, "Bbbbbbe vvvvvv vvvvverrrrrr cccccccccareful."

Izzy cautiously stepped into what had been his life's meaning. He tested the floor, and gingerly stepped through the wet ashes to a rack of wet wrinkled suits, covered with black soot. They were ruined- beyond any hope of being salvaged. He examined some of the labels. Izzy loved labels. The fine clever woven labels of a generation before were becoming increasingly superfluous. In a way, he thought sadly, he was like one of these labels- superfluous.

No longer were the suits made in the good old U S of A. Now it was China, Mexico, Honduras, the Phillipines, Sri Lanka, even Viet Nam. He shuddered, thinking of suits now made in Viet Nam. These were the sources of the suits now sold in men's shops, even in exclusive men's clothing stores. And India! Suits galore came from India. What happened to all the old Southern textile mills? The cut and sew shops?

He sat down in what remained of his favorite old office chair, ignoring the soot and ash, thinking only of what had once been.

He was totally dejected as he thought about Mart-World. That was the future. He began to cry, soft silent tears, as he got up, his bottom coated with black sooty goo, and began to walk out of the store for the last time.

He heard some sounds where the front door had been. It seemed like a lot of noise. He began to hurry out of the office. Even though it was a tad early, irrationally he thought maybe it was a customer. He was astonished to see several people dressed in suits looking around, and a young man with what looked like a TV camera on his shoulder, a couple of long wires trailing out the door to a white van waiting in front of the store.

One of the suits spied him. "Are you Mr. Isadore Shapiro?" he asked.

Izzy nodded. The man had a perfectly glued pompadour and went into a big spiel about the lottery and the good fortune of Mr. Hamish O'Halloran and his sad demise. "Anyway, since you are the administrator of Mr. O'Halloran's estate we are proud to bring you a check for $1,000,000.00," he brashly, and incongruously announced, given the circumstances. The cameras were rolling as they focused insensitively on the appropriately stunned Izzy.

The check for the million was cardboard and about as big as a billboard. That wasn't the real check, of course. It was all for show. Then they asked him about the beneficiary of the estate, which they already knew, the producers having done their homework.

Izzy mentioned, "Da Demple of God," and they were off to find Pastor Ronnie, and get a much more appreciative recipient and a more colorful and entertaining interview. The entourage was gone amidst much commotion, leaving the stunned little man holding a real cashier's check made out to the estate of Hamish O'Halloran. He sat down on the walk in the front of the store, blankly looking at it.

After a while Nat came up to him. Izzy was still sitting on the concrete walk, dejected. "What's the matter Pop?" Nat knew immediately something wasn't quite copacetic. Izzy just smiled and handed his son the cashier's check for a million dollars. "What's this, Pop?" he asked.

"Id's fifdy dousand dollars for us, Nad, dad's whad id is. Fifdy dousand dollars. Dad's de commission I'm a ged from dis check. Id's de loddery dad O'Halloran won. Id is bad luck, Nad, really bad luck. Ve godda deposid dis check in da esdade accoun'."

Chapter 26

A few days later an important looking certified letter from the Old Rome Fire and Casualty Company arrived. Nat had taken the slip and gone down to the post office and signed for it. With great anticipation Izzy tore open the envelope expecting a big fat check as compensation for the terrible loss of his store and all its inventory. But no, in the universal ways of insurance companies everywhere, it was a terse letter denying the claim.

> Dear Sir;
>
> Our investigation has revealed that the destruction of the insured premises was due to governmental action. Please refer to paragraph 2 of page 6 of the Exclusions, attached to your policy, entitled Governmental Action Exclusion. We therefore respectfully must deny your claim.
>
> Sincerely,
>
> Claims Department

"Whad is dis?" Izzy angrily shouted to himself, for no one else was around just then. "Whad guvmin agshun? He was furious, so it didn't take him long to go where he usually went when he was furious these days. In less then five minutes he was seated in Jimmy G's waiting room, impatiently tapping his foot, angrily reading and rereading the letter, and periodically smacking his forehead with his palm, crying "Oy vey."

Izzy was seriously getting on Hazel's nerves what with the constant movement, tapping of his foot, and talking to himself in Yiddish. She was just about to put a stop to it in the inimitable manner of stern Hazels in every law office, when the door opened, and Jimmy G emerged. He immediately picked up on Izzy's snit.

"What now? Whatcha got dere, Iz?" said Jimmy, as Izzy started waving the letter at him, sputtering. Jimmy reached out and grabbed the offending document. He had read it before he even got into his office.

"What dis is, Iz, is insurance companies. Dey don' make da big dough by payin' claims, even legit claims. Dey always fine some reason ta try ta weasel out. Dis one, I'm tellin' yiz, Iz, dey'll pay. Dey jes wanna make us woik fer it. Don' worry about it. Leave it ta me, Iz. It'll take a while but dey'll pay up. Jes' bring me da insurance policy. I'll do da rest."

Izzy was back in five minutes with the insurance policy, scorched edges and all. It had somehow survived the fire intact, securely ensconced in the old safe, which as, guaranteed, could survive heat of 1700 degrees. Jimmy dashed off a letter demanding payment, or else, threatening treble damages for unfair and deceptive trade practices and attorney fees, and promising to give the story to every newspaper in this part of North Carolina where the Old Rome Fire and Casualty did most of its business. He sent a copy to the state's Insurance Commissioner, that dreaded ombudsman and protector of the state's good citizens, who held the key to the vast riches insurance companies gleaned in the state. The Commissioner had the power to shut an insurance company's doors in a flash, and they all knew it. Jimmy prayed the old commissioner wasn't in the pocket of Old Rome Fire and Casualty.

"Vy'd dey say gummin agshun eggsclusion, huh, Jimmy, vy?"

"OK. Listen, up, Iz. Dey figger since dem two bozos what caused da fire wuz cops, da insurance company can claim gummental action, see. Mos' a da time, pipple jes give up, ya know. Don' follow tru wid da claim. Don' worry,

196

dough. I doubt da police chief or da mayor is gonna back 'em up on dis one. Dem cops wuz actin' on dere own. Total mavericks. Completely outside o' dere aut'ority. So dere ain't no gummental exclusion, Iz. Dey'll pay. Dey don' wanna bad fait' claim lodged against 'em. Or treble damages and attoiney fees. Dat'll really scare 'em."

Izzy was still sorely irked, but his anger had subsided, and he was pleased with Jimmy G's confidence. But the more he thought, the more he worried. That's what Izzy did -worry. It was his forte, his default state.

He looked up to the sky involuntarily. This was not part of the accursed estate. This was his own store, the store he nurtured and spent a generation developing. "Vy, God? Vy iss all dis crap happenin' do me?" He apologized to God for using the word, 'crap'. That wasn't nice. But suddenly he knew the answer. He didn't remember actually hearing God speak, but he positively knew the answer. Izzy was astounded. It was merely time. Time for a change.

Chapter 27

Guilt! Detective Sergeant O'Malley, being a good practicing Catholic, had been infused with a healthy sense of guilt at an early age by ruthless and sadistic nuns. They ran the Catholic school he attended like a concentration camp. The guilt carried through to adulthood in the form of a relentlessly nagging conscience, which he steadfastly tried to ignore. After the episode at O'Halloran's, where he was lucky to escape with only that ersatz Heidelburg dueling scar, try as he might, O'Malley could not shake the ever-rising guilt. It covered him like a lead blanket.

Everywhere he went the guilt nagged at him. He tried to rationalize it away. *He hadn't stolen anything, had he? No one lived there, after all, it was just an empty house.* But as soon as he processed these thoughts, the good side of his conscience fought its way in. *You're a cop, for cryin' out loud. Protector of the people. You burgled a house! B and E, pure and simple. Somebody owned that house, and it wasn't you.* O'Malley crossed himself involuntarily, just at the thought of his perfidy, vowing once again to go to confession.

After meeting with Gus Seay, O'Malley left the police station, vaguely considering going to Our Lady of Perpetual Care in Greeneburg to make his confession. But as he reached the street, he stopped short. There on the other side of the street was, of all people, Isadore Shapiro. The very sight of the decent old Jew filled O'Malley with a new infusion of guilt, just as the old was subsiding. God was testing him, he just knew it. As Izzy walked across the street toward him, the guilt escalated to near panic.

"Misder O'Malley. Oy vey. Wad happened do your face?" he inquired.

"Oh that. I was on my back workin' on the engine of my car and dropped a wrench and it fell on my cheek," he recited the excuse he had prepared for just such an occasion. It was feeble, he knew, but it was all he could come up with when the Lieutenant first asked him about it, so he had to stick with it. Izzy seemed to accept the excuse, but O'Malley sensed a little suspicion on his part, nevertheless, for the cop knew the excuse was pretty lame. Perhaps his own emotions were somehow transmitted to Izzy, especially since he felt his face flush when he lied to Izzy. The confessional was calling.

"How's de invesdigation goink?"

"Well, we got those three dimbulbs with all their cuts and bruises, but we're pretty sure there were others. We're still lookin' for a perp dressed in black who some neighbors saw crawlin' away from the scene. Was anything reported missing, Iz?"

Shapiro winced at the uninvited familiarity. "No. Nuddings. Bud dere wass nuddings of value in de house, anyvays."

O'Malley desperately wanted to ask him where the things of value were, but he knew such a question would give him away and expose him as the budding thief he was. They nodded at each other, Izzy's face clearly evincing the suspicion that O'Malley was certain he felt. The guilt came surging back with a vengeance.

Izzy went into the courthouse which was, as I said, next to the police station. O'Malley watched him like a hawk as Izzy went up the stairs and walked in. He then got into his car and carefully drove off. He had to pass the place of his egregious sin on his way home. He had just about gotten there when he almost drove off the road. There coming down the steps of O'Halloran's house was Izzy Shapiro.

It can't be. I just saw him going into the courthouse. What? Am I going nuts? O'Malley said to himself out loud, as he made the sign of the cross twice in a futile plea for divine assistance. He closed his eyes tight and shook his head, half expecting Izzy to disappear when he reopened them. But he didn't, for Izzy was still there, standing in front of O'Halloran's house looking confused, when O'Malley opened his eyes. He felt he was obliged to greet him, but Izzy just looked at the detective as if he had never seen him before, which, of course, this particular Izzy hadn't.

Once again, O'Malley crossed himself, involuntarily. He thought about his strained relationship with the church and was certain this chaos was his part of his punishment. The spectre of Izzy Shapiro was going to haunt him the rest of his life. He determined to get back to church and make his amends. He would once again be a good Catholic, rejoin the Knights of Columbus, say his rosary and go to confession every Saturday. He was going to get right with God.

But O'Malley desperately needed a drink. A shot and a beer, that would sure help straighten out his addled mind. He drooled at the thought, and his instincts were taking him to Sullivan's Bar like a homing pigeon.

But the ways of the Almighty are strange indeed and instead of pulling into the familiar parking lot of his favorite pub, he pulled into the parking lot of Saint Brendan's R.C. Church, one of the very few Roman Catholic churches in the area. He was confused as he got out of his car. This isn't where he wanted to go, but since he was here he might as well go in.

The church was empty. Empty that is, of people, yet when O'Malley went into the nave of the church, he was convinced he was not alone. Guided by an unseen hand, he walked up to the front of the church and knelt at the altar rail. Prayer came easy for him in this holy place, this place of sanctuary from evil and temptation. It was the prayer of confession that flowed freely from his heart. Purged of the crushing weight of his sin after this personal act of contrition, O'Malley felt a huge sense of relief. He could breathe easier, now. He felt forgiven. God was back in his life

But as he left the comfort and sanctity of the church, the guilt returned, dowsing him like a bucket of cold water. There in front of the church was the ersatz Isadore Shapiro. O'Malley stared at him unabashedly, and Isadore stared back. O'Malley felt like he was going crazy. Isadore had changed clothes, or had he? He was totally confused. He couldn't remember what Izzy was wearing when he saw him at the courthouse or coming out of the Pine Street house.

O'Malley flipped Izzy a feeble wave, quickly got in his car and took off. He immediately drove home, stripped to his skivvies and went straight to bed, shivering under his covers like a frightened child

Chapter 28

It took the beleaguered detective almost a week to recover from the sight of Izzy Shapiro everywhere he went. After suffering a few migraines and gulping down the appropriate medicine, he had pretty much returned to normal, at least what was normal for him.

Every so often, Detective Sergeant O'Malley liked to wander out in public, be seen, so to speak – keep his fingers on the pulse of the community, don't you see. Let the folks know he was actually doing his job and looking into things. Although he would much rather have leaned back in his comfortable old desk chair and rested his feet on his desk for a little shut-eye, if he had his druthers.

Nevertheless, he decided it was time. He wandered over to the Court House Coffee and found himself a nice, unobtrusive booth which gave him a good view of the patrons, where he set up shop. Shop was just a cup of coffee and pastry, naturally, and a newspaper which he pretended to read as he surveilled (don't you just hate that word if it is in fact a word) or rather observed, the patrons.

After a while, during which nothing happened other than what you might expect to happen in a coffee shop near the courthouse, late in the morning, for no one came in who looked guilty of anything. Usually the guilty ones went home or got out of town as quickly as they could after being fortunate enough to leave the courthouse.

O'Malley was a little surprised to see none other than Mr. Gus Seay sidle into the coffee shop. Seay gave a perfunctory, if rather cool, nod to O'Malley as he sat in a nearby booth. The first thing Seay did was take out his lap top computer and go to work.

O'Malley considered how different his style was from Gus Seay's. O'Malley learned from watching people, their expressions, their movements and mannerisms. He could deduce a lot by just examining the demeanor of a person, for despite his innate laziness, he was a pretty good detective.

Seay was methodical, precise, but impersonal. He looked for square pegs and round holes – things that didn't fit his known scenarios, but he was not at all comfortable dealing with actual people themselves.

After Gus had been industriously bent over his lap top for a pretty good while, O'Malley was surprised to see a man come into the coffee shop and sit at one of the front tables next to the window with his back against the wall. The man had guilt indelibly etched all over his face, perhaps not actual guilt, more like the remnants of cuts and scratches.

O'Malley knew at once who he was. Not his name, perhaps, but O'Malley sure knew who he was. It was the mysterious burglar in black, who had joined the ignominious perpetrators in the closet during the break-in at O'Halloran's.

O'Malley studied him carefully, taking in every noticeable element of his features. Gus, meanwhile, was so intent on his monitor screen he was oblivious. The man was an average sized, middle aged man, with intense blue eyes, and short cropped gray blond hair. He was well muscled, his definition quite apparent under his jeans and solid black T-shirt.

The man knew that O'Malley was watching him, and even though he sensed that O'Malley was one of his co-burglars, he started to sweat. Hypocrisy aside, O'Malley was still a cop with all the powers of that office, and the man in the black T-shirt was just a burglar, notwithstanding his (outdated) private investigator's license.

The PI had become obsessed with the coins after he had been given the assignment by the museum, long ago. He had followed trail after cold trail, each one a dead end. But he had found and identified some other stolen coins, and the underworld that profited in that traffic, from the thieves themselves to the fences and insurance companies that racketeered in them. And since his ethical compass must have been skewed by the gold and silver metal, the burglar in black became one of them. Still, in the back of his mind he was haunted by the rare coins stolen from the museum, not a trace of which had surfaced in all these years.

As the two were staring at each other, Gus Seay let out an uncharacteristic, "hah!" as an image popped up on the screen in front of him. He immediately looked up at O'Malley, who was of course, now watching him intently. Sheepishly, Gus looked back at his screen, and then scanned the faces of the coffee shop patrons to see if any one else was looking at him. One was, and Gus breathed an involuntary gasp as he realized the customer staring at him was the same man as the image on his lap top screen.

Despite his physical frailty, Seay was a pretty courageous fellow. He immediately jumped up and quickly moved toward the suspect, his hand reaching for the shoulder holster well hidden under his jacket. O'Malley, sensing what was about to happen also jumped up, but years of lethargy and donuts impaired his agility to a surprising degree.

Sensing he was trapped, for his egress was quickly blocked by the fastidious little man reaching for a weapon, and the big detective who loomed large in another direction, the suspect jumped up on a table and in a single move leaped feet first into the plate glass window. Like a movie stunt man crashing through a faux plate glass window, he landed on his feet, did an obviously practiced tumbling parachute landing fall, and took off running.

O'Malley knew his physical limitations, and stopped after a few steps, heaving a big sigh. It probably was pure relief at not having to run after the fleet footed burglar. He watched resignedly, as the frail museum investigator ran almost delicately down the street, waving his .25 caliber Beretta, and frantically hollering, "stop, thief" in his high-pitched voice. It was a pretty comical sight.

O'Malley sat back down, smiling, and sipped his now tepid coffee, as a bored waitress ignoring all the hub-bub, swept up the glass. Interspersed among the sounds of tinkling broken glass as it was swept into the metal dustpan, one could still hear the squeaky sounds of the little detective's voice as he futilely chased the physically fit felon.

Something in the dark recesses of his mind nagged at O'Malley. It definitely had to do with the burglar Seay was chasing, but what was it? It seemed like it had something to do with the man's black T-shirt. He had been dressed all in black when he burgled the O'Halloran place, even wearing a black ski mask. You couldn't even see his blond hair. That was it- the black shirt and the blond hair. He had seen a wanted bulletin some time back about a blond-haired burglar who wore all black when he did his break-ins. What was that alias? Black blondie or Blond blackie? That was it- Blond Blackie Blair, aka Arnold Potts.

O'Malley had always marveled at how some crooks could shed their real names like snakes shed their skins. Some of them did it so often they forgot what their own birth name was. It did create havoc with the system, but with the computer age and the police information network, it was getting easier every day to track down the name changers.

O'Malley quickly dropped a few bucks on the table, took one last sip of his now cold coffee, and made his way back to the station. In a few minutes, he had the man on the screen in front of him. It was definitely him, Arnold Potts aka Robert Owen Blair, aka Blond Blackie Blair. He had all the man's vitals but more importantly, a DMV search gave him the make and model of the car he drove – a black 1999 Toyota Corolla with a current registration.

O'Malley leaned back in his worn old chair and began to put his feet on the desk when he had an inspiration. He jumped up and moved relatively fast, at least for a man of his girth, got into his car and started driving around the neighborhood of the courthouse. He had been thinking why the thief would have been hanging around the courthouse and why he would have taken such a chance to expose himself by coming into Court House Coffee in broad daylight.

A block off Main Street he found what he was looking for. The black Toyota Corolla was unobtrusively parked on the street, under the shade of a large maple tree. The crook had not stayed on the lam as long as he had without some smarts, the big cop thought. When he took off running from the coffee shop, he would do his best to lead Seay away from his car. When he lost his pursuer, the crook would circle back.

O'Malley figured he had some time. He let the air out of the left rear tire of the Toyota and opened the driver's door. It was unlocked. It was ironic, he thought, how often thieves left their own cars unlocked, easy pickings for car thieves. Sure, they needed unobstructed access in the event they needed a quick getaway, but really, they just had so much trust in the honesty of their fellow man.

He popped the hood and pulled a few wires. He drove down the street a little way and turned his car around to face Blair's Toyota. He too parked under the shade of a large maple tree, for it was Maple Street after all, and waited.

After about a half hour during which O'Malley tried to come up with the answer to that pesky 'why' question, he saw his man trotting down Maple Street. He started his car and waited. It was definitely Blond Blackie Blair who slipped into the driver's seat of the Toyota. O'Malley grinned because he could just make out the angry expression on his face when the car wouldn't start. He hopped out and lifted the hood just as O'Malley quietly pulled up even with him.

"Havin' trouble, Bud?" he asked through his open window. Blair turned, a surprised expression on his face, which became even more surprised as he recognized Detective Sergeant O'Malley and his no-nonsense, non-issue .357 magnum pointed right at him.

"Down on your knees, Bud. Hands in the air." He got out of his cruiser as the perp reluctantly complied, and announced, "Arnold Potts aka Robert Owen Blair, you are under arrest for burglary."

The jig was up. Even though he knew he could still out run the cop, Blair was spent after running two miles to escape the persistent pesky little museum investigator. Blair, aka Arnold Potts or vice-versa, knew who he was, and of course, knew what he had done. He knew the cop had been there. Blair was thinking now of how he could cut his losses and use his knowledge of O'Malley's perfidy for his own benefit. He gave the officer no problems as he submitted to the arrest and listened to the standard recitation of his Miranda rights.

O'Malley was still bugged by the question as they drove around the block to the jail. In a conversational tone, O'Malley asked, "What made you come into Court House Coffee today, Blond Blackie?" But he was disappointed as the burglar remained quiet, a trace of a smile on the corners of his mouth as he held up five fingers, the universal signal of perpetrators to cops the nation over that they were invoking their Fifth Amendment right to remain silent.

Chapter 29

Things had slowed down in Pine Ridge after the furor of the fire in Shapiro's store. Jimmy G had had it with drugs and thugs, and the low lifes in criminal court. He was thankful for the respite. But his mind was always racing, always worrying, always thinking, thinking, thinking. It started on the streets of Brooklyn because he was a little guy. He had to constantly out think, and out fox the myriad thugs who were out for him. In third grade, he got depantsed by a bunch of fifth graders. He was mortified and vowed that would never happen again. He was too small to put up much physical resistance, so he became hyper vigilant, hyper cautious, and hyper clever.

Of all his cases, O'Halloran's Will was the most intriguing. The Temple of God left a taste in his mouth like chewing aluminum foil. He would do whatever he could to disabuse the public of its supposed worthiness. That would leave the Institute for the Treatment of Canines Humanely (ITCH) as the beneficiary. Jimmy thought about the Institute and began to wonder about the dogs. What happened to them? They had not been seen in quite a while. Now that he had a little time he decided to do a little investigating.

He slipped off his fancy orange and purple tie with the gold border and hopped on his bicycle. Yes, that's right, his bicycle. Pine Ridge was a small town, with a measly twenty-mile per hour speed limit through it. He could make better time on the bike, parking wasn't a problem, and it gave him a little desperately needed exercise. But more importantly, it really threw people off when he arrived somewhere on his bike, and Jimmy really liked that; that stunned expression on people's faces when the middle-aged man hopped off his bicycle.

And Jimmy sure threw off Billy when he arrived on his bike at the local Institute for the Treatment of Canines Humanely (ITCH), that afternoon. Billy, who was out front sweeping the sidewalk, when the lawyer rode up, gaped at the little man with greasy unkempt hair, purple pants and orange shirt as he hopped off his bike.

Jimmy got right to the point. "My friend, Rex, said you took in some dogs here. Dey came from da ol' lawyer's house on Pine Street."

"Oh, yeah," said the naïve young man. "Sure, I remember those three dogs. The big shepherd that looked more like a wolf bit me when I tried to give him the "U" shot. I grabbed his rear leg and he turned and bit me hard, real hard, like a bear trap snapped my arm. That wolf was growling like a grizzly. He took off outta here like a shot. I don't know what happened to him, but I never saw a dog open a door like that before."

"Whadda ya mean open a door?"

"I mean actually open a door. The big dog ran up to the door, almost stood up and put his paw on the door handle pushing it down. He opened the door and pushed it open and ran away. Never saw him again. I ran after him a little bit, but he was gone. I really didn't want to catch him. My hand hurt like the devil. That sure was a big dog."

Jimmy considered the garrulous young man. He was very nice, eager to please. He hadn't asked Jimmy for any credentials, not that there was such a thing as a dog- keeper privilege that would require him to keep what the dog did in confidence.

"Wha hoppen to da udders?" Jimmy asked, "da udder dogs wot came here wid da big wolf?"

"Oh, we U'd them. They was pretty scroungy mutts. Nobody woulda wanted them."

"Whaddaya mean, U'd dem?"

"You know, euthanized them. Put them to sleep. We didn't have any room here at the Institute. They were pretty good-sized dogs and would have eaten a lot, and our funds are a little low, you know. We probably couldn't have adopted them out. They were full grown, and you know, people like puppies. Not hungry, scroungy looking, full grown curs, with matted fur. Plus, they weren't housebroken at all. Whew, just thinking about the piles they left. Maybe we could have leased them out to a fertilizer factory."

Jimmy rode back to the office with a whole lot less enthusiasm than he had when he went there. As usual, his mind was racing as he thought about the current state of events. *So the Institute for the Treatment of Canines Humanely (ITCH) had not taken care of the dogs. Killed two and lost one. That was a pretty lousy record of taking care of their charges,* he thought. *Looks like the Institute for the Treatment of Canines Humanely (ITCH) was out. What would happen if the Temple of God was really found to be unworthy, who would get O'Halloran's estate then?*

He shuddered as he realized that if that turned out to be the case, the estate, this very large estate, would most likely escheat to the state, and he sure didn't want that. There didn't appear to be a single heir anywhere else, at least none that anyone knew about. He would have to get Hazel working on that problem.

All of a sudden Jimmy's zeal in the representation of the Estate of Hamish O'Halloran waned precipitously. But he was ethically bound to do his best. He grimaced. He would do his best even if it meant that the state of North Carolina would be the one to benefit. At least Izzy would get something out of it. He liked Izzy. Izzy was honest, dogged, and, for once, Jimmy had a client with integrity

Chapter 30

After an afternoon of worrying and fretting, Izzy was exhausted and schlepped up the few steps leading to Nat's house where he had been staying. He dragged himself into the living room and collapsed onto the sofa. Almost immediately, he fell into a deep, virtually comatose sleep. The warm afternoon sun shined in, causing a sheen of fine sweat to appear on his face.

He dreamt a disturbing, unsettling dream. He was being hounded by wolves nipping at his heels as he ran, at least in this dream, with agility and speed, barely eluding the howling, snarling animals. As the pack grew and they seemed to be closing in all around him, it started to rain, a salty wet downpour. But something was happening; the wolves seemed to be backing off. They were still chasing him, but he no longer had the feeling of impending doom. Then he saw a huge, ferocious dog, much bigger than the wolves, and it seemed to be standing guard, leaning over him, protecting him. The rain kept falling but Izzy had the odd sense that it was just his face that was getting wet.

Slowly, Izzy emerged from the Stygian depths of his tortured sleep. His eyes began to focus but it was still dark, the dampness on his cheeks and brows continuing unabated. He slowly began to realize the source of the unnatural wetness. He was being licked to death by a huge, slobbering wolf. He screamed, not quite the blood curdling scream of imminent death or disfigurement, but a pretty good scream for a grown man, nonetheless.

He bolted upright, his spine pressed solidly against the back of the couch. The wolf, startled by the scream and sudden movement, backed off a few steps. Izzy's heart was pounding, racing. He thought he was having a heart attack.

He was panting, gasping for breath as the wolf looked at him querulously, its head cocked in an uncertain manner, its expression one of disappointment.

Just then, Nat walked in. "What's the matter Pop?"

"Nad!" he gasped. "Dank God. Save us from dis creadure."

"Oh, Pop. That's just a big dog I found, or maybe he found me. Don't worry, Pop. He won't hurt you. He's the best natured dog I ever saw. He is so thankful if anyone scratches him behind the ear or pays him any attention at all. He just showed up a couple of days ago, Pop. I gave him a good bath and fed him and ever since he's just been hanging around. His name is Caesar. It's on the tag on his collar. There's no address or phone number, though."

Izzy gaped at the huge dog, who was returning the stare with a big smile on his face. No kidding, an honest to God smile. Dogs do smile, you know. It was not a wolf after all, just a huge, hairy German Shepherd, with weird golden eyes. It was the biggest dog Izzy had ever seen, but of course, he was not really a dog person and had never seen an Irish wolfhound. Instinctively he stretched his hand out, and the dog started wagging his tail, took a step forward, sniffed it, and then licked it. Sensing no more fear or potential harm, the dog moved in for some serious behind the ear scratching. The two were becoming fast friends.

Izzy pondered. Could this be the same dog that the Institue for the Treatment of Canines Humanely (ITCH) was supposed to be taking care of? He examined the brass tag on the luminescent orange collar. The tag just announced "Caesar." There was no other identification, no address, no number to call. This was just too much to be a coincidence. It had to be O'Halloran's Caesar.

Nat had taken a load off his feet. Lounging in a big, well worn leather overstuffed chair, he said, "What is it, Pop? You're looking kind of strange."

"Dis dog, Nad. Dis big dog I dink is O'Halloran's dog. De Insdidude is supposed do be dakink care of de dog bud id's ride here, an id doesn' look like id's goink anyvere. You van' keep de dog, Nad?"

"Sure, Pop. I do. It kind of keeps me from being lonely, and he sure seems to like it here. He really likes to climb up on that old couch and settle in next to me while I watch a little TV in the evening."

A few years before Nat had married a nice Jewish girl from New York, Susan was her name. She hated bucolic Pine Ridge with a passion and longed for the stylish chaos and stress of the New York City scene. When Nat started losing his hair, that was it for Susan. She went home to New York to visit her mother and never came back. Good thing they didn't have any kids. Nat was a little sad at first but quickly got over it and was actually glad she was gone after a while. It was more peaceful that way.

Chapter 31

"The wheels of justice grind exceeding slow," the old adage goes. To anyone who has ever been involved, it is a frustrating, maddening, and above all, ineffective process, but it is our process, and it is the best anyone has thought of to date. So after one of those maddening interstices in which nothing at all seemed to be going on, it was time. The trial of the century was ready to start. Pine Ridge was about to learn whether the Temple of God was in fact truly worthy.

Not only was everyone in the little town in a tizzy, the press had descended upon Pine Ridge from every metropolis in the state and then some. The parking area on Main Street anywhere near the courthouse was jammed with media vans and trucks. Cameras, microphones and all sorts of media paraphernalia were being shoved in the face of anyone who looked important or seemed to have the slightest connection with the case.

True to form Jimmy G, spotting the mob of reporters and cameraman, ducked around back tugging Izzy along reluctantly. He snuck into the courthouse through a back door without being spotted, breathing a sigh of relief. He was always worried a made guy might be lurking in the shadows.

Mr. B.S. Fotheringham, III, and his publicity seeking client, pulled up in front of the courthouse in the Temple's powder blue Lincoln stretch limousine with the gold trim. Flashbulbs a popping, B.S. himself regally exited the vehicle, posing all the while. When Pastor Ronnie Conner joined alongside him, they condescendingly greeted the crowd and made a truly regal entrance into the courthouse, followed by a retinue which included Margaret Young, not looking too shabby, a host of Armitrage Grace toadies carrying boxes filled with important looking documents, and last but not least, Donna Conner brought up the rear, in more ways than one.

B.S. was positively basking in the notoriety. He super-confidently announced his certainty of victory to the big three television reporters. He was just dripping with aplomb and sophistication. Boy, did he look good. He just knew that everyone in the nation needing a high priced, slick lawyer was looking up his telephone number just then and checking their account balances. B.S came from the old school of attorneys that felt that any publicity at all was good publicity.

But not all the TV cameras were focused on Mr. B. S. Fotheringham, III. No, some of them were distracted by Margaret Young, all dolled up and looking about as good as she could, which today, with a dab of makeup and a can of hairspray, was pretty darn good. Those cameramen seemed to agree as they panned their cameras slowly upward, starting with her very high heeled pumps.

Despite his penchant for a little publicity himself, Judge Martin, to his credit, barred the cameras from the courtroom. Oh, he loved to chat up an attractive, bright, young reporter or television commentator as well as the next guy, but he made certain not to compromise that elusive quality, justice, no matter what he thought of the individuals involved in the case he was presiding over, or their attorneys. And in this case, it was quite difficult for Judge Martin not to show his bias.

It was customary for the Judge to get to the courthouse early on days court was in session. The parking space reserved for the Judge was right next to the rear entrance, so he made it in unobserved, while the media paraded out front like a pack of hungry hounds waiting for something to happen. He was a little disappointed at missing the opportunity for a little press, but the good judge supposed it was all for the best.

He settled back comfortably in the quiet of his chambers and looked over the file. Just a wisp of a suspicion nagged at his subconscious. What was it? What was wrong with this case? Just then, Bailiff Burton came in bringing the Judge his morning coffee. Each morning before court, the two of them would sit in the Judge's chambers, drink their morning coffee, and talk about the local legal gossip. Every so often Bailiff Burton would get up and take a peek out of the chambers' door looking over the people in the courtroom. As it approached 9:30 the Judge got up and put on his robe. "Are they ready, Bailiff?"

"There's still a lot of commotion, but there's a bunch of lawyers out there, seem to be arguing behind the Plaintiff's table. And Judge, I never saw this before. One of the lawyers has a dog with him."

"A dog you say? Hmm. OK. I'm ready. Open Court, Mr. Burton."

Burton strode out into the courtroom and announced in his booming baritone, "All rise."

The courtroom was packed. Spectators lined up against the wall – standing room only. There was a lot of shuffling, jostling and rustling as everybody stood up.

"Oyez! Oyez! Oyez," he thundered in the tradition of opening courts since the time of William the Conqueror. Judge Martin, being an aficionado of legal history, had many years before explained to Bailiff Burton that *Oyez* meant hear ye or listen up, in old French, so the bailiff wouldn't be embarrassed at bellowing out the unfamiliar words in front of a courtroom full of people. Thereafter, the Bailiff was smug and actually emboldened with the arcane knowledge.

Judge Martin regally entered the Courtroom in all his judiciousness. Burton bellowed, "Be seated," and everybody did, with more jostling and rustling, all except for the five lawyers, avariciously eying the four seats at the tables. It was oddly reminiscent of a game of musical chairs with the lawyers frozen in place as the music stopped.

"Who are you?" Judge Martin directed his question at an unfamiliar man, obviously an attorney, standing with the others behind the four chairs at the attorney's tables. He was tall and slender, graying at the temples. A good looking man with sharp features and prominent eyebrows, he responded confidently: "The name is A. Benfield Suggins, Assistant Attorney General, Judge. I am making an appearance on behalf of the state of North Carolina, the residual beneficiary. After the Temple of God is determined to be unworthy by these fine folks of Pine Ridge, and the Institute for the Treatment of Canines Humanely (ITCH) has failed or is unable to perform the required conditions because it is incapable of doing so, it is the State's contention that the entire net O'Halloran estate escheats to the State of North Carolina, there being no residual beneficiary."

The courtroom erupted in gasps of astonishment, followed by a plethora of murmurs at this statement, but they all fell silent as the Judge's gavel banged like a gunshot. "Hmmmm," muttered the judge as he stroked his chin pensively. "All right. Here's how it's going to be. B.F., you and Margaret sit there at the Plaintiff's table. You, too, Mr. Chase, and get that dog outta here. Enough of the cases I hear anymore are dogs. The way I see it, you all are the Plaintiffs and have the burden of proving that your client is worthy, or that your client, Mr. Chase, has met the conditions imposed by the will if the Temple's not found to be worthy. Kind of makes you wish you hadn't filed this suit, doesn't it, B.F.? Then the burden of proof would have been on Mr. G, here, in a declaratory judgment action." The judge chuckled a bit at his own cleverness. "OK, Mr. G, you and Mr. A. Benfield Suggins, here, sit at the defense table. You're supposed to be impartial in this, but I bet the state man is just salivating at the opportunity to do a little cross examination, aren't you Mr. Suggins?"

The state man gave a wry little smile, but Judge Martin didn't give him a chance to respond. "Gentlemen, and you too, Miss Young," the judge said in a manner that was a little too obviously less than avuncular, "Your clients will have to sit in the chairs behind you. Bailiff! Bring up another chair for Miss Young."

After a few minutes of lawyerly rearrangement, which is sort of a controlled chaos, everyone was in place, and a lot of scowls were apparent indicating the dissatisfaction of the attorneys, but really, nothing would have satisfied any of them just then.

They soon settled into their appointed seats ready to try the case. Judge Martin just stared out at the sea of expectant faces. Nothing silences a courtroom more than the icy stare of the venerable Judge waiting for order in the Court.

A morbid silence descended over the courtroom. All eyes were now on the stern-faced Judge. "All right folks. Now that I have your attention let me deal with a few preliminaries. Have all the parties exchanged witness lists?" Everybody nodded approvingly, proud to admit they had complied with one of the Court's written rules for a change. All except Mr. Suggins who rose unsteadily.

"Uh. Judge. I don't have anyone's witness lists. I just made an appearance in the case today, and, um, I guess I should move to continue the trial so I can be brought up to speed."

There was a collective groan from the courtroom. Not another delay.

"No, suh, Mr. Suggins. Not today. The wheels of justice grind exceeding slow, so they say, and I am not going to add to that slowness. The way ah see it, the state is just a grandstander, a spectator. Ah'll let you participate to a degree, just out of courtesy, but remember the state is just a residual beneficiary if no one else qualifies as a beneficiary. So we're goin' forward with the trial today, Mr. Suggins. Y'all got copies of your witness lists? Give 'em to Mr.

Speedy. Mr. Speedy go make a copy for our esteemed ASSISTANT Attorney General." The Judge sarcastically emphasized the word "assistant" just to make sure Mr. Suggins understood his lowly position in the pecking order.

After that was done, and in record time considering it was Mr. Speedy making the copies, Judge Martin announced in his practiced Southern drawl, "Aw right. Mr. Speedy call twelve to the box."

Speedy stood and slowly announced the names of twelve town folks. Bailiff Burton directed them to their assigned seats in the jury box, and a motley crew they were. Of course, you always have a truck driver, a nurse, and a teacher on the jury. That's standard. But there was a young girl with a promising exposed midriff, a wan, haggard looking, inarticulate boy-man, with multiple tattoos depicting your traditional violence, sticking out from his ragged T-shirt, enough piercings to set off any metal detector, and the bored, hurt look of the perennially unemployed with no idea why no one would hire him. There was a bespectacled black student, a very old lady who literally appeared to have one foot in the grave, and a few others of the totally nondescript type who inched through life without setting off any alarms. Your typical Southern jury!

B.S. officiously cleared his throat, but the Judge said, "I'll do the preliminaries, heah. Folks, how many y'all attend the Temple o' God here in Pine Ridge?" Eight jurors raised their hands. The Judge wrote down their seat numbers. "Now folks, how many y'all make a contribution to the Institute for the Treatment of Canines Humanely (ITCH) here in Pine Ridge?" Two more elderly folks cautiously raised their hands. "Aw right, then. How many y'all been convicted of a felony, or got any reason, any reason at all, you cain't be fair and impartial or jes' don't wanna sit on this heah trial?" One person half raised his hand, sheepishly.

"Aw right then evahbody 'cep' Mr. Creegan in seat numbah six go on back to youah seats in the courtroom. Make way for them, folks." Eleven would be jurors rose and returned to the audience, guilty expressions on their faces trying to look like they were innocent.

The Judge repeated this routine several more times until he finally had twelve people who weren't felons, or devotees of the Temple of God, or contributors to the Institute for the Treatment of Canines Humanely (ITCH), or had a criminal record or some secret reason why they didn't want to be jurors.

"Aw right. Now the Jury is with the Plaintiff. B.F., go ahead and do your voir dire."

Fotheringham was well practiced in the art of jury selection, but the judge had deflated his planned voir dire. He wasn't going to be able to slide in a secret Temple of God devotee. He asked a few perfunctory questions and after getting some bland answers he accepted the panel, acting as if he was some benevolent provider, giving them all a bone. Rex Chase seemed a little confused, as if it was his first jury trial which it may well have been. He quickly passed the twelve.

Now it was Jimmy G's turn. He had watched the faces of the jury and didn't like what he saw on a couple of them. He came right to the point.

"Any o' youse related to Mr. B. F. dere, or frien's wit' 'im?"

A handsome young man in a turtle neck sweater and a tan suede sport coat glared at Jimmy, but raised his hand. "He's my uncle. My mother's brother," he said curtly.

Jimmy then turned his attention to an attractive middle-aged woman with gray hair in the front row. She had a confident bearing, almost sophisticated. They looked at each other for a few seconds, the woman's condescending expression daring Jimmy to ask her questions. He decided he didn't want to know, or perhaps he decided he didn't want the others to know. In any event he did not ask her a single question, but just smiled at her for a few seconds. He excused the two of them from the panel.

The judge repeated the drill a few more times, calling replacements for the excused jurors. B. F. and Mr. Rex Chase asked a few perfunctory questions. After Jimmy passed them they finally had a jury.

"Aw right, said the Judge amiably. Then let's have your opening statements. You first B.F."

B.S. Fotheringham, III, rose slowly, dramatically, buttoning his expensive suit coat as he approached the expectant jurors. Brother, we should have such a man as president! What charisma! What bearing! What a presence! Without notes or props he faced the jury confidently. He never had notes because he just didn't know what he was going to say until he opened his mouth, but it always came to him. Tall, broad shouldered, he was wearing a perfectly tailored, suit of the finest worsted wool, a brilliant fine Egyptian cotton white shirt, the French cuffs of the sleeves extending two inches beyond the cuffs of his coat revealing exquisite, ornate golden cuff links, he was the epitome of what everyone hoped their lawyer would be.

The jury was spellbound. His oration was magnificent, convincing, terrific, as he spelled out the extreme and unimpeachable worthiness of the Temple of God. Pastor Ronnie positively beamed, and it seemed like a genuine halo framed his perfectly coiffed, suspiciously black, hair. Fotheringham summarized with a flair, a perfect end to the magnificent speech, and sat down in his chair with supreme confidence, and with the absolute knowledge that he had wowed the jurors, every last one of them.

If the vote had been taken then, it would have been a slam dunk. Not only would the entire jury have found the Temple to be worthy, everyone in the courtroom would, probably even Jimmy G. But, alas, the law has its processes. No vote would be taken just yet.

Then, after a halting and ineffectual statement by Rex Chase, it was the estate lawyer's turn. Jimmy G stood to a sea of hostile faces. "Folks," he said meekly, his Brooklyn accent already grating on the unaccustomed Southern ears. "I gotta a'mit. He's pretty good. He's real good." Jimmy gave a nod in the direction of the Temple's esteemed lawyer. "But he ain't a witness. No, he ain't. He wan't even unner oat.' So I ast ya. Jus hol' off until ya hoid de evidence." He pronounced each syllable in "evidence" as if it was a separate word. "Fact is, I ain't got nuttin' against dis here Temple. I don't know nuttin' about it. Nuttin' at all. So le's hear wat de witnesses gotta say about it unner oat.' Den we'll decide if de Temple is woithy. Whadda ya say?"

He sat down with a plop, but Jimmy G had effectively made his point. With that brief little statement, he had taken an awful lot of wind out of the grand sails of the Temple of God.

The first witness was a little old lady. She looked like an honest to God church lady. She was dressed neatly, tastefully, in a blouse and skirt with a cardigan sweater. Holding her old fashioned purse with both hands demurely in front of her, she took the stand. Even her white neat hair had a blue tint to it, just as you would expect in a church lady. Her wire rim glasses rested precariously on the tip of her cute little nose. She couldn't have been a better looking witness if she had been type-cast by Hollywood. Immediately everyone's hearts went out to her.

"Please state your name ma'am," B.F. directed with authority.

"Ruby Graham," she said shyly.

"Tell us how Pastor Ronnie Conner and the Temple of God helped you."

"It was three years ago. I was destitute. I had nothing, no home, nothing. My husband was dead. I had no income, no money, and Pastor Ronnie came to my rescue. He saved me. He is an absolute saint. He bought me this nice little bungalow, just perfect for a poor old widow. He helped me get Social Security. The Temple pays my electric bill, buys my groceries. I was saved by Pastor Ronnie and the Temple of God."

Everyone loved Ruby. Just on that testimony alone the whole courtroom would have voted that the Temple was the most worthy of worthies in God's whole kingdom. The jury turned their attention to Jimmy G and stared at him, glared at him was more like it. They dared him with their eyes to cross examine Ruby Graham. He was in deep trouble.

"Cheese. Dat's tough," began Jimmy G, with mock sympathy. "How'd ja come inta getting' in touch wid da Temple, anyways, Miss Graham?"

"Oh! Through my nephew. He's a deacon or something in the Temple. He made the arrangements."

"Uh huh. How long ya been a widder, Miz Graham?"

"Objection," B.F. bellowed, his voice like a bull horn echoing in an alley, the sound reverberating off the walls. The Judge glared at Jimmy G, his expression clearly asking for an explanation.

"Well, Judge," said Jimmy feebly, in response, "She brought it up. Don' I get a little cross examination here?"

"Overruled for the time being." Judge Martin glared at Jimmy disapprovingly as the little lawyer squirmed in his seat.

"Twenty-eight years," she said meekly, her voice barely audible.

"Oh. Twenny-eight years, huh?" Jimmy emphasized the long time of Ms. Graham's widowhood. "How'd he die, yer husband?"

"Objection." B.F. was less forceful for some reason.

The judge interjected, "Is there a point here, Mr. G?"

"Yeah, your Honor. I'll get to it inna minute. Jes' one or two more questions."

"Overruled. See that you do, Mr. G. Keep it on point."

She was fidgeting now, was Miss Graham, squirming even. In a voice even quieter than before, she said, "He was the victim of a poisoning."

"Wadja say? I din' hear watcha said."

"He was the victim of a poisoning. He was murdered." She said this loud enough that everyone in the courtroom could hear, and everyone gave a little gasp.

"Oh. Cheese. Dat's too bad. Was it a accident or was it a poisoning on poipose?"

The jury, the audience, and even the Judge was listening intently, curious now. B.S. forgot to object, he was so interested.

"On purpose," said Ruby Graham, tears now dampening her cheeks, genuine tears. The jury was now steaming at Jimmy G. How dare he intrude into her privacy like this; into the most delicate and hurtful part of her life!

"Dey ever catch who did it?"

Silence. The jury slowly turned their glares from Jimmy, and looked squarely at Ruby Graham, waiting to hear the response. So did his Honor, B. S., and the all the other lawyers.

"Dey ever catch who did it? Ya gotta answer dat one."

Ruby erupted angrily. "Yeah they did. I did it, OK? I killed the rotten bastard. I did it and I'm glad. I did twenty-five years in the joint for it. I served my time, OK? I paid my price."

Oops! There was a stunned silence, as the jury, the judge and the audience took this in. B.S. turned angrily to Margaret and whispered something in her ear. She immediately turned beet red and pointed to Pastor Ronnie Conner. It didn't take a lip reader to understand what she said.

Judge Martin called for the morning recess. It couldn't have come at a worse time for B.S. Fotheringham, III, for now the jury had a few more minutes to really think about this damaging testimony, and let it sink in.

The grand Temple of God was helping a murderer. And helped her get Social Security benefits, too. How could that happen unless she was getting the benefits based on her husband's earnings? There was a lot of thinking going on in the minds of the twelve during that break.

B.S. was hot in a conversation with Margaret when the Judge came back into Court and the Bailiff's booming baritone brought him to attention. "Court's back in session."

Before B. S. resumed his case, he turned around and leaned over to Margaret, his face a bright red which was a really nice contrast with his gray, mostly white hair. He was still so angry it looked like steam might actually be emanating from his ears. It was just that he didn't know who to be angry with, for after all, it was his case, his responsibility. He should have spent some time preparing the witnesses, for he was the experienced trial lawyer here, wasn't he?

Ruby had been a disaster. What could possibly be worse than that?

Margaret pointed to the second name on the witness list. She whispered to B.F., "I didn't have a chance to vet her either, but Ronnie says she's wonderful." She pointed to the girl, a plain, short, brown haired girl, with horn rimmed glasses and a pug nose. She seemed so very young, so very fresh faced, so very innocent. B.F. decided to chance it. He just had to do something to pull his smoldering case out of the fire.

He announced to the Court, "Plaintiff calls Miss Susie Swann." The girl rose coyly, hesitantly. She looked around with an expression of embarrassment on her pure face. As she walked up to take the stand, everyone couldn't but help to notice her clothes. She was wearing what was as close to a Catholic school girl's uniform as it could be without actually being one; plaid skirt, white knee socks and a white blouse. She looked bookish, nerdish even, but virginal. Yes, positively virginal.

Susie sat in the witness chair and nervously pushed up her eye glasses with her forefinger.

"Tell us, Miss Swann, just how has the Temple of God helped you?"

"Well, I've known Pastor Ronnie just about all my life, of course. As long as I can remember anyway." She looked over at Ronnie as if he was God. "One day he came in where I work, and we just got to talking. I told him how bad I wanted to go to college, but my Mom- my Mom is a single Mom and I have a little brother – just couldn't afford to send me. I was working, but I hadn't even been able to save up enough for tuition. The next day Pastor Ronnie made some telephone calls and now I'm a sophomore at State College in Greeneburg majoring in psychology. I'm so happy." She giggled, "Pastor Ronnie and the Temple made it all possible. They pay my tuition, books, room and board – just about everything."

B.F. was relieved. It was perfect – Susie, the cute little librarian look, the testimony, everything. He turned to Jimmy to signal that she was his witness now. Satisfied, he leaned confidently back in his chair.

But the gods of chaos lurk everywhere, and B.F. had let down his vigilance. As he smugly leaned back in the chair, a comfortable leather office type chair on wheels, his center of gravity shifted, the chair shot forward and he went flying backwards, butt over teakettle, as they say, his feet pointing skyward. In an unbelievably athletic move for such a distinguished middle-aged man, he spun in the air like an Olympic diver in a desperate attempt for salvation and to avoid at least some level of painful embarrassment.

The result was unexpected, and even more unfortunate, for he landed on his knees, his head face down, securely planted dead center in Margaret's lap. Her reaction was to instinctively place both hands on the back of his head, holding him there, a look of astonishment on her face. After a few seconds in this interesting but embarrassing position from which the hapless B.F. inexplicably failed to even attempt to extricate himself, she jumped up, aghast. B.F. was tossed unceremoniously to the floor as she frantically brushed the front of her rather tight skirt, in a symbolic but involuntary attempt to remove some imaginary vile residue from this violation.

Judge Martin just shook his had sadly, and called another ten-minute recess, as he marched off into his chambers, just a trace of a smirk fighting to emerge from his clenched lips. He forced hiumself to retain his composuire, for judicial propriety, don't you see.

When Court resumed, Judge Martin directed his attention to Jimmy G. "You may cross examine the witness, Mr. G."

Pastor Ronnie scooted up into the seat next to his lawyer and whispered something to him. He stayed in the seat while Jimmy began his cross examination.

Jimmy looked at the incredibly sweet young thing. Something wasn't right about this. He wasn't sure what it was, so he decided to proceed slowly, see where it led.

"So you been goin' to dis Temple a long time, Miss?"

"Oh yes. Since I was just a little girl."

"How often ya attend soivices?"

She hesitated. She was under oath she remembered. She could be truthful on this one. It really shouldn't matter. "I haven't been to any services in quite a while, what with my work and school, you know."

"Hmmm. Now how long's dat?"

She hesitated again. This wasn't helping her or anyone, she realized. "It's been several years now." There was quite a murmur and rustling as a great number of people in the audience commented on this to each other. Judge Martin merely banged his gavel and silence resumed.

Jimmy had an inspiration. "Yer Mom. Where's she woik?"

B.F. didn't know either and wondered, too.

Another hesitation, this one a little longer. Susie copped a bit of an attitude. "She is the secretary to the treasurer of the Temple of God," she announced, just a little too arrogantly. Then to ameliorate that a little bit, she added. "She has been there a long time."

"Hmmm. An' you, where were you woikin' when you ran inta da Pasta dere?"

Uh oh! Susie did not like this, not one bit. But she couldn't avoid answering. Maybe a little waffling would be OK. "I was working at a club in Greeneburg," she answered tersely. Jimmy picked up on it for it was a little too terse.

"What club's dat?"

"A gentlemen's club. An exclusive gentlemen's club." Maybe that was too much of an answer, she worried. She looked out at the sea of faces in the audience. They were interested. Yes indeed, they were very interested. They sure were.

"Hmmm. What club's dat?" Jimmy asked, repeating his question for clarity.

"Objection," B.F. jumped up. "Asked and answered."

The Judge looked questioningly at the odd little lawyer.

"OK. Yeah Judge, but she still din't tell me da name of de club," he responded to the implied but unasked question from his Honor.

"Does it matter, Mister G?"

"Yeah, Judge, I kinda t'ink it does."

"Aw right, we'll see, but don't belabor the point Mr. G."

"Yeah, yer Honor," duly admonished, Jimmy turned to the witness. "Wad's de name of da club where youse ran inta Pastor Ronnie, Miz?"

She hesitated, the longest pause so far. "The Pleasure Dome," she announced with just a bit of pride, while those reprobates in the audience familiar with this particular establishment snickered.

"Wadda ya do dere?"

"Objection, irrelevant," B.F. was sensing the resurgence of the disaster that had been plaguing him during this whole trial.

"Actually, Mr. Fotheringham, I think I'll let the witness answer the question. What do you do there, Miss?" asked the now curious judge.

Another pause. "I'm an entertainer." The judge motioned her with his hands, a clear direction to spill it. "I'm a dancer. I dance with a pole." The audience was aghast once more, and the murmuring and rustling was intense. The judge banged the gavel twice, and they all settled down. Jimmy took over the questioning again.

"Lemme get dis straight. You woik at a gentlemen's club, an' yer a dancer. Dance wid a pole. Do ya take off yer clothes when ya dance?"

B.F. erupted. As it was to everyone else in the courtroom, the answer was obvious even to him. This disaster was as bad as the first one. No, worse, because Susie had stated that is where she ran into Pastor Ronnie.

"OK. That was your last question, Mr. G." The Judge turned to the girl, her face a mask of defiance. "Do you?"

"Yes, I'm a stripper, OK? I wear a wig, a skimpy costume, and I strip for the horny men. And they pay me a lot of money to do it. They stuff twenties in my G string," said Susie with a petulant air, the "What's it to ya, Bud?" unsaid, but clearly implied.

B. F. laid his head on the table, hiding it in his hands. At first Pastor Ronnie gave Susie a less than paternal little smile, no, it was more of a leer, but he quickly changed his expression when he thought about the repercussions. But it was too late, for a couple of members of the jury had caught the look.

Susie sat in her chair with a vengeance, crossed her legs, her arms, and stared ahead defiantly. B.F. had visions of money with wings, flying off in a direction far away from him. The only witness that could resurrect this fiasco was the Man of God, himself. He reached over to Ronnie and put his arm around the pastor's shoulder, as if he was his best friend, and whispered something to him. It was a long, congenial, ostentatious whisper.

B.F. announced from his chair, without standing, "The Plaintiff calls the right Reverend Ronnie Conner." The lawyer withdrew his arm from around the Pastor's shoulder, just as the Man of God turned in his seat and rose. The awkward concatenation of the two movements resulted in B. F.'s very fine, ornate gold cufflink becoming entangled in Pastor Ronnie's perfectly coiffed, hair sprayed hair, which latter remained entangled in said cufflink when the pastor rose to his full height.

The crowd gasped. The hair piece was stuck to the wretched cuff link like a squirrel in a spring trap. The pastor was bald as a cue ball. With ears.

This time it was the Judge who put his head in his hands. It took a few minutes for the initial surge of whispering, rustling, and snickering from the spectators to tone down to a point where they would even hear the gavel. "Aw right folks. It's not yet lunch time, but I think we've had enough drama for one mornin'. Ah'm gonna adjourn Court for lunch. Come back this afternoon at 2:00 sharp. Mr. Burton, adjourn Court." The Judge rose, and Bailiff Burton announced that Court was in recess until 2:00 p.m.

Chapter 32

Miz Tilly slowly regained her strength after she had returned from the hospital. Being in her familiar surroundings, no matter how humble they might be, was quite therapeutic, better than all the fancy pharmaceuticals the doctors might prescribe which, of course, she could not afford anyway. After a few days, she could amble about the house using the high backed overstuffed chairs decorated with hand knitted doilies to support herself.

She was sitting in one of these overstuffed chairs, having just awakened from one of her many naps. It was the middle of the afternoon, and she had heard a noise coming from the back of the house. But rather than be afraid, for in her mind, there was nothing in the world to fear, she called out, "Dat you, Darren? Come here, boy."

It was in fact Darren, who, having just come home from school, like any red blooded American boy, was looking for something to eat. He shuffled obediently into the parlor, his mouth crammed with a piece of buttermilk pie he had found in the refrigerator. Unable to articulate, he mumbled, "Yem, Mum."

"Darren, be a sweet boy an' fetch mah sewing kit."

He did as he was told, and in a few minutes, returned with a round bucket shaped sewing kit supported by three spindly legs. He placed it near his great-grandmother and shuffled back into the kitchen for another piece of the enchanting pie.

After a minute or two, Ms. Tilly shouted, "O' Lordy me. Darren, boy, could you come in here, puh leeze?"

Darren shuffled back into the parlor, his mouth stuffed with another piece of buttermilk pie, "Yem, mum," he mumbled inartfully, his articulation handicapped by the pie being savored.

"Darren, looka heah. Dis a 'portan' paper ole Missah O'Halloran lef' fer me ta take keer of fer 'im." She held up a large sealed manila envelope. There was no writing on it except the name *O'Halloran,* written in big block letters with a black magic marker. Be a good, boy, wudja, an' tek this heah 'portan' paper to de judge. He'll know what to do wid it."

Obediently, Darren took the envelope and ambled over to the courthouse. He didn't know where exactly to go or where the judge lived in the courthouse. He thought the judge actually lived in the imposing building, and that's why he was so important.

He was stopped at the door of the courtroom by a burly sheriff's deputy, in charge of security at the courthouse that day. He had seen the boy about town, and knew he wasn't one of the young thugs who often habituated the lower courts. After Darren informed him of his mission, the deputy accompanied the skinny young boy to Judge Harley Martin's courtroom.

Darren cautiously entered, peeking around the partially opened door. Judge Harley Martin was just heading for his chambers, having adjourned court for the afternoon recess. A few of the Court personnel were standing around, including Assistant District Attorney, Billy "Benedict" Arnold, who had been a motivated spectator. Because the ADA looked important in his conservative suit, the boy cautiously sidled up to him, reverently holding the envelope in both hands in front of him.

When he caught Mr. Arnold's eye, Darren said politely, "'Scu' me, Suh. Ah gotch 'is heah 'portan' paper. Mah Gran said give it to de Judge. Said he'll know what ta do." He held it up for Arnold to see.

When Arnold reached for it, the boy quickly withdrew the envelope, tightly clutching it to his chest. Intrigued by the name "O'Halloran" boldly printed on the face of the envelope but realizing the boy's reluctance to let it out of his hands, he said, "OK, son, you, me, and the deputy here, will go see the Judge."

They proceeded toward the Judge's chambers and cautiously knocked on the door. After a longer than normal interval, the word "Enter," came loudly from within. As they opened the door, Judge Martin was just zipping up his fly and coming out of his private bathroom. "What do you three want?" he snapped, a little tired and irked after the unusual goings on in court that day, but nevertheless, curious at the assemblage before him.

Billy Arnold said "Judge, this boy has an envelope he says is an important paper for you. It's something with the name 'O'Halloran' written on it.

"Oh?" said the Judge, exhibiting curiosity, "Lemme see it."

Darren stepped forward deferentially, his head bowed. "Mah Gran, Miz Shan Tilly, said it's a 'portant paper Missuh O'Halloran give her ta tek keer of."

He handed the envelope to Judge Martin who unceremoniously collapsed back into his big chair and quickly opened the envelope. He started reading it while the three stood before him, each with an expression of anxious curiosity on their faces.

The frown that initially graced his judicious visage slowly disappeared. He started laughing. He laughed, and he laughed, and the more the three in front of him looked bewildered and anxious, the more he laughed, a genuine laugh from the core of his being.

Finally, after wheezing and coughing a few times, the laugh attack subsided. He said to Mr. Burton, the bailiff, in between several gasps for breath, his face as red as the proverbial beet, "Bailiff, we are going to recess court for the day. Tell everyone we'll resume court tomorrow morning. When the jury and spectators come back after the recess apologize to them for me. At nine-thirty sharp, we're gonna have a special session of court. I want you to personally inform Mr. B.S. Fotheringham, III, and Jimmy G, and the other lawyers, that they are to be in Court at that time, with their clients. Not that I need to remind them after the shenanigans of this day." He emphasized, "with their clients." And tell Molly McMasters, too. And tell her to bring the entire O'Halloran estate file."

He started laughing again. Unable to speak since he had relapsed into actual hysterical laughter, he waved them out of his chambers, clutching the manila envelope and its contents tightly to his chest.

As they shut the door behind them, the judge's laughter still reverberating, Billy turned to Bailiff Burton and asked, "What in the world was that all about?"

"I dunno. It sure is strange, but I gotta get going. I got to find all those birds and personally tell 'em to be in Court tomorrow morning."

Chapter 33

When court was about to resume the next morning at nine-thirty, the courtroom was packed. Word of the strange envelope and its mysterious contents had gotten around like wildfire in Pine Ridge. Curiosity infused the people like a raging, contagious disease.

Crowded around one of the tables, B. S. Fotheringham, III, and his efficient associate, Margaret, were mystified. Pastor Ronnie Conner was there too, in all his splendor, a new peruke firmly glued in place, and seated directly behind him was his wife, Donna, who was plastered. Plastered with layers of makeup and perhaps a valium or two too many. Mr. Rex Chase was there too, looking quite sad because he had to leave his dog at home.

At the other table, Jimmy G was nervously running his fingers through his greasy hair. Next to him, Izzy was totally at sea, even more mystified than normal at the arcane procedures of the Court. Rounding out the group was the state man, Mr. A. Benfield Suggins, a supernumerary if there ever was one.

People were crammed into the pews, and the walls once again were lined with spectators, reporters, and even television cameras, which was unusual because Judge Harley Martin was notorious for forbidding the distracting elements of the media from his courtroom. But for today's hearing he had not only given them permission, he had personally informed the press and news media. There was a loud undercurrent as hundreds of whispering voices spoke in muted tones, speculating on what was to come. Suddenly, the loud baritone voice of the bailiff silenced the crowd.

"Oyez, oyez, oyez. The Superior Court of Pine Ridge County is now open for the hearing of a special session. The

Honorable Harley Martin, Judge, presiding. Be seated. Silence in the Court."

Judge Martin breezed into court, his robe flowing imperiously. He sternly faced those present in the courtroom and took his seat. So did everyone else.

When the rustling stopped, he appeared as if he was about to speak, but instead he was silent, apparently struggling over something. Then, suddenly, he boomed, "Ladies and Gentlemen. Yesterday, a young boy brought a document to my office. Are you here, boy?" he asked, looking around the courtroom. Not seeing him, for Darren had dutifully gone to school to be sure he got another perfect attendance certificate this semester, the judge coughed into his hand.

"Anyway," he continued, unperturbed, "that boy brought me this document." He held it up for all to see. He turned to Molly McMasters who was uncomfortably seated in the seat normally occupied by Mr. Speedy, the Court Clerk, who stood against the wall behind her, a disgusted expression on his face since his routine has been interrupted and his prized seat at the left hand of the Judge was usurped by his boss.

"Madam Clerk, let me see the will in the 'Estate of O'Halloran' file," Judge Martin demanded with a flair. She quickly opened the file, turned to the will, which along with all the other papers, was securely clipped in the file.

The judge inspected the will, and then loudly announced to all present. "This will," he said holding up the file, "is dated ten years before our good friend, Mr. Hamish O'Halloran, tragically and unexpectedly died."

The judge put down the file and then picked up the other document he had shown the court. Looking at it, Judge Martin started to snicker. Then he erupted into a paroxysm of laughter, startling the crowd. Tears streamed from his eyes and he almost fell out of his plush, high backed judge's chair, before being able to bring himself under control, and taking a sip of water the bailiff had thoughtfuly brought him.

"But this document," he held up the document that Darren had brought him, "this document is what appears to be the actual Last Will and Testament of our dearly departed friend Hamish O'Halloran." He stopped and giggled a bit. "It is dated just three days before he died. And it looks to be properly witnessed and notarized." He started giggling again.

"Mr. Fotheringham. Mr. G. Ah am dismissing this case. The worthiness of the Temple of God is no longer at issue. This will Ah have here in my hand is Mr. O'Halloran's real last will, and in it, he leaves the bulk of his estate to someone named Ms. Shan Tilly Rice. Attached to the will is a letter explaining it all. Miss McMasters, in the event our good friends of the press would like one, please make copies of the will and the letter for dissemination to the press. And you might want to make a copy for all the attorneys who are interested in this case. A will, after all, is a public document after the death of the propounder. Mr. Burton, please adjourn Court." And with that, Judge Harley Martin got up and left the courtroom, giggling like a school girl.

Naturally, the press was all over Ms. Molly McMasters as she left to run into her office, stunned at what had just occurred, tears streaming down her face. She personally made a bundle of copies of the will. Her mind, a vacant expanse, as she dealt the copies of the will out to the myriad hands seeking them. She went back into her office, closed the door, and cried.

Chapter 34

The next morning the local news papers printed copies of the the actual last will and testament of Hamish O'Halloran, and the letter of explanation attached to it. The will was short and simple. It read:

> Being of sound mind, I, Hamish O'Halloran, hereby publish and declare this to be my last will and testament. I hereby appoint Mr. Isadore Shapiro to be the executor of my will to administer my estate. I have no family or heirs at law.
>
> At first, I thought I would leave my estate to an organization that would do good with it. I know something of what the estate is worth. The coins I received from my Aunt Gertrude. She was a widow who received nothing from her husband's estate, since he left everything to his children by a former marriage. But Aunt Gertrude's grandfather, my great grandfather, was an interesting man, as my Aunt described in the attached letter. But after some considerable thought I finally determined there is no such organization that will truly do good and only one such person. I have not been treated well by those who I see in the course of my employment. There are only two members of my profession who I deem worthy of consideration. I therefore direct my executor to provide a sufficient sum to the Legal Lunch so that Mr. Sparrow, and Assistant District Attorney Benedict Arnold may eat their lunches there for free as long as they wish.
>
> The remainder of my estate I leave to my housekeeper, Ms. Shan Tilly Rice, the only truly decent and honorable person I know. Everyone else is out for whatever they can get, however they can get it.

To Miss Shan Tilly, I say; Thank you. Send Darren to college, get some health insurance, and take care of yourself. Your buttermilk pie is terrific.

This, the 19th day of July, 2005.

/s/ (Hamish O'Halloran)

The attached letter was more interesting, for, you see, it constituted genuine provenance for the gold coins, or as close as anyone was going to get to genuine provenance. It was hand written, and dated 1951. Signed by Gertrude O'Halloran Lafferty.

Dear Hammy,

I am leaving you this box of coins which belonged to your great grandfather, Sheamus O'Halloran. He was born in Ireland in 1828, and came to America when he was nineteen years old. He was obsessed with gold. He married your great grandmother, my Grandmother Maggie, and left her with a small male child when he was twenty-one to go prospecting for gold in California. He never came back. He died in a mining explosion at the gold mine in Bodie, California in 1885. My grandmother went out there to collect his belongings. There were only a few insignificant items but there was a key to a safe at the Bank of Bodie. She retrieved this box of coins which I think are mostly gold, and had it ever since until she gave the box to me on her death bed. But in the box was a letter which provided that his heirs could never sell the coins until the last surviving heir had died. I'm sorry I couldn't leave you more. But please know that I love you.

Aunt Gertrude

EPILOGUE

Life went on in Pine Ridge. It always does. After a few days of sensationalism in the press, the media lost interest and went home. The town reporter continued to report instances of the more prosaic things in small town America: things like drunk driving, teenagers vandalizing mailboxes, and pushing over grave stones. Fun stuff such as that which brought out the "tsk, tsks" from the old folks, decrying the up and coming generation anew. No matter what, old folks always looked at the young as lost souls, their profligacy just one more profanation of the good old values of the generation of the old folks, values which were fast disappearing in the younger folks.

Of course, life sure changed for Miz Shan Tilly Rice. She had suitors galore, but she pushed them all aside. Except for one, that is. Lester McAlester, she kind of kept around like a pet. They called him Sarge, but no one really knew why. He never said much, didn't ask for anything, just did a few things around the yard, and was so very, very polite to "Miz Rice." Every week he brought her a bouquet of freshly picked wild flowers. He was meticulous in making sure all the ants and bugs were washed off them, and that no poison ivy or poison sumac mistakenly got included in the big bouquets. Occasionally, she invited him in for a piece of buttermirk pie. That was reward enough for the retired old veteran, with his grizzled, knobby hands the size and color of baseball mitts. They never got married, and he never moved in. There was no need to. The two oldsters had a great, silent, mutual respect for each other, and their relationship was just fine the way it was.

Darren went to college. He wasn't a world beater, but his essential goodness led him to divinity school at a Baptist college, not too far away. His training made him a fine preacher, a very fine preacher, and he helped out a lot of folks, really helped some decent, deserving folks.

O'Malley retired, well, he kind of had to, since he was having the visions and all. He never could get the image of Izzy Shapiro out of his mind. The image of Izzy Shapiro was everywhere O'Malley went. So he moved into a rusty old trailer in a really isolated spot on Manchese Island on the coast and spent his time fishing. Every once in a while, he caught a big rockfish and felt wonderful for days. After a while he was convinced that catching a twenty-pound striper was the greatest feeling in the world, much, much better than coming up with a fist full of gold coins you couldn't use.

Jimmy G ended up with a nice fee, a new suit, and all the business he could handle. Even though he was an Eye-talian lawyer from Brooklyn, the folks in Pine Ridge afforded him a lot of new found respect. The suit was a bit too shiny for the likes of the Pine Ridge snoot set, but Jimmy didn't care. It was sort of purple, no, more like lavender. It was somewhere in between puce, mauve and pink. It was godawful, but he liked it. It went well with his orange and lime green ties or so he thought.

Izzy! Now Izzy Shapiro is another story. Izzy made enough administering the estate to retire. He did everything properly, and with Jimmy's help, everything in the estate fell into place like the tumblers of a lock. He could often be seen around the streets of Pine Ridge walking his big wolf looking dog. Caesar was devoted to the old man, and Izzy was delighted to have an uncomplaining, loyal companion he could talk to. The dog's only vice was to tear off after a jack rabbit or 'coon once in a while. But he always came right back, for he never actually got close enough to catch them.

A new IRS agent made another run for Izzy, but as soon as the agent got a parking ticket, he quickly left town. He had heard about what had happened to the Agent who went by the name of James Smith. Everybody at the IRS did. So they kind of stayed away from Pine Ridge for almost a whole generation after that.

Mart-World paid a bundle for the house on Pine Street after the oil well they found on it ran dry, and the royalties stopped. Nat got a job as a merchandise manager for them and met a nice quiet Methodist girl. It was strange, Izzy thought. He liked her much better than Susan, even if she wasn't Jewish. They had a few kids and they raised them Unitarian.

It was kind of sad about the Temple of God, though. The Rolley children came out of the woodwork demanding their property. Fotheringham's firm, Armitrage Grace, made a pretty good buck on that case too. But in the end, they lost that one.

Pastor Ronnie somehow lost his charisma. People passing on the street would snicker and point at his toup, which never really healed after the Fotheringham "hair raising." In the end, he sold his Hummer and Lincoln and bought a nice Toyota SUV. Donna Conner left him for another televangelist, but the few flock he had left were loyal.

Ronnie read up on Dante's *Inferno* and became somewhat of an expert on the seven deadly sins, especially the sin of pride, which he used to preach about all the time. He was proud of his new-found humility. Most of the Temple's workers left and got real jobs.

Billy "Benedict" Arnold and Mr. Sparrow continued their routine at Court House Coffee in the morning, and the Legal Lunch at noon. They could often be seen sitting together, seldom speaking, comfortable with the steady, reliable presence of each other, but they were mighty glad to have been included in the O'Halloran legacy. The benefit caused them to have a new- found respect for the memory of the eccentric old lawyer.

Yes, Pine Ridge was Pine Ridge once again, bucolic, safe and boring. Friends and relatives of the residents of the little town often said, "Pine Ridge is a great place to live, but I wouldn't want to visit there."

FAR FROM TURNING OVER IN HIS GRAVE, THE SOUL OF THE ICONOCLASTIC LAWYER LOOKED DOWN FROM ABOVE, SMILING. IT PLAYED OUT JUST AS HE HAD HOPED. NO, BETTER, WAY BETTER.

CPSIA information can be obtained
at www.ICGtesting.com
Printed in the USA
LVOW11s0743200418
574235LV00001B/71/P